VENETIAN MAGIC

VENETIAN MAGIC

Jean Morrant

CHIVERS
THORNDIKE

This Large Print book is published by BBC Audiobooks Ltd, Bath, England and by Thorndike Press®, Waterville, Maine, USA.

Published in 2006 in the U.K. by arrangement with the Author.

Published in 2006 in the U.S. by arrangement with Jean Hall.

U.K. Hardcover   ISBN 1–4056–3538–X (Chivers Large Print)
U.S. Softcover   ISBN 0–7862–8145–6 (British Favorites)

The text of this Large Print edition is unabridged.
Other aspects of the book may vary from the original edition.

Set in 16 pt. New Times Roman.

Printed in Great Britain on acid-free paper.

British Library Cataloguing in Publication Data available

Library of Congress Cataloging-in-Publication Data

Morrant, Jean.
    Venetian magic / by Jean Morrant.
       p.   cm.
    "Thorndike Press large print British favorites."—T.p. verso.
    ISBN 0–7862–8145–6 (lg. print : sc : alk. paper)
    1. Venice (Italy)—Fiction. 2. Large type books. I. Title.
    PR6113.O755V46 2005
    823'.92—dc22   2005021965

VENETIAN MAGIC

CHAPTER ONE

Turning swiftly away from yet another dark, inviting gaze, Kate had to admit the busy railway station in Venice was not the best of places for a girl to linger unescorted. Perhaps it had been rather foolish to insist there was absolutely no reason for anyone to meet her, confident she could find her own way to the house. Thank goodness she had taken the trouble to write down the directions her aunt had repeated so patiently.

Moving away from the increasingly persistent young man, she glanced at the instructions which would enable her to complete the journey. Relieved to find the man at the ticket office comprehended her destination, she made her purchase and went towards the pontoon to await the waterbus.

A tremor of excitement rippled through her as she scanned the Grand Canal to the buildings opposite; the tall houses with their peeling façades rising from the water, their shutters closed to the late April sun. Beyond them stood historic buildings crowned by bell towers or shining domes. She was already intrigued by this brief initial glance of Venice and hoped her holiday in this unique city would help erase the dreadful memories of her recent accident and the heartbreak which had

1

followed.

Her excitement mounted as the waterbus pulled away from the landing to chug along the canal amidst boats of varying shapes and sizes until it was time to disembark and make her way towards Campo Lucia. She knew her elderly aunt would be concerned if she failed to arrive in reasonable time, and didn't wish to cause any distress to the lady who had made this exciting visit possible.

Tiring rather quickly in the heat, and wishing she'd chosen to travel in a cool dress rather than the dark blue trousers and jacket she was wearing, she crossed a narrow bridge, pausing on the other side to put down her heavy suitcase. Convinced her aunt's house must be in the immediate vicinity, she spread her map on the stone parapet and was just about to check her position when a foreign voice cut sharply into her thoughts. Having quickly learned to ignore them, she kept her back turned against its owner until a sudden change to perfect English startled her.

'Boy! Are you aware you are trespassing?'

Swinging round to confront her accuser, she removed the baseball cap she'd been wearing, asking sharply, 'Are you speaking to me?'

The tall man advancing towards her appeared quite taken aback, as her hair tumbled around her shoulders, his dark brows lifting in surprise.

'My apologies, signorina, I see I was

mistaken. Even so, you are trespassing.'

Her eyes narrowed.

'What made you decide to address me in English?'

'The label on your suitcase,' he pointed out, his voice edged with mockery as he added, 'A common tour company logo, I believe. One could hardly miss it!'

'Then it should have been sufficient to tell you I had merely lost my way and had absolutely no intention of trespassing!' she shot back, infuriated by his manner. 'And now, perhaps you will be kind enough to direct me to Signora Rossini's house. It can't be far from here.'

'Quite so, signorina,' he agreed, stepping forward to take her heavy case. 'In fact, just across the bridge.'

She followed him back over the bridge and round the next corner where he set down her case in the first doorway. Thanking him in her limited Italian, she glimpsed a hint of a smile flickering around his mouth.

'Prego, signorina. In future I suggest you avoid placing yourself in such a vulnerable position. Someone could have led you in the wrong direction, particularly if he was not so unfortunate as to mistake you for a boy.'

Shrugging off the unpleasant thought, she turned back to the heavy wooden door and pressed the bell. A muffled ringing came from within, soon followed by the sound of footsteps when the door opened to reveal a dark-eyed maid.

'Signorina Macleod?' the young woman enquired with a smile, and beckoned Kate into the spacious hallway. 'Please, come in. Signora Rossini is waiting.'

Once inside, it took Kate a moment to adjust to the semi-darkness. Only a faint ray of sunlight penetrated the small, dusty window, revealing the water-marked plaster of bare walls. But the light increased as they ascended the marble steps when Kate looked up to see her Aunt Margaret on the landing, a gentle smile playing on her lips.

'Kathrine! I'm delighted to see you. It's years since you were here!' the signora exclaimed, bestowing kisses on her niece's cheeks as they embraced. 'Come along, you must be exhausted,' she said ushering Kate into a chair. 'Did you have a good journey?'

'Yes, thank you, very straight forward.'

'Good. Rosa will serve tea when she has recovered from the excitement of your arrival. She has been longing to meet my niece from England.'

'On my way here, I was mistaken for a boy by someone you may know.'

'I don't believe it!' Margaret Rossini laughed. 'Who could make a stupid mistake like that?'

'The gentleman who showed me to your door. You see, I took a wrong turning, went

4

over a bridge just round the corner from here when this man very quickly informed me it was private.'

Her aunt nodded.

'That would be Signore Ferrari's man, but I hadn't realised you could speak Italian.'

'I didn't need to, he spoke English!'

Her aunt frowned.

'How strange. Perhaps he guessed who you were and wanted to appear friendly.'

'Quite the reverse, actually,' Kate said with a short laugh. 'In fact, I considered him to be rather arrogant.'

The signora chuckled.

'Never mind, tell me about yourself, Kathrine. Do you enjoy living in London, or do you miss being at home with your parents?'

'Please, call me Kate, everyone else does,' Kate said, then hesitated a moment before she continued. 'Yes, I miss Edinburgh and the family, and since moving south to complete my training I don't have the opportunity to go home quite so often. I expect Mother keeps you informed.'

'Yes, Kate, your mother writes regularly, but it's not quite the same as having one's family close by and you were only a child when I left Scotland.'

'If it hadn't been for my exams I would have come here with mother two years ago, when Uncle Benito died.'

'That was a sad time for me and there are

5

moments when I feel extremely lonely so I'm pleased to have you here. Beni was a wonderful man,' she declared wistfully then, in an attempt to shake off her sadness, told her, 'You know, I surprised everyone when I allowed a handsome Italian to sweep me off my feet!'

'I can quite understand why. He was very handsome,' Kate commented as she spotted the wedding photograph on the cabinet beside her aunt's chair. 'How old were you then?'

'About your age, my dear, twenty, I believe.'

'I'll be twenty-three on the first of May,' Kate corrected.

'But you look much younger. Now tell me, how do you enjoy being in the nursing profession? And how are you after your accident?'

Kate was reluctant to reveal the unhappy events of the past weeks, but realised her aunt was bound to be curious. Her aunt noticed her reluctance to talk about what had happened.

'I sensed there was more to it than just a slight accident, Kate, but if it's painful to recall . . .'

'No, I've got to face up to it, and no doubt you're wondering why I'm not on duty. Quite frankly, I simply had to get away.'

'You most certainly had! That pretty little face of yours is much too pale and I now realise it has been more serious than I was led to believe.'

6

'Yes, it was,' she admitted, lowering her eyes, 'that and losing my job, and it's completely over between Greg and me.'

'Oh, my dear, I didn't realise it was anything quite so definite. To lose your private nursing position must have been upsetting for you, and then to lose Greg as well.'

Kate sighed.

'I'll admit I was dreadfully upset at the time, but while I was in hospital I decided against returning to private nursing, and then, on top of that, Greg stopped visiting.'

'Oh, Kate! You must tell me what actually happened, and how badly hurt you were.'

Again Kate hesitated, carefully considering her reply.

'We were driving home after a party,' she began finally. 'The car skidded into a wall and I was knocked unconscious. I had a head injury but it turned out to be less serious than first suspected. You should have seen the sight I was, all the bruising. I'm almost back to normal now.'

'But surely that wasn't the reason Greg neglected you,' her aunt said in astonishment.

Kate shrugged.

'I really don't know. Perhaps he thought I'd be disfigured though, amazingly, I have only one small scar.'

'But it all must have been a dreadful experience for you.'

'I'll admit I was heartbroken at first yet, on

reflection, I can't think why. As soon as I began to recover, I realised Greg wasn't the person I thought him to be. I just want to forget him,' Kate said, forcing a bright smile. 'I would like to hear about you, Aunt Margaret, and Venice, of course. From the little I've seen it looks fascinating, and I'm longing to explore.'

'I don't get about as well as I used to,' the signora said as her maid brought in tea. 'However, I'm sure Rosa will take you.'

'I shall be happy to accompany the signorina,' Rosa agreed, giving Kate a shy smile as she set down the tray.

'You will find plenty to occupy your time, and most likely we shall receive an invitation to visit my neighbour, Marco Ferrari, whilst you're here. I believe he's away on business at present but you'll have an opportunity to meet him on his return. He's a charming fellow, and quite influential in the city, wealthy, too. You'll like him,' the signora added quickly.

'What exactly is his business?' she asked, a trifle overawed by the prospect of meeting her aunt's influential neighbour.

'Collecting art is one business he's involved in,' her aunt told her. 'And finance, expert advice, that kind of thing. He's the descendant of a well-known Venetian family whose ancestors were silk merchants, so dealing in financial matters is in his blood. Beni's family were business acquaintances of theirs, and as we are neighbours Marco and I became quite close.'

Kate smiled.

'I'm pleased you have friends nearby. Do you visit each other often?'

'Occasionally. Of course, his home is very grand, much larger than this,' she declared with a sweep of her hand. 'The old, established families had beautiful houses.'

'Sounds quite exciting,' Kate agreed. 'But this house is lovely, too,' she added as her gaze travelled appreciatively round the large salon, a soft sigh escaping her as it came to rest on the high ceiling with its elaborate cornice framing the fading painted scenes.

'In great need of restoration,' her aunt commented wistfully, following her niece's gaze. 'Like many of the old buildings here, the crumbling outer walls betray little of the beautiful interiors, but the upkeep is almost impossible to maintain. Now, I'll take you to your room. Consider this your home for as long as you care to stay.'

'That's very kind of you,' Kate said, following her across the shining terrazzo floors to the large bedroom which had been prepared for her.

'This room's terrific!' she cried, her eyes shining. 'I just know I'm going to like it here.'

'I do hope so,' the signora said, her warm gaze resting thoughtfully on her niece for a moment before she tilted her head to say, 'I believe I hear the telephone so I'll leave you to unpack.'

Once alone with her thoughts, Kate realised how little the memories of Greg had troubled her since her arrival. Also, she was thankful it hadn't been necessary to disclose every detail of the accident, or the reason for her present lack of employment. She uttered a sigh of contentment; at last she could put it all behind her, determined to enjoy what lay ahead.

But her enthusiasm for the coming weeks was quickly dampened when her aunt returned to the room.

'Kathrine, the call is for you.'

'For me?' Kate said, surprised, then laughed. 'Oh, I expect it's my mother making sure I've arrived safely.'

'No, it's a man. He didn't give his name, and I don't recognise the voice.'

Puzzled, Kate went into the hall and picked up the telephone.

'Kathrine Macleod speaking.'

'Kate, it's me, Greg. Glad I've found you.'

'Greg! Why are you ringing me here?' she said crossly. 'I thought we decided to make a clean break.'

'We?' he said with a laugh. 'I think you mean you decided, but I know you didn't mean it.'

'Oh, yes, I did!' she shot back. 'Anyway, how did you know where to find me? I didn't tell you where I was staying.'

10

'A telephone number is easy enough to find, though there are a few Rossini's in the book.'

'The book?' she echoed. 'You went to the trouble of getting hold of an Italian telephone directory?'

'No problem, Kate, there are plenty of them here, in Venice.'

'You mean you're in Venice right now? Why have you come here?'

'There's something we've got to discuss.'

'I have nothing to discuss with you,' she said and immediately hung up.

CHAPTER TWO

Next morning, Kate flung aside the bed covers to dash across to the balcony overlooking the canal. She watched a boat on its gentle journey, the slow throb of its engines echoing between the high buildings. As it disappeared from sight under a stone bridge it suddenly occurred to her it was the same bridge where she had paused to check her map the previous day only to be accused of trespassing by some arrogant manservant.

The place opposite must be the one her aunt had spoken of, the home of her friend, Signore Ferrari. But the building appeared grim and forbidding, its windows heavily shuttered, and by its outward appearance she couldn't begin to imagine the beautiful interior described to her.

Across the bridge, beyond wrought-iron railings, stood a solid, wooden door set in an arch of grey stone. Nearby, a lower archway reached down to water level, its inlet stoutly guarded by a rusting iron grille. She supposed, being elderly, Signore Ferrari cared little for the outward appearance of his home, his main concern being security during his absence.

'Oh, you're out of bed already! I trust that means you slept well. Not a very exciting view from this side, I'm afraid,' Kate heard and turned to find her aunt had entered the room.

'Come, let's enjoy the hot rolls and coffee Rosa has prepared. I suggest you go shopping with her this morning to help get your bearings, then you can explore to your heart's content.'

After breakfast, finding the weather agreeably warm, Kate chose to wear a sleeveless cotton dress. She hoped to acquire a tan during her stay but gave in to her aunt's suggestion to take her wide-brimmed hat for protection against the midday sun, realising it might also act as a shield against the possibility of being spotted by Greg.

She was worried still as to why he had chosen to come to Venice, and wondered if she had been wise to allow her aunt to believe his phone call had actually come from England. Thankfully, she hadn't been asked to explain the reason she was unemployed, though she felt a trifle guilty over keeping her aunt in ignorance of both these matters. Perhaps it would be better to bring it into the open, when the opportunity arose.

She and Rosa were soon on their way through the busy streets. Eventually, she got her first glimpse of Saint Mark's Square. Ahead stood the Basilica of Saint Mark, its façade a varying mixture of designs, the ancient doorway crowned by glittering mosaics. Rosa smiled at Kate's wondering gaze.

'It's fascinating!' Kate exclaimed breathlessly. 'There's so much to see I can't take it all in at once.'

'Next time we will enter the Basilica,' Rosa promised. 'But now I do the shopping. You will not get lost?'

'Don't worry, I'll return in time for lunch,' Kate assured her laughingly.

Rosa disappeared into the crowd which thronged the narrow street leading away from the piazza, leaving Kate to follow a different route where she feasted her eyes on the sparkling jewellery and pure silk fashions. In another shop a display of glassware made by local craftsmen caught her eye and she paused to admire the treasures within knowing her mother would appreciate such a delicate souvenir. The items looked rather expensive, but maybe there would be something less pricey inside.

Taking off her sun hat, she entered the shop, her tread inaudible on the thick carpet. Carefully picking her way around the huge ornaments displayed, she paused to view a dainty crystal posy bowl on a shelf behind the window display. Then, just as she reached up to see the price ticket, her eye was caught by someone passing outside—someone tall and sandy-haired, very like Greg.

Startled, she gave an involuntary gasp and stepped back from view. But the resounding crash which followed startled her even further when, to her horror, she realised the brim of her hat had caught one of the delicate glass ornaments, sending it crashing on to its marble stand.

At the sight of the shattered object, her eyes widened in shocked dismay. Obviously, this had been one of the more expensive articles on display. The assistant's horrified expression told her as much before he uttered a sound.

'Oh, my goodness, what have I done!' she gasped.

'You have broken it, signorina,' came his stern-faced reply. 'It was,' he continued, with emphasis on the last word, 'one of our best pieces.'

'I'm so sorry. It was an accident. I'm quite prepared to pay for the damage, though I don't consider it entirely my fault. There's hardly room to move in here,' she said with

14

more spirit, but kept her eyes on the window, the brief glimpse of Greg uppermost in her mind.

'The card does say not to touch,' he pointed out.

'Card or no card, it was an accident,' she said heatedly, 'and I have every intention of paying.'

An icy chill ran down her spine when the assistant stated the value of the broken article, and a quick calculation told her the price was out of her reach. She would have to make an arrangement with the bank, assuming she dare venture outside without the risk of encountering Greg.

Glancing nervously from the doorway of the shop, at first she saw no sign of him. But the moment she turned in the direction of home she came face to face with his sneering countenance.

'Causing a bit of a commotion in there, weren't you?' he remarked. 'What was the trouble?'

'Nothing you need concern yourself with,' she replied with forced lightness, 'so there's no point in you hanging around here.'

'But I did telephone,' he said as she made to brush past him. 'Didn't your aunt tell you?'

Not wishing to linger in his company, she asked sharply, 'When?'

'About an hour ago, though I must confess she did her best to dissuade me from seeing you.'

'I only wish she'd succeeded,' she shot back, wishing now she'd had the sense to reveal Greg's arrival in Venice when he telephoned the day before.

'Well, how've you been?' he asked casually.

'How have I been?' she hissed, her cheeks crimson. 'I don't know how you have the nerve to ask! I still have nightmares over that dreadful night. Can't you understand, I don't want to see you ever again.'

'Oh, Kate,' he broke in, 'I know I've been a cad, and I realised my mistake as soon as I found you'd left. I was so desperate to see you I got the first plane out of London, and I want to make it up to you, if you'll allow me.'

'No, Greg, it's no use. We have already agreed not to see each other again,' she said as coolly as she could manage.

'No, as I reminded you yesterday, it was you who decided.'

'Whoever it was, I didn't expect to see you here, and I'd prefer it if you don't phone again. I mean it, Greg, just keep out of my life!'

'Whether you like it or not, I'm staying,' he said with a derisive curl of his lip. 'There's a bit of business I must discuss with you.'

'I don't want to hear it, Greg. In fact, should we chance to meet again, I shall ignore you completely.'

'Not after you've heard what I have to say,' he began, but Kate had already started to

16

hurry away.

Disturbed by her encounter with Greg, she rushed back to the house, to find her aunt standing by the telephone. Her heart sank. Did it mean Greg had rung again?

'Ah, Kate, here you are! I've got some quite exciting news.'

'Aunt Margaret, before you say any more I'd like to apologise. Yesterday, I chose not to mention Greg was in Venice as there was no point in worrying you unnecessarily, but I now know he has telephoned again.'

'Yes, dear, just after you left this morning.'

'I'm really sorry about that, but he won't trouble you further as I've told him I want no more contact.'

'Very wise, just what he deserves,' the older woman declared. 'But it is Marco's call I want to tell you about. He rang just a few moments ago to invite us to a dinner party he is giving this evening. I was sure you'd be pleased as it will give you an opportunity to see inside the palazzo.'

'Oh, yes, great!' Kate responded, relieved to know it hadn't been Greg pestering her again. 'But I thought you said he was away.'

'Had to return early, something to do with the security of the art exhibition he's planned. I'm not sure of the details. He's been away buying pictures, you see, so I expect it's connected with that.'

'Oh, I see. Well, I've been looking forward

17

to meeting him, and I hope you can advise me about what I should wear.'

'I notice you've brought one or two very pretty dresses, so choose the most feminine as I suspect he's not in favour of the modern trend in fashion which some young people are wearing here.'

'Never worry, I won't let you down.'

'Apart from meeting that awful Greg fellow, did you enjoy your morning?' the signora enquired as they went into the sitting-room.

'Yes, I had a good look round the piazza,' she replied, relieved her aunt didn't pursue the subject of Greg.

'If Marco takes a liking to you he may offer to accompany you to places of particular interest.'

'I don't suppose he'll want to act as tour guide,' Kate replied, 'particularly to someone of my age.'

'Why not? He's very proud of Venice, and I can't see that age matters.'

'But he may not be so keen to offer if he hears of my fiasco this morning,' Kate put in, and went on to relate what had happened in the glass shop. 'Of course, I intend to pay for the damage.'

After taking the short rest her aunt prescribed, Kate decided on her dress for the evening. She laid it on the bed in readiness and, hopeful of adding a little height to her own five feet two, selected matching high-heeled sandals. There was time to spare before she changed and, anxious to gain a little more knowledge of the Italian language in preparation for the coming evening, she sought Rosa's help. But Rosa was too excited about the impending visit and held Kate's dress against her admiringly.

'Tonight you will meet Signore Ferrari and see the beautiful rooms and paintings. I am so happy for you.'

'I'm quite looking forward to meeting him,' Kate agreed. 'By what my aunt says, he sounds a very nice person.'

'Oh, yes, he is, and I am pleased he has returned, though I hope the signora did not come with him,' Rosa said, laying Kate's dress on the bed.

'I didn't realise he was married.'

'No, they are not married. He employs her for the art,' Rosa declared, yet her lip curled as she added, 'But she wishes to be his wife, I can tell!'

'But maybe Signore Ferrari likes her,' Kate tried to reason. 'People of his age often marry purely for companionship, you know.'

Rosa's only reply came in the form of a derisive snort as she swept from the room.

After taking a shower, Kate slipped into the blue dress, smoothing the silky material over her slender waist. At the dressing table, she applied a hint of eye shadow above her wide grey eyes, and flicked her hair forward to frame her face. She found her aunt, awaiting her in the main salon, looking splendid in black, her silvery hair coiled softly on to the crown of her head.

'You look lovely, my dear,' she complimented Kate as they left the apartment. 'Blue suits you.'

'Being invited to a palace is exciting,' Kate whispered, shaking off her feelings of anxiety as they crossed the narrow, stone bridge, 'but how shall I address him? Does he have a special title, or do I simply say signore?'

'Good gracious, no, he wouldn't expect it,' her aunt assured. 'Just be your normal self, nothing more.'

This evening, the huge, wooden doors set in the high, stone wall stood open with the unexpected delight of a fountain playing gently into a garden pool before them, sheltered by a magnolia tree, its wax-like flowers already in bloom. Kate could hardly believe the dismal wall would enclose such a pretty courtyard.

'Come along or we shall be late,' the signora urged as she led the way towards the impressive marble steps. 'Most of the guests will arrive by boat. I noticed one or two moored by the bridge, but it is difficult to reach the front entrance now the steps are partially submerged, particularly earlier in the year.'

'Is it true the sinking may be arrested?' Kate queried.

'Possibly. As I understand, a great number of architects and engineers have been involved in making plans to prevent it,' the signora informed her as they passed between tall glass doors.

Kate paused on the threshold of the magnificent room, allowing her gaze to travel up to the two immense crystal chandeliers which hung from a ceiling filled with beautiful frescoes in delicate colours.

'It's beautiful,' she whispered. 'I never dreamed of anything like this!'

She crossed to the balcony, leaning over the stone parapet to view the busy Grand Canal. Truly a palace, she thought, spotting the blue and gilt mooring posts by the partly submerged steps leading to the imposing entrance below.

Kate turned as the sound of voices drifted out from the main salon where guests assembled to sip an aperitif. She was convinced her limited knowledge of their language and culture would cause her to feel an outsider. However, just as she prepared to join them, a voice which she immediately recognised sounded close behind.

'Ah, Signora Rossini, I have been searching for you!'

The signora drew Kate to her side.

'Just arrived, Marco,' she said, 'but first let me introduce you. Signore Ferrari, this is Kathrine Macleod, my niece.'

Speechless, Kate looked up to meet the

man's smiling blue eyes when, barely able to conceal her embarrassment, she managed to utter a formal greeting.

'Let us dispense with formalities, Kathrine,' he suggested as his outstretched hand found hers to grip it warmly. 'My name is Marco, and I welcome you to my home.'

Kate had compressed her lips in case they should have fallen apart in surprise, and in a daze she heard him say to her aunt, 'So this is the young lady of whom you have spoken. This becomes our second meeting,' he continued with a twinkle in his eyes, 'although I had absolutely no idea who you were on first acquaintance.'

'You've already met?' Kate's aunt intervened, casting Kate a faintly reproachful glance.

'Yes, but I didn't realise it at the time,' Kate admitted, her cheeks growing warm under his mocking gaze. 'Naturally, I presumed . . .'

'The fault was entirely mine,' he offered quickly. 'Come, let me get you an aperitif.'

Kate listened while he discussed his plans for the next exhibition, emphasising his words by gestures of his well-shaped hands. Undoubtedly, he was the most handsome man in the room, tall and dark, and wearing a white dinner jacket with the true bearing of a cultured man. How could she have mistaken him for a manservant!

He turned to catch her stare, the shadows

from the wall lights accentuating his high cheekbones, and his gaze stayed teasingly upon her as she sipped her drink, until someone caught his attention.

'Ah! I see the last of my guests have arrived,' he said, inclining his head slightly as he moved away.

As he crossed the room her aunt drew closer.

'So it was Marco you spoke to on the day you arrived?' she said.

'Yes, I'm sure he thought I'd lost my way on purpose, and he had the cheek to lecture me!'

'At the time he wasn't to know who you were,' her aunt pointed out, 'but now you appear to be giving a good impression.'

'For your sake, I'm pleased, but he shouldn't presume,' she objected. 'Now I suspect he's laughing at me.'

'Nonsense!' the signora exclaimed. 'He's a true Venetian gentleman.'

Kate sighed. Perhaps she had been over-sensitive. She shouldn't have allowed herself to be provoked by his previous manner. She sighed thoughtfully yet, as he advanced towards them, she couldn't help but admire his good looks and grace, and as his hand rested lightly beneath her elbow, she experienced an unaccountable sensation of pleasure.

'Come, meet everyone before we dine,' he said, urging her towards one of the most strikingly elegant women Kate had ever seen, whose crimson lips parted in a smile as they drew near. But the smile never reached her eyes, and very soon Kate was meeting that cold, dark stare.

'Camilla,' Marco was saying, 'I would like you to meet Signora Rossini's niece, Miss Kathrine Macleod. Kathrine, this is a friend, Signora Verdi.'

'Ah, so you are the young lady from England,' Signora Verdi drawled in heavily-accented English, her bejewelled hand touching Kate's only briefly. 'I hope you are enjoying a taste of Venetian culture and trust you have not felt too ill at ease.'

'Camilla!' he reproached softly. 'I hope you are not suggesting . . .'

She turned to him with an expression of innocence.

'No, caro, merely sympathetic. It must be quite daunting for Miss Macleod to adjust to our ways and language so soon after her arrival.'

Kate bit back the first retort which came to mind and replied stiffly, 'To the contrary, I find it most relaxing.'

Shooting her a cool, disinterested glance, the signora turned to Marco with an endearing smile and reverted to their familiar tongue.

Returning the conversation to English, Marco asked, 'Where is this art expert you brought with you, Camilla? Kathrine may like to meet him.'

24

With a bored expression, Camilla turned away, raising her hand to draw someone forward.

'Signore Jonathan Webb from New York,' she said as the man disengaged himself from the centre of the group nearby. 'Jonathan, meet Miss Kathrine Macleod.'

Puzzled, Kate met the narrowed gaze of the man who came to a sudden halt before her.

'I believe we've already met,' she started to say, searching her memory for where she had encountered him before.

'You already know each other?' Marco asked in surprise.

Before she had the chance to respond, Jonathan Webb merely raised his dark brows to reply without interest, 'No, I have not met this lady.'

CHAPTER THREE

Feeling somewhat foolish, Kate watched as Jonathan Webb moved away, soon lost from view in the crowded room.

'I must have been mistaken,' she said, though still convinced she had met this man somewhere before, even if his manner had been cool.

'It may be someone your aunt has mentioned,' Marco suggested. 'She knows so many people here. Quite a number of the gentlemen present are business acquaintances,' he continued as they went towards the dining-room, 'but tonight I shall mix business with pleasure. When Signora Rossini spoke of your visit it was my wish she should bring you here. Little did I realise we would meet on the day of your arrival, so already I feel we are quite well acquainted.'

'It was kind of you to invite me,' she murmured, attempting to give him her full attention, although still puzzled over the American. 'I'm pleased to have the opportunity to see inside such a splendid house.'

'The pleasure is mine, signorina,' he said, adding with a hint of a smile, 'And never again will I mistake you for a boy.'

Kate felt extremely aware of his masculine presence as he held her chair, seating her between himself and the elderly businessman who had been chatting to her aunt. She couldn't fail to notice the admiring glance he bestowed upon her as he took his seat. Recalling the moment they'd first met with sudden humour she smiled, unfolding her napkin.

'What is it that makes you smile, Kathrine?' he queried softly, pronouncing her name in such an attractive way she lost the desire to ask him to shorten it.

'I was remembering the first time we met,'

she disclosed, 'when I inadvertently trespassed on your property.'

He lowered a dark brow, simulating disapproval.

'And you assumed me to be a manservant at the palazzo.'

'I believe we both assumed,' she countered, seeing the light of amusement in his eyes, 'though, naturally, as a friend of Signora Rossini I imagined you to be a much older person.'

'Ah, but in this country men of all ages treasure the beautiful things in life,' he rejoined with a roguish smile, 'and a pretty face is one of them.'

Kate felt extremely vulnerable under his gaze, and was relieved when the gentleman seated on her other side engaged her in conversation. Then, as the next course was being served, Marco caught her attention again.

'As you are new to Venice, perhaps you will allow me to escort you through the city and reveal to you its many treasures. Providing Signora Rossini approves, of course.'

'Thank you, signore, I'm sure she will.'

'Marco, please,' he reminded her, and went on to say, 'I think it better you do not go alone. The tourist season is upon us when an unsuspecting young lady may fall into the trap of the shrewd, and sometimes unscrupulous, Venetian.'

'Really?' she said, her eyes widening. 'I wouldn't have thought it was that kind of place.'

Chuckling at her expression of disbelief, he nodded.

'Oh, yes, believe me, the torment of money unspent—palms itch at the very thought of it!'

'Now you're teasing me,' she reproached with a smile.

"I must also protect you from the Romeos,' he continued. 'My countrymen do not always take "no" for an answer.'

'You've no need to worry about me, Marco. I'm quite old enough to take care of myself.'

He smiled.

'I doubt your age will save you from the pitfalls I have mentioned. Venice is a city steeped in romance from which very few visitors escape, and once the magic has worked its spell even you, mia caro, will not be immune!'

'I came for a rest and to see the treasures you spoke of, not in search of romance,' she declared firmly, finding his manner faintly irritating.

In reply, he raised the sparkling crystal glass he held.

'To your holiday,' he said, smiling, 'and may you not be disappointed.'

There had been no sign of Jonathan Webb at dinner, nor was he anywhere in sight when they gathered for coffee and liqueurs in the salon. Kate had felt curiously uneasy as she puzzled over the American, and it was only when her aunt mentioned Marco's forthcoming art exhibition that her mind was jolted by a sudden recollection of where she had met him before. It had been in a London gallery when Greg had introduced her to members of the art world. Jonathan Webb had been amongst them.

She remembered him now, the rather arrogant, self-proclaimed expert of the group, but she didn't recall him having the accent of an American. It seemed odd that someone Greg had once introduced to her should also be in Venice, and pretending he had never met her previously.

As Kate drank her coffee she saw Camilla take a possessive hold on Marco's arm. But as he circulated amongst his guests she noticed him gently disengage her hand from his sleeve before coming to a halt at her aunt's side.

'Camilla forgets I have other guests,' he apologised, and went on to say, 'I suggested to Kathrine it may be helpful if I were to accompany her on her explorations. You know how difficult it can be for anyone alone.'

Signora Rossini nodded.

'Very wise, Marco,' she agreed. 'I shall know she is in good hands.'

'Then I am at your disposal, Kathrine,' he said, just as Camilla came to a halt beside them. 'Perhaps you will let me know a convenient time.'

'Do not forget your exhibition, caro,' Camilla reminded him. 'It will not leave you much free time. I am sure Miss Macleod will be quite safe. Most tourists manage perfectly well without a personal guide.'

Kate caught Marco's frown of disapproval before her aunt intervened.

'One can hardly describe my niece as a tourist. She's staying at least a month, maybe longer.'

'Then we have plenty of time,' Marco said, 'and your aunt will feel more at ease if you allow me to escort you.'

'Thank you, but I don't want to take up your time when you have an exhibition to arrange,' Kate said uncomfortably.

With a casual shrug Marco turned away leaving Kate to wonder if she should accept his invitation, or was he a typical Latin of the kind he himself had warned her against?

Kate spent many disturbed hours throughout the night, troubled by Greg's appearance in Venice, and the chance meeting of Webb, someone curiously forgetful of their past introduction. She wondered, was it merely a coincidence, or was there a connection between the two men which brought them both to Venice at the same time? And what possible reason would Webb have for pretending they were total strangers?

When morning came at last, she

remembered she had to call in at the glass shop, hoping this time there would be no Greg in the vicinity. Relieved to see no sign of him as she made her way to the shop, she made a careful entrance, nervously avoiding the delightful but delicate wares on display.

'I promised to come back,' she began brightly when she spotted the assistant, 'although I don't intend to cause any trouble today.'

Her voice faltered to nothing as a tall figure she immediately recognised emerged from the rear of the shop.

'You don't intend to cause trouble, signorina?' Marco queried. 'Is there a problem of some kind between you and Luigi?'

She uttered a sigh of annoyance when she realised he appeared to be awaiting an explanation for the reason for her visit. But it was the assistant who spoke first in rapid Italian and Marco's firm lips quirked with amusement as Luigi gestured to the spot where the broken ornament had fallen.

'I assume he has told you his version of what happened yesterday,' she began with a cool glance in the assistant's direction, 'and I hope he mentioned that I have already offered to pay.'

'I understand from Luigi it was merely an unfortunate accident, so I beg you not to distress yourself further,' he assured kindly.

'But I must explain to the proprietor,' she

insisted, opening her bag to gather the few notes from within. 'I don't have sufficient money on me, so if I leave my name and address, will you be kind enough to vouch for me?'

His hand covered her own briefly.

'Please, close your purse. I will explain to the proprietor.'

Then, after speaking briefly to Luigi, he took her arm.

'Let me escort you back, otherwise you may get lost again.'

Grateful for his presence in case Greg should pass her way, she stayed beside him as they left the shop, but once outside in the narrow street she came to a halt.

'I don't wish to give the impression I'm using my aunt's friendship with you as a reason for not paying,' she declared firmly. 'I would have preferred to speak to the proprietor myself.'

'It is not necessary, Kathrine,' he said, a hint of laughter in his voice. 'Signora Rossini will explain.'

The following morning, Kate was out shopping with Rosa when Marco telephoned. On her return she learned her aunt had accepted an invitation from him on her behalf, to act as Kate's guide.

'Oh, no, I'm sure he was only being polite,' she declined, still piqued by Camilla's remarks.

Signora Rossini flung down her newspaper.

'I think I know Marco well enough to decide whether or not he was being polite!' she said exasperatedly. 'He has an unlimited knowledge of Venice's history which is exactly what you wanted, isn't it?'

Kate hesitated uncomfortably.

'I know, but must it be today?'

'Last night you accepted so, naturally, I assumed you'd be eager to go. I trust you haven't allowed Camilla to discourage you.'

'She gave me the impression he was merely being polite and I sensed she thought I was trying to ingratiate myself with him.'

'You shouldn't listen to anything she says. She behaves like a spoiled child. Even widowhood hasn't matured her and she continues to have tantrums if she doesn't get her own way,' her aunt disclosed. 'Between ourselves, Marco tolerates a great deal because of his close friendship with her late husband, Carlo, who was a brilliant artist. Carlo was an orphan, and it was Marco's parents who took him in and paid for his education, including his years at the art college. He and Marco grew up together, almost like brothers.'

'I see,' Kate said, curiously relieved. 'That explains a lot. I must try to be more sympathetic.'

A thoughtful, little smile played round the signora's mouth.

'Quite frankly, I suspect Camilla is not the

broken-hearted widow she professes to be,' she said with an expressive lift of her shoulders. 'But, there again, it is none of my business.'

Kate couldn't account for her unexpected feeling of elation when Marco arrived. She was just adding the final touches to her make-up when she caught the sound of his voice drifting from the salon.

'I have brought the launch round to the bridge,' he was saying. 'Perhaps a tour of the Canal Grande would be a good way to start, yes?'

'Everywhere is new to Kate,' her aunt was enthusing. 'She was thrilled when I told her of your invitation.'

Kate smiled to herself, and when she entered the salon to see Marco standing by the open window, the sting of Camilla's tongue ceased to trouble her. His casual, but immaculate attire suited him well. A fine black sweater above well-cut grey slacks added a look of lithe grace to his muscular form.

'You are ready to leave, Kathrine?' he asked as his gaze lingered on her appreciatively.

'Please, call me Kate.'

'I prefer to call you Kathrine,' he said, repeating her name in his sensual Latin voice.

Her heart seemed to skip a beat but she managed a croaky little, 'If you wish,' and allowed her hand to rest in his as they descended the stairs.

Out in the brilliant sunshine, they made their way to where his launch was moored.

'Today, I grant you the freedom of my bridge!'

He laughed, bringing a smile to her face.

'From this point we will take a gentle cruise along the Grand Canal, then I suggest we call at a little café in a quiet backwater where you can tell me all about yourself, and the reason behind your sudden decision to visit Venice.'

Kate shot him an anxious glance as he helped her into the launch, wondering how much he already knew, or could it be merely friendly curiosity on his part?

'I'd prefer to talk about Venice,' she said, releasing his hand. 'I understand you're an authority on the subject.'

'Just as you wish,' he conceded. 'I shall enjoy having your company whatever topic of conversation we choose.'

After making sure she was comfortably seated, he started the engine and cast off, pulling smoothly away in the direction of the wide canal.

'This is wonderful,' she breathed as she relaxed to take in the view. 'I didn't expect to do my sightseeing by private launch.'

'Bene! Enjoy yourself,' he said, raising a hand. 'Here is the Rialto Bridge, and the Ca da Mosto, thirteen century, much older than my home.'

'But your home is beautiful, Marco,' she

enthused. 'Well, the part I saw.'

'Then you must come again, to see the rest of the palazzo. Perhaps dinner one evening, but this time without my business acquaintances.'

'But the signora, she may object. I mean . . .' she began, then turned away to hide her confusion as a gleam of amusement sparkled in his eyes.

'Do you mean Camilla?' he queried, his free hand turning her to face him. 'Why do you mention her?'

'Well, I understand your exhibition will be held quite soon. She may need to discuss it with you.'

'You must not regard her too seriously,' he advised. 'She's inclined to be a little outspoken at times, though quite competent when it comes to organising an exhibition.'

Furious with herself for mentioning Signora Verdi, Kate asked casually, 'And the American she introduced to me, Jonathan Webb I believe was his name, will he be employed to advise on the display?'

'I haven't employed him. That is for Camilla to decide. According to her, he had seen the exhibition advertised and volunteered his assistance.'

'Oh, I see,' she said quietly and returned her attention to the buildings.

Marco continued in his rôle of guide as they cruised along between the slender gondolas, water buses, and water taxis, each ploughing their way along the street of sun-dappled water. Eventually, he steered the launch into the maze of narrow backwaters, slowing the engine to a soft purr as the sounds from the busy canal faded. Expertly manipulating the controls, he pulled in at a mooring beside a short flight of worn, stone steps. Kate watched whilst he secured the boat until, aware of his gaze, she glanced away to follow the silent glide of a passing gondola.

'Would you like to ride in a gondola?' he asked pleasantly, breaking the uneasy silence which had fallen between them.

'Oh, yes,' she replied with a spark of enthusiasm. 'They're so elegant, and very kind of, well . . .'

'Romantic,' he supplied. 'Could that be the word you search for?'

'Mm, I suppose it is.'

Marco chuckled.

'And have you come to Venice in search of romance?' he asked, his blue eyes meeting hers as he lifted one foot on to the steps. 'Will you allow the magic of Venice to capture your heart?'

'I believe I told you once before, romance is the last thing I have in mind,' she declared lightly, even though she found his close scrutiny rather disturbing.

Marco merely smiled and reached down, about to take her hand when, quite unexpectedly, a boat shot round the corner just ahead of them, the roar of its powerful engine echoing between the tall buildings. There was a bump, and a spray of water hit Kate as she lost her balance, falling heavily against the side of the boat.

In seconds Marco had jumped down beside her, helping her back on to the seat, his expression one of deep concern as he asked, 'Are you hurt?'

For a few moments she was speechless and remained in the supporting curve of his arm. When eventually she managed to shake her head, he let out a sigh of relief.

'Take it easy,' he advised quickly. 'I'll fetch a blanket from the locker otherwise you will soon feel cold. I wish I'd seen the crazy fool who did this. I would report him to the authorities!'

'Please, Marco, don't worry, I'll be all right when I get my breath back,' she managed to gasp. 'Accidents will happen.'

'This was no accident,' he exclaimed. 'It was extremely irresponsible behaviour! There are speed regulations on the canals, and for safety's sake they should be adhered to.'

By now, a small group had gathered at the water's edge, all wide-eyed with interest, their voices increasing in pitch.

'Signore!' one called. 'You need an ambulance for your loved one?'

'No, no, grazie, but maybe a little brandy

will help,' Marco suggested when the proprietor of a nearby café rushed to the scene.

'Ah, Signore Ferrari!' the man exclaimed, his hands raised in a dramatic gesture. 'Two large brandies, immediately!' he cried, dashing off to attend to Marco's wishes.

'Did you witness the incident?' Marco asked the group of onlookers. 'Maybe one of you recognised the boat, or who was at the helm?'

They looked at each other and shrugged, then one man volunteered, 'No, signore, just the gold flash along its bows, rather like the form of a bird, nothing more.'

Kate felt Marco tense.

'Grazie. You have a keen eye, signore,' he said. 'I was too concerned for my passenger to notice, but I intend to find the idiot responsible!'

CHAPTER FOUR

'Signore, to help restore your strength,' said the café proprietor as he placed a tray on the steps and with a nod of acknowledgement, Marco pressed a glass into Kate's hand.

'Try this. You'll feel much better.'

Kate found the amber liquid warming and soon her trembling had almost ceased. But she noticed the lines of tension were still visible in

Marco's expression as he spoke sharply into his mobile phone before returning to his position at the wheel.

'I shall take you back to the palazzo,' he decided, starting the engine once more and turning the boat on the narrow canal. 'You must get out of those wet clothes.'

'They are a little uncomfortable,' she admitted with a rueful smile, 'but I'll be fine after I've dried off.'

Alongside the palazzo's private mooring, Marco secured the launch and lifted her from it, disregarding his own discomfort as he negotiated the partly-submerged, slippery steps.

'I deeply regret this happening,' he said as he set her on her feet.

Still in the circle of his arm, Kate looked up, smiling.

'I'll just think of it as a sort of initiation ceremony,' she began to say, but then she saw his eyes darken and he drew her closer, holding her gaze as his lips came down to capture hers.

The unexpected kiss startled her, brief as it was.

'Kathrine,' he murmured. 'I find you so very tempting.'

Inside the palazzo, Marco gave instructions for his housekeeper to take Kate to one of the large dressing-rooms where she could change into a thick towelling robe while her dress was dried and pressed.

'But I could go home and change,' she protested. 'I don't want to give your staff extra work.'

'It is no trouble, really,' he insisted, 'and, as you are here, you may like to continue your tour of Venice in my library. A quiet rest would be advisable as I'm sure you must be feeling rather shaken after your experience. We can take out the launch another day, that is, if you won't feel too nervous.'

She smiled.

'I'm sure I won't. It will be something to look forward to.'

He glanced down at his sodden footwear.

'I also must change,' he said with a rueful smile. 'See you in the library in about twenty minutes.'

In the well-appointed dressing-room, Kate took off her damp dress and handed it over to the housekeeper, and after washing the canal water from her hair in the adjoining bathroom she dried her wet hair, her thoughts dwelling on Marco.

During the short time they had spent together, he had been an informative and entertaining guide but, after the incident on the canal, she had noticed his expression become strained, and his manner towards her became almost protective. But was it that same protective instinct which had prompted him to kiss her? Kate thought not, yet the touch of his

41

lips lingered in her thoughts as she wrapped the towelling robe around her and prepared to join him in the library downstairs.

Marco had already selected a number of books which were on the reading table. Some illustrated Venetian art and others had details of the city's architecture, all of which Kate found so interesting time passed almost unnoticed.

'You will dine with me?' Marco invited when she remarked on the hour.

She glanced down at the robe she was wearing and said with a smile, 'I'm hardly dressed for dinner.'

Marco grinned.

'Don't worry, I shall enjoy having a meal without any traces of formality.'

'Then I will go and change into my very informal gown,' she told him and returned to the dressing-room to find her dress already waiting.

During dinner, he described the places she had yet to visit and her enthusiasm for the unique city increased throughout the meal. But as they sipped coffee from dainty, gold-rimmed cups she sensed the conversation was drifting towards the reason she was in Venice, and she broke in.

'My aunt was right, you're quite an authority on Venetian architecture.'

He gave a modest shrug.

'I'm pleased the day has ended a little better

than anticipated after the accident on the canal.'

'Accident or incident?' she queried. 'Surely no-one would have done that on purpose.'

'Perhaps you are right,' he agreed quickly, though not too convincingly she thought, 'and as you didn't suffer any serious consequences, I think it better we forget it ever happened.'

She nodded, though was secretly surprised that he should now brush aside a matter which had made him so angry at the time. Glancing at her watch, she gave a reluctant sigh and got to her feet.

'I had no idea it was so late.'

'I'm sure the signora will guess where you are,' he assured her, rising from the table, and then his expression turned a little anxious when he suggested, 'Perhaps it would be advisable not to mention the accident. It may upset her.'

As she left the palazzo by way of the garden where the sweet scent of flowers hung on the still evening air, he paused to look down on her, his eyes glittering in the faint light.

'Were you shocked by what happened earlier?' he asked softly.

'You mean on the boat?'

He chuckled.

'No, no, I was referring to the moment when I kissed you.'

'No, Marco, not shocked, just a bit startled.'

'You looked so helpless, so tempting.'

'And wet,' she put in with a wry smile.

'Kathrine,' he whispered softly and kissed her again.

Kate closed her eyes as his arm tightened about her, her heartbeats quickening at the pleasurable sensation of his warm lips on her own.

'Yes, so very tempting, mia caro,' he whispered as he drew away from her. 'May I call you tomorrow?'

'I'll look forward to that,' she responded happily.

He brushed her cheek with his fingers as he drew open the heavy door.

Later, as she undressed, she recalled this moment with Marco and asked herself why a mere kiss should have put her mind in such turmoil. Dare she allow that magic moment to be repeated, or would it only take her headlong into further heartbreak?

The following day Marco telephoned whilst Kate was writing a letter home and she heard her aunt invite him to lunch.

'You see, it is Kate's birthday,' the signora continued, and by her smiling responses, Kate guessed he had accepted.

She uttered a contented sigh. The morning post had brought numerous cards, including a cheque from her parents, and her aunt had given her perfume. But the most unexpected gift was from Rosa who had shyly thrust a parcel into her hands. On opening it, Kate had been delighted to find a small blue crocheted bag of unusual design, the top drawn together by a thin, gilt chain.

To her relief there was no word from Greg, so it seemed their last conversation had deterred him from attempting to contact her further.

Marco arrived promptly at one, dressed more formally than on the previous day, and as he strode across the salon to greet her, she silently admired the light suit he was wearing.

'May I wish you a very happy birthday, Kathrine,' he said, handing her a single red rose, its long stem encased in ribbon and silver foil.

Delighted by the romantic gesture, Kate thanked him and breathed in the sweet fragrance from the perfect bloom.

As they were served a dry, sparkling wine to celebrate the occasion, Marco glanced at the cards and gifts on the table beside him.

'You haven't been forgotten,' he remarked. 'Someone must miss you.'

'Yes, I expect my parents do, although I'm not sure I won't want to leave here when the time comes,' she confessed with a sigh.

'No-one else?' he said softly, regarding her with a question in his eyes.

'No, no-one,' she confirmed on a faintly bitter note.

'Then let us make the most of your time here,' he suggested. 'Perhaps you would enjoy riding in a gondola later this evening. Venice is spectacular after dark.'

Kate experienced a glow of pleasure at this suggestion but noticed he seemed to avoid any conversation concerning the previous day. She wondered about those moments in his arms, and the kisses they'd shared. Had it been merely a gesture for which he held little regard? She had found his kiss curiously exciting and, on reflection, Greg had never caused her heart to pound in anticipation of the next embrace.

After coffee was served, Rosa announced a call for Marco. With a sigh of exasperation, he went to the telephone where his conversation was brief, his tone impatient, and Kate observed his taut expression when he returned to the table.

'It is most unfortunate, but something has occurred which calls for my attention. I hope you will excuse me, signora.' Turning to Kate, he said, 'Do forgive me. I hope this will not delay our outing.'

'Of course. It will be something to look forward to, whenever you're free.'

'Marco appeared quite angry,' Kate remarked to her aunt once they were alone. 'I wonder what's wrong?'

'I expect Camilla is having one of her tantrums. By what I could gather from his conversation, it seems she wants a plan of the palazzo immediately so that the display of pictures can be decided upon. As if it couldn't have waited until lunch was over,' Aunt Margaret sighed. 'Poor Marco, he never has a moment's peace.'

'Perhaps all this attention to paintings reminds her of the past, particularly if some of them were painted by her husband,' Kate remarked. 'She may still be upset over his death.'

'Upset? Pah!' the signora brushed the suggestion aside. 'No, Camilla's not in the least sentimental about Carlo's work. She now thrives on having a string of admirers, particularly those who are wealthy.'

'And is Marco one of them?' Kate found the courage to ask, her sympathy for Camilla decreasing.

'Marco has a strong sense of duty, but he's too shrewd, even for Camilla's clever wiles, to be swayed by beauty alone,' with a surreptitious smile the signora added, 'Do remember, it was to you he gave the rose.'

'What on earth has a rose got to do with it?'

'An old Venetian custom, my dear. When a man gives a girl a single red rose on the first of May it is because he wishes to further their acquaintance.'

'Surely you don't think Marco . . .' Kate stammered.

'I most certainly do!' Aunt Margaret interrupted with a chuckle. 'He's not the kind of man who makes frivolous gestures.'

47

Kate shook her head.

'It's a charming custom, I agree,' she said then, in an attempt to quell the surge of happiness within her, added, 'but I don't want to get too involved with anyone.'

'Given time, your bitterness will subside, you'll see,' came the wise response. 'I suspect you already like Marco more than you care to admit.'

'Even so, I wouldn't risk placing my aspirations on an old Venetian custom,' she said, and to avoid the older woman's keen gaze Kate crossed to the window overlooking the canal.

By the narrow bridge she noticed a launch was moored with a dark-haired man lounging at the wheel, idly smoking a cigar. She assumed the launch had brought Camilla to the palazzo, and let her gaze travel the length of the boat. But when she caught sight of the bold insignia on the bows, she drew a sharp breath, recalling the observations of the man who witnessed the accident on the canal the day before. She was looking at an emblem in the shape of a golden hawk, and he had likened the one on the offending boat to that of a large bird!

Kate's first thoughts were to bring it to Marco's attention, then checked herself. Half of all the craft in Venice could be displaying such an emblem, and this just happened to be Camilla's. With a wavering sigh she returned

48

to her chair, her mind on the raven-haired beauty. She wondered, had Marco presented the rose in the hope of furthering their acquaintance, or was he, a mature and more experienced man, merely flattered by her attention?

However, that evening, when he telephoned to ask if she was still willing to take the promised gondola ride, she couldn't suppress the delight which rose within her and accepted without hesitation.

Barely twenty minutes later, Kate opened the door to her smiling escort, immaculate in his dark suit as he walked beside her to the water's edge where a waiting gondola gently buffeted against its moorings. With the aid of Marco and the straw-hatted gondolier, she boarded the shining black craft with its flower-filled vases and sank into the velvet cushions. Once Marco was seated beside her, the gondolier took up his position, grasping the long pole to pilot his craft.

It was quiet on the canal, with only the warning cry of a passing boatman or a distant peal of laughter breaking the silence over the dark, softly-rippling water. Gliding along gently, she noticed the occasional light shining in a window set high in the peeling wall of a canal-side hotel, or from the many low bridges straddling the water. And Marco laughed at her gasp of amazement when the gondolier appeared to duck his head in the nick of time as they passed beneath.

'Renato has travelled these waterways all his life. He never makes a mistake,' Marco told her, sliding his arm along the back of her seat, his hand gently covering her shoulder as he drew her towards him. 'Later, we shall return by way of the Canal Grande when it will be brightly lit and busy, in contrast to this stretch of water.'

'It's just wonderful,' she declared with a happy sigh. 'I couldn't have wished for anything nicer on my birthday.'

'Tell me,' he asked softly, 'is it proving to be as romantic as you anticipated?'

'Oh, yes, much more romantic than the waterboats. They're always so crowded.'

He nodded thoughtfully.

'Yes, I often watch them from my window, laden with people, heading in all directions. Tell me, Kathrine, in which direction are you heading? What do you expect from life?'

'Oh, Marco, what a question!' she exclaimed laughingly. 'I couldn't possibly give you an answer without giving it more thought.'

'But you are young and pretty,' he observed. 'There must be someone special who shares your romantic aspirations, who awaits your return.'

She gave an emphatic shake of her head.

'No, I've told you before, no-one. Why do you ask?'

He smiled and drew her closer until her

head rested against his shoulder.

'I needed to know,' he whispered, causing her a shiver of pleasure. 'I haven't been able to get you out of my thoughts since you arrived. I want to know everything about you, Kathrine—your work, and the accident, what happens in your life.'

Lost for words, Kate remained silent when, to her relief, the gondolier began to sing, his clear voice rising on the warm, evening air. She was beginning to appreciate just how easily this unique city could capture the heart of an unsuspecting visitor, just as Marco had predicted. But what would he have to say if he were to learn of the cloud of suspicion she had been under, the reason she'd felt obliged to leave her employment? In addition to that, there remained the possibility Greg would incriminate her in the claim for damages resulting from his reckless driving.

'An old Italian love song which Renato sings so very beautifully,' Marco commented, bringing her thoughts back to the present as the singer's voice rose to end the song in a long, high note.

After a brief exchange with Marco, the gondolier pulled over to a mooring and hopped ashore, his sudden movement rocking the slender craft.

'I have asked Renato to return later,' Marco told her. 'There is a small restaurant nearby and not too many people realise its existence so it is both quiet and unspoiled.'

He indicated a narrow, dimly-lit alley a short distance ahead and rose to help her ashore. Hand in hand they walked along the path beside the canal, to where the restaurant was situated in a tiny square. Once inside, they were shown to a table in a secluded alcove where candle-light provided a soft, intimate glow. Seated opposite, Marco translated the menu and explained the dishes, helping her to make her choice.

'What a cosy little restaurant,' she remarked after he had given their order, 'and so very Italian.'

'Venetian,' he corrected gently. 'Only local dishes are cooked here.'

Raising his glass, he drank a toast to her birthday, his gaze lingering upon her across the table.

When the first course arrived, Marco was unable to suppress his amusement as she attempted to copy the deft manner with which he tackled a plateful of spaghetti. Laughingly, she allowed him to instruct her in the art of twirling the long strands into manageable mouthfuls.

'You learn quickly,' he commented with a chuckle. 'Did you enjoy it?'

Kate was about to reply when the murmur of other diners was drowned by a shriek of female laughter followed by the sound of breaking glass.

'Tourists?' she queried with an amused glance.

Marco uttered a sigh of annoyance.

'No, I think not,' he said coolly when the woman's voice demanded the cost of the breakages be charged to the Ferrari account.

'And order a motoscafo, there's a good guy,' Kate heard a male voice demand in the pseudo-American drawl she instantly recognised.

Glancing sideways she saw Camilla, closely followed by the unmistakable form of Jonathan Webb. Her heart sank when she realised they were heading in their direction, Camilla's dark beauty and flame coloured dress catching everyone's attention as she swept along.

'Marco!' Camilla exclaimed as she drew near. 'And Miss . . . er . . . I am forgetting your name,' she ended with the briefest of glances at Kate.

Marco rose and murmured a polite greeting to include Camilla's escort who hovered a short distance behind.

'You should have told me you were here,' Camilla continued in a petulant tone. 'We could have dined together.'

'Katherine and I were discussing Venetian cuisine,' Marco told her in a reasonably pleasant tone.

Camilla wrinkled her nose.

'How terribly boring for you, caro.'

Marco broke into a torrent of Italian which Kate couldn't possibly follow. But she did realise he was growing extremely angry and only seconds passed before Camilla swept out of the restaurant, followed by the scowling Jonathan Webb. Quickly regaining his composure, Marco returned to his seat, spreading his hands in a gesture of despair.

'Again, I find myself apologising for Camilla's rudeness. I notice her American friend made no comment so I assume he doesn't speak Italian.'

'Please, don't feel responsible,' she said, and wondered if she should admit to the possibility she was already acquainted with Webb, but Webb had been so insistent they had not met, she might appear foolish if she mentioned it now.

'I'm afraid I do,' he said, his hand covering hers briefly, 'and I will not allow your evening to be spoiled by anyone.'

Kate shot him a quick smile and attempted to continue as if nothing had happened, but however charming an escort Marco continued to be, she noticed a certain tension about his manner and a lack of humour in his inscrutable blue eyes as the evening progressed. On the return journey along the wide canal between floodlit churches and palaces, Marco's arm rested casually across the seat behind her, his hand only tightening on hers to help her to her feet when the gondola drew alongside the bridge by the palazzo. He had seemed rather preoccupied since dinner, and she was certain Camilla was responsible.

CHAPTER FIVE

Kate had hardly dared to hope for Marco's telephone call which came the following morning, and when she hesitated over his invitation to take her sightseeing, it was almost as if he read her thoughts.

'Camilla is busy organising the exhibition so it is unlikely she will be around,' he assured her.

A short time later, they were strolling from room to room in the Accademia where she saw the masterpieces of Tintoretto, Veronese and many other famous artists. With Marco beside her to explain their history in detail, her appreciation grew.

'Of course, you can't expect to view all the works displayed in one visit, but we shall come again,' he promised, about to continue when someone tapping on the office window caught his attention.

'Will you excuse me, Kathrine? The secretary would like a word about the exhibition,' he explained. 'I'll be with you in a few minutes.'

He directed her towards another room to

view a compelling Veronese canvas which covered an entire wall. Content to continue, she followed the arrows indicating the route visitors should take. But when she turned into the next room she came to a sudden halt, finding herself facing Greg.

'What are you doing here?' she demanded, the colour draining from her face. 'You have no right to pester me.'

'Pester you?' he derided. 'Oh, Kate, what kind of welcome is this?'

'What do you expect?' she retaliated. 'I thought you would have gone home by now.'

'No, not yet. We're in a spot of bother,' he said, 'or perhaps I should say, you are.'

'Exactly what is that supposed to mean?'

'It's rather a long story,' he told her, handing her a card. 'I've booked into a hotel not far from here, so meet me there tonight when I'll have more time to explain,' then on a cryptic note he went on to add, 'You see, they've issued a summons, and you're involved.'

He hesitated, his grin widening as he noted her stunned expression.

'I'll fill in the details later. See you there around seven.'

Kate stared after Greg's retreating figure in dismay, and she barely had a chance to gather her wits before she heard Marco's voice coming in her direction. She thrust the card into her bag.

'You didn't get very far,' he observed with a smile. 'Which picture captured your attention?'

'I've taken my time with them all,' she managed with forced enthusiasm, 'but perhaps that one is my favourite.'

'Yes, it's quite beautiful,' he agreed. 'Are you ready to move on?'

She nodded, and they left to go in the direction of Saint Mark's Square to view the Doge's Palace with its impressive stairway rising from the courtyard, and the Great Council Chamber above.

'You're very quiet, Kathrine. Is something troubling you?' he paused to ask as they came back into the open.

'No, I'm fine,' she assured him quickly, 'just a little overawed, maybe, but I'm glad you're here to explain everything.'

'The pleasure is mine,' he said, squeezing her hand gently. 'Perhaps you would like to look round my home after lunch. It also represents a tiny piece of the history of this city.'

'Thank you, I'd love to,' she agreed without hesitation. 'My aunt has told me about your fabulous art collection, and the lovely Venetian glass.'

He smiled over her enthusiasm.

'But first we shall enjoy a quiet meal together,' he decided, 'then you may take your time looking around.'

To Kate's dismay, the quiet lunch Marco proposed didn't turn out as planned. They had only just made a start on their first course when the dining-room door burst open and Camilla rushed in, followed closely by Marco's manservant who hovered anxiously in the doorway.

'Marco, I have to see you,' Camilla said, ignoring Kate completely as she went to his side. 'If I'm to move freely around the palazzo to arrange this exhibition I shall need your keys. Georgio seems reluctant to part with his without your permission. Will you speak with him, caro?'

With a brief nod, Marco dismissed his manservant, and turning to Camilla, he asked coolly, 'Couldn't this have waited until later? I had planned to take Kathrine round the palazzo after lunch.'

'But what about me!' Camilla exclaimed furiously. 'You know how awkward Georgio can be, and I can't think of lunch with this on my mind!'

'Sit down and be quiet!' he directly sternly. 'Starving yourself won't solve anything, and I think you owe Kathrine an apology for this interruption.'

Camilla appeared to resign herself to the fact that Marco wasn't to be moved by her angry display, and, forcing a brief smile in Kate's direction, she sank down on a chair.

'Forgive me,' she said, spreading her red-tipped fingers, 'I should not depend upon Marco so much.'

Kate acknowledged this with a stiff smile but as the meal continued she found it to be less enjoyable than she had anticipated. It wasn't the food, which was delicious, it was Camilla's incessant chatter dampening her appetite. But Marco reminded the dark beauty to include Kate in the conversation. He had spoken sharply in Italian, but by Camilla's petulant response Kate guessed what he had said.

'Is preparing for an exhibition hard work?' Kate asked the woman politely when the ensuing silence had become almost impossible to endure.

Camilla gave a harsh laugh.

'Hard work, yes! But I enjoy it if it is for someone special,' she replied.

To this Marco merely raised his dark brows. Kate was relieved when the meal came to an end so that she could take her leave, suggesting she come to view the palazzo another day. But he wouldn't hear of it and took her on the promised tour of the vast number of rooms, each containing remarkable pieces of Venetian glass and antique furniture.

Descending to the lower apartments surrounding the courtyard, they had just reached the foot of the steps when Georgio caught their attention from the direction of the rear entrance.

'Rose wishes to speak with you,' Marco translated after his short exchange with Georgio. 'I have asked him to allow her to bring the message to you personally.'

Murmuring her thanks, Kate looked expectantly towards the doorway to see Rose crossing the courtyard.

'Signorina, there is a gentleman on the telephone who wishes to speak with you,' the girl announced breathlessly.

Going towards Rosa, Kate frowned.

'Are you sure? I wasn't expecting anyone to call.'

'But it is your fiancé, Signore Courtney,' Rose said.

Kate came to a sudden halt and gaped at the smiling girl.

'My what? Courtney, did you say?'

'Si, Si, your fiancé. He is waiting to speak with you.'

'But he's not my fiancé!' she stammered as she turned to meet Marco's cold stare.

'Come, come, Kathrine, don't keep the girl dithering here,' he cut in. 'Your fiancé is waiting!'

And with that final icy reminder he swung round on his heel and quickly mounted the stairs.

'You are happy to speak with Signore Courtney, no?' the maid asked as they left by way of the stone bridge.

'No!' Kate almost sobbed, but seeing Rosa's

60

crestfallen look, added quickly, 'But you did right to let me know.'

'I usually answer the telephone when Signora Rossini is resting,' the girl explained and Kate knew that if her aunt had taken the call she would have dealt with Greg herself.

As they walked the short distance to her aunt's house she recalled Marco's icy stare of only moments before and her heart sank. What could he have thought? Dismally, she entered the house and made her way slowly upstairs to pick up the telephone.

'Just a reminder, be at my hotel at seven, or else,' she heard Greg say before she slammed down the receiver.

That evening, seated opposite Greg in the lounge of his hotel, she saw his old confidence return, the gleam of triumph in his eyes irritating her almost beyond endurance.

'Well, what was it you wanted to tell me?' she prompted sharply. 'My only reason for being here is to discover why the summons concerns me.'

'Before we discuss that, have a glass of wine,' he suggested. 'I don't want you having hysterics.'

'Which is most unlikely,' she responded coolly, concealing the tension she felt. 'In fact, I'm beginning to think this is just a ruse to get me here.'

'You won't say that when you see the papers I brought with me, but that will keep. Now, what will you have?' he asked, signalling the waiter. 'I'm not discussing anything until I've had a drop of wine.'

Despairingly, Kate selected a drink, and waited with increasing apprehension for the time when he would choose to enlighten her. Finally, she took a steadying breath.

'I understand we are here because you have something to tell me, so will you please get on with it,' she reminded him.

'We can't discuss it here,' he said curtly, rising to his feet. 'Come with me. The papers are in my room.'

'Then you can bring them down,' she directed. 'I can read them here.'

'Don't be stupid,' he retorted. 'They're private.'

He came round to draw back her chair, indicating for her to follow him from the dining-room to the brightly-lit reception area where he asked for his key. With mounting trepidation, Kate waited a short distance from the desk whilst the receptionist attended to Greg. Somehow, she doubted he was being frank with her yet would he have come all this way unless the matter was serious?

She was just reminding herself to be on her guard when the sound of a familiar female voice caught her attention and she quickly averted her head just as Greg strolled up, his room key swinging from his finger.

'As you're so impatient, let's go,' he said,

ushering Kate ahead of him as he turned towards the stairs.

Imagining the impression Camilla would have seeing them go upstairs together, she hesitated at the door of Greg's room.

'I think it would be wiser to discuss this downstairs. The lounge was almost empty.'

'I'm not going to eat you!' he exclaimed, grinning as he turned the key and indicated for her to enter. 'Anyway, I'd like to know more about this Italian pal of yours.'

'I thought you already knew, after all, your friend Webb was at the palazzo the other evening.'

'Don't know anyone of that name,' he denied and hurried on to say, 'I'd like to get a look at Ferrari's place, you know, do a spot of socialising. Any chance of you getting me in?'

'Certainly not! Greg, you really are the limit, and if I have any say in the matter I'll advise Marco against letting you in, so you'd have to ask him yourself.'

'Marco, is it? You haven't wasted much time. Actually, I thought you could find a way for me to have a look round. I'm interested in these old buildings but I can't be bothered with formal introductions. I notice Ferrari appears to enjoy a luxurious lifestyle, but I thought all those musty old palaces had been turned into museums.'

'Not this one. I've seen it myself and it's beautiful!' she returned crossly, then with a sigh of impatience reminded him, 'But I'm not here to talk about palaces, particularly when they're private.'

His eyes narrowed.

'But if I were to drop a hint about why you lost your job in England, I think he'd welcome me with open arms.'

'You wouldn't dare! I've a good mind to tell . . .'

He held up a silencing finger, and his lip curled in a sneer as he returned sharply, 'Ah, but you won't, not after you've heard what I've got to say.'

'Well, for goodness' sake get on with it. I'm tired of hearing your voice.'

'Ah, yes, the papers,' he said, withdrawing them from his briefcase, handing one to her. 'Read this first. It's the summons I received.'

'But it doesn't concern me!' she cried incredulously. 'Surely you haven't brought me here for that!'

'Then you may find this fax from my solicitor more interesting,' he returned with a sneer. 'And perhaps now you will listen to me.'

Kate's initial feelings of disbelief were quickly dispelled when he confronted her with the copy of the typewritten sheet. It appeared Greg was contesting the summons for cost of the damage he'd caused on the grounds he wasn't driving the vehicle at the time of the accident, naming Kate as the person who was.

'But you were driving!' she cried, completely

aghast. 'Surely you're not going to put the blame on me. I wasn't in the driving seat.'

He looked at her and grinned.

'If you remember, I was rather tipsy at the time, so I had to stick to my original story. In addition to that, I have no chance whatsoever of meeting those costs, plus my licence is already endorsed. You'd get away with it easily,' he continued with confidence. 'You know the owner of the building. Make an offer for compensation and say you were blinded by the lights of an oncoming vehicle, a dog ran out, or some such tale. You'll think of something.'

'But the road was deserted!' she gasped. 'And besides that, I haven't a licence.'

'You damned fool!' he cried. 'Why didn't you tell me this before?'

'You never asked,' she replied quickly, and reminded him, 'Anyway, you always said you would never trust women drivers!'

He calmed a little.

'Well, I suppose that could mean you'll get a small fine. At least you haven't a licence to lose.'

'Now look here, I didn't agree to you saying I was driving,' she returned hotly. 'You'd already told them that before I was fully conscious.'

He gave a hiss of impatience.

'Damn it, Kate, I had to give some sort of explanation, but I didn't think we'd hear

65

anything further.'

'No, Greg, you, not we,' she intervened sharply. 'I've suffered quite enough without having to lie for you as well.'

'Come on, sweetheart,' he cajoled, reaching for her hand. 'I know you won't let an old friend down.'

'Some friend!' she cried bitterly. 'Tell me, where were you during the time I was in hospital? No, Greg, you're, no friend of mine so you can count me out!'

He caught up with her as she reached the door, and forcing a smile on his flushed face said, 'Surely, you're not going to turn against me now.'

'Get out of my way!' she hissed, pushing him aside. 'If you try to stop me I'll scream the place down.'

'You'll regret this!' came the harsh response, his smiling expression quickly fading. 'Just you wait!'

Ignoring him, Kate hurried in the direction of the stairs, her anxiety increasing as his threats penetrated her troubled thoughts. What was she to do if Greg persisted with this story? And would anyone believe her should she deny it? She made her way back to the house, unhappily contemplating the steps she must take to prevent Greg involving her in this case.

*   *   *

'I can't imagine what Marco must have thought when Rose announced Greg as my fiancé,' Kate said as she faced her aunt across the breakfast table the following morning. 'I've got to give some sort of explanation, otherwise he may get the wrong impression.'

Signora Rossini nodded.

'I agree, he's bound to think it rather strange. Marco's reaction has really upset you, hasn't it?' she ended shrewdly.

'Yes, it has,' she admitted, though reluctant to mention the reason Greg had phoned.

She saw no point in involving her aunt in the matter of the summons, confident she could deal with it herself. But now, as she made her way to the palazzo, she could think of no suitable way to explain the call.

'Buon giorno,' she said brightly when Georgio opened the door. 'I would like to see Signore Ferrari.'

'The signore is working at his desk,' the man replied, inclining his head briefly as he beckoned her inside.

Thanking him, she made her way up the wide staircase, glancing down on the courtyard below as she reflected on how her opportunity to see the lower rooms and boathouse had been so dramatically interrupted. Fear rose within her as she recalled Marco's icy expression at the time. But it also added strength to her determination to put things right between them, and remembering which was Marco's study from her tour of the first floor, she knocked on the solid wooden door.

'Entri!' a voice commanded and she drew a steadying breath before entering the room to find him engrossed in the papers on his desk.

'Si?' he said, without glancing up.

'Good morning,' she murmured shakily and noticed his hand stiffen.

He continued writing for a few seconds before he slowly raised his head. As he got to his feet she met his stony gaze and continued hopefully.

'I'd like a word with you, if you're not too busy.'

He sighed and gestured to the papers before him.

'I do have a great deal of work to get through before lunch,' he said tersely. 'Can't it wait?'

'I only intend taking a little of your time,' she replied, gathering courage. 'You see, I feel I must explain.'

'There's no need for you to explain anything, Kathrine,' he broke in. 'I believe we concluded our tour of Venice so you are at liberty to spend the remainder of your holiday just how you wish. You are under no obligation.'

'Please, allow me to explain!' she cried in dismay. 'I didn't know Greg would phone me here.'

'Greg? Your fiancé?'

'He's not my fiancé. He was just being stupid,' she said, forcing a smile. 'In fact, I was furious with him for interrupting my visit. I was really looking forward to seeing the boathouse and . . .'

'Perhaps another time,' he broke in without enthusiasm, returning his attention to the desk. 'I believe you have already made another friend.'

'Friend?' she said blankly, then exhaled slowly as it dawned on her what he meant. 'Oh, you mean the man at the hotel? No, that was Greg, but I assure you I won't be seeing him again.'

He glanced up slowly, fixing her with an icy-blue stare.

'Why?' he demanded, the vehemence of his tone startling her. 'Is he not satisfactory?'

'How dare you!' she gasped. 'How dare you infer there is anything between us? You are the most presumptuous . . .'

'Presumptuous!' he echoed, his lips curling disdainfully as he leaned towards her. 'I understand you were willing to go to this man's room, so I consider my presumptions are well founded.'

'I was what?' she cried, meeting his stony expression.

He held up his hand.

'Please, spare me the need to repeat this sordid information.'

'But if you will only let me explain.'

'I prefer not to discuss your personal adventures,' he said coldly before he quickly turned away from her to go and stare through the window.

The heated colour left her face.

'I'll bet your informant almost choked over her dinner in her hurry to bring that tit-bit of gossip to you!'

Marco spun away from the window.

'So, tell me, what am I to think?'

'If only you would listen,' she reproached brokenly. 'I left the hotel soon after Camilla saw me, but you haven't given me the chance to explain.'

'Maybe not,' he admitted. 'Quite frankly, I was angry. I understood you to be unattached.'

Her heart gave a tiny jolt.

'And is that important to you?' she queried, her head held high.

For a long moment he merely held her gaze then, as if to avoid the question, said, 'Naturally, I wouldn't wish to cause any friction between you and this friend of yours by imposing upon your time. Even so, I had no right to lose my temper.'

'Quite,' she murmured on a note of disappointment, 'but, as I told you before, he is no particular friend of mine.'

'Yet you are still acquainted with this man?' he queried quietly, his dark brows lifting.

'I was,' she replied with emphasis, 'but that

70

is all in the past. Even so,' she continued as she reached for the door handle, 'I don't wish to impose upon your time by discussing my personal life.'

CHAPTER SIX

Kate's heart was heavy as she left the palazzo to hurry along the canal side. Marco had apologised, but there was a coolness in his manner towards her, and all because of Greg. She had considered revealing the reason for her meeting with him but, as she was in no way responsible for the accident, felt it was not necessary for her to explain.

She also had thought of mentioning her suspicions regarding Webb, but since Greg appeared ignorant as to whom she was referring, she had begun to wonder if her memory deceived her. However, although she hadn't realised it at the time, another matter had become clear. Greg had been aware of her visits to the palazzo but, unless Webb had told him, how could he know?

Once she was well away from the palazzo her pace slowed. She was enveloped by a feeling of despair over both her friendship with Marco and Greg's intention to involve her in the summons. When she finally returned home, hopeful of going to her room unobserved, Signora Rossini waylaid her to enquire if she had seen Marco.

'Yes,' she managed with forced lightness, 'and I've been for a stroll.'

'With Marco?'

'No, but in this lovely weather it seemed a shame to be indoors,' she rushed on then faltered, knowing tears were imminent.

'Oh, my dear!' the signora exclaimed gently. 'Come, tell me what troubles you.'

'I'm sorry,' Kate said, fumbling for her handkerchief. 'I'd rather not discuss it.'

'Just as you wish, but I assume I'm correct in thinking Marco was not too happy with your explanation of Greg's presence.'

Brushing away her tears, Kate nodded.

'He wasn't. In fact, he was quite insulting so I don't know why I'm allowing myself to get so upset about it.'

'A typical Latin reaction. He's jealous!' her aunt declared with satisfaction. 'Exactly what did he say?'

'It seems Camilla saw me go up to Greg's room at his hotel. Obviously, she exaggerated the situation, so he now presumes I spent the night there.'

The signora clicked her tongue reprovingly.

'But going to Greg's room was rather foolish, particularly after you told me it was over between you.'

'It is, and it wasn't anything like that. You must believe me.'

72

'I do, but did you convince Marco you and Greg are not . . . er . . . lovers?'

Kate sighed.

'I don't know, but when the time comes for me to go home, I'd hate to leave with him having a bad opinion of me. It's so unjust.'

'But you still haven't explained why you went to Greg's room in the first place,' the signora pointed out.

'I only went to look at some papers he had with him, nothing more.'

The signora cast her a shrewd glance.

'Concerning the accident?'

Kate gave a guilty start.

'How did you know?'

'I think I'm right in assuming there was far more to that accident than you've admitted.'

Kate sighed.

'In a way, yes, but nothing you should worry about.'

The signora threw up her hands in exasperation.

'Of course I shall worry, unless you care to tell me about it.'

'I feel I must tell someone,' Kate confessed in a shaky voice and reluctantly related the latest development in the matter of the pending summons, ending on a sorrowful note. 'And Greg has such a plausible tongue, who's going to believe me?'

Signora Rossini nodded thoughtfully.

'Mm, somehow, he's got to be made to own

up, though I don't like the sound of the threat he made. What possible connection could it have with your last employer?'

Kate sank into a nearby chair.

'I suppose you may as well know,' she began with a sigh. 'As you may be aware, I had taken a private post, nursing a lady who was terminally ill, and I really enjoyed working there. It was a perfect place to live, a beautiful house and gardens, and I got on with the family really well.'

'Why did you leave? Were they not nice people to work for?'

Kate pursed her lips for a moment, then went on.

'Yes, but then something occurred and I felt obliged to leave. You see, something quite valuable went missing and suspicion fell on me.'

'Oh, Kate, surely they didn't suspect you of stealing?'

'They didn't actually accuse me, they had no proof, but their manner towards me changed. I wouldn't dream of stealing from a patient.'

'I know that, but what an awful situation this must have been for you, and then for Greg to bring it up again now.'

Although Kate experienced some relief at unburdening herself, she still felt dismayed over Marco's hurtful remarks. Whatever reason her aunt had provided to excuse his behaviour, it didn't help to ease the fact his manner was now less friendly towards her. Why did it trouble her so much, she asked herself repeatedly as sleep eluded her that night. Could she be falling in love with this handsome Venetian?

Kate spent the following two days indoors, reluctant to go out in case she should encounter Greg. But, when Friday came, she agreed to accompany her aunt to the home of a close friend who lived on the other side of the Grand Canal.

The beautiful house they visited was not unlike the palazzo, though smaller, and it was only when the guests had assembled to go in to dinner that she caught sight of Marco across the room. Her heart gave a tiny lurch when she realised he was heading their way, and very soon he was standing beside them, tall and immaculate in a white dinner jacket.

'Signora Margaret, Signorina Kathrine,' he greeted them, smiling as he took her aunt's hand, though merely raising a dark brow in Kate's direction. 'I trust you are well?'

Kate gave him a tremulous smile, while her aunt immediately entered into conversation, issuing Marco with an invitation to lunch the following week.

'Unfortunately, I shall be away,' he said with a shrug of reluctance. 'I have business in Florence, but possibly the following week-end?'

'Of course, Marco, perhaps you will contact

me on your return,' the signora suggested then, as though it had just occurred to her, went on to say, 'Kate tells me she has not yet seen your wonderful paintings, or the boathouse. She was most disappointed to miss the opportunity last time, weren't you, dear?' she prompted, turning to her niece.

'Oh, I don't expect you to . . .' Kate began, but he raised a silencing hand.

'Why not join me for tea tomorrow?' he invited, and before she had a chance to decline, went on to insist, 'I'll expect you both around four.'

Kate's opportunity to resist was thwarted when the glamorous figure of Camilla appeared at his side.

'Ah, caro, you are here,' the woman purred, flashing her dark eyes in Marco's direction before she turned to Kate to enquire casually, 'Your fiancé is not here this evening, Miss Macleod? I was hoping to meet him.'

'Sorry to disappoint you, but I don't have a fiancé,' Kate returned, her manner equally casual, and taking her aunt's arm, suggested, 'Perhaps we should find our seats.'

Throughout dinner, although seated some distance from Marco, there were times when she could sense his eyes resting upon her and wondered what was in his thoughts. Had he felt obliged to invite them to tea tomorrow merely because her aunt had reminded him her previous visit to the palazzo had been curtailed, or had he extended the invitation in the hope of seeing her again? She wouldn't have thought him the kind of man who needed to arrange some social occasion purely to satisfy his wishes. He was far too self-assured for that.

The meal seemed endless and she had to make an effort to concentrate on the conversation around her as they relaxed over coffee. When at last it was time to leave, she breathed a sigh of relief. Being in the same room as Marco, with Camilla at his side, had made the occasion almost unbearable.

The next day, promptly at four, Kate and her aunt presented themselves at the palazzo. Wishing to keep the occasion informal, Marco had arranged for tea to be served in a small, comfortable salon overlooking the courtyard. The main topic of conversation was the weather forecast when he expressed his anxiety over the storm warning and the possibility of flooding as a result.

His expression was serious as he said, 'I dislike the thought of being out of Venice should this occur.'

The signora voiced her own dismay.

'It worries me, too, but I'll keep my eye on things as usual whilst you're away. Don't forget to leave the telephone number of your hotel.'

'I'll take my mobile with me. You have that number.'

Immediately tea was over, Marco suggested

they go and view his more valuable paintings which were hanging in a room just off his study near the head of the rear staircase.

'I don't like having to keep them hidden away like this,' he said as he went ahead to unlock the door. 'Such beauty should be available for all to see. They will be on show at the exhibition when I'm at home, and as you know I am in the process of having alarms fitted. Meanwhile, until I can ensure their safety outside this room, viewing is reserved for close friends.'

Kate gazed in wonderment at the pictures hanging there, some framed in heavy gilt, beautiful scenes of Venice, the Italian lakes and mountains, and others in plain dark frames which, he told her, were the most valuable of the collection. A few of the painters were known to her, but others, many of them priceless works, were not, yet Marco could relate their history in detail.

'It is like having, your own art gallery,' she said with a sigh of admiration as they left the room. 'You must feel very proud to own such a collection.'

'I enjoy having beautiful things around me,' he said with a smile as he locked the door, 'but I would like to share my pleasure with others. Once the fitting of alarms has been completed and in working order, I intend moving them into the grand salon.'

He tossed the key into the drawer of his

desk.

'Unfortunately, such drastic measures are necessary as paintings can so easily go missing. To improve security is the only way.'

She nodded.

'Yes, indeed, as you say, more people can enjoy them that way. But I thought you already allow certain visitors to look around the palazzo.'

'Only historians, or those who are really interested in our architecture,' he told her as they left his study to go towards the stairs. 'Only when I'm here, of course, and always by appointment.'

'Very wise,' she agreed as they descended the steps, the same route she had taken on that terrible day when Rosa had come into the courtyard below to announce Greg's telephone call, but now, with Marco guiding her attention to the area of the palazzo which was new to her, she cast aside that awful memory and listened to what he had to say.

'These are the servants' quarters,' he explained when they reached the ground floor, 'or rather, they were in years gone by. Now we are more considerate and put them on a higher level so they do not have to worry about the floods.'

'Does the water rise so high?' she asked in amazement as she looked into the dimly-lit rooms, shuddering in the cool atmosphere.

He laughed at her incredulous expression.

'Sometimes, in the spring when the tides are high,' he told her as he led the way over the stone-floored courtyard.

To the right of the rear entrance, under a vaulted ceiling leading towards the boathouse, stood an old gondola, its ornamental trappings green with age. It reminded Kate of films she had seen of the past when lovers took refuge in such a vessel, stealing unseen kisses as they glided along.

'It was used by my family years ago,' Marco said as he beckoned her towards a heavy, wooden door at the end of the wide passage and drew back the huge, metal bolt. 'In the past, most families owned their own gondolas but now usually they hire one. But now let us turn to modern means of transport. Come, see where I keep the launch,' he said and swung the door wide, standing aside for her to enter.

Down a short flight of steps, Kate's eyes travelled along the ceiling which fell to a mere seven or eight feet, and a floor sloping to a water-filled cavern below where daylight filtered in through a rusting iron grille. The heavy grille dropped below water level, protecting the palazzo from intruders. And there, in the water, lay Marco's launch, its gentle buffeting increasing each time boats passed on the canal outside.

'It looks very deep,' she commented, her voice echoing eerily round the damp stone chamber.

'Not so deep as when the floods are with us,' he told her. 'The entrance is completely obliterated, so all boats must be left tied up outside.'

Kate shuddered and turned away.

'I can understand why you are concerned over the weather forecast, particularly as you will be away. When exactly do you expect to return?'

He shrugged.

'Friday, at the earliest. I have a number of meetings to attend.'

'But won't Georgio be here if the waters rise? I expect he's used to it.'

'I've agreed to Georgio taking a few days to visit his sister in Padua,' he disclosed as they made to leave the watery cavern.

'You leave this huge place unattended?' she asked in surprise.

'Why not?' he queried. 'It is quite secure.'

And to add emphasis to his statement he drove the bolt in the heavy door firmly home.

'So I see.'

She laughed as they retraced their steps to where Signora Rossini waited.

It was just after Kate had thanked him for the interesting tour that Marco suggested a visit to the Isle of Murano the following day. Suppressing a surge of delight, she merely smiled.

'But you're going away on business,' she reminded him.

'Not until Monday, so tomorrow is a day for pleasure,' he said, casting the signora a questioning glance.

'Not for me, Marco. I intend to rest,' the signora protested laughingly, 'but I'm sure Kate will enjoy it.'

Turning to Kate, he raised a dark brow.

'So, it is just the two of us, yes?' He smiled. 'Can you be ready soon after lunch?'

CHAPTER SEVEN

Immediately after lunch the following day they set off in Marco's launch. During the morning Kate had been undecided about taking this trip. After all, only the previous week Marco had more or less stated his services as guide were no longer available, so she found his present attitude confusing. However, her spirits rose to the welcome breeze which swept over her as they left the busy canal to cross the lagoon.

'I am sure you will find it interesting,' he said as they disembarked. 'We can visit both the Guistinian Palace, and one of the factories.'

'I'm sure I shall. It is something I've not seen before,' she agreed.

'Our glass-manufacturing industry is world famous, dating back to the thirteenth century,' he told her. 'The heat of the furnaces must have been almost unbearable at that time.'

Standing on an earthen floor, fanning herself with her straw hat, Kate watched the craftsman. She was amazed to see how deftly he manipulated the rod he held after he drew it from the furnace to urge its tip of molten glass into the desired shape.

'Oh, Marco, just look at that!' she cried, marvelling at the final result.

'A skill which comes from years of practice,' he said. 'Are you pleased we came?'

She shot him a smiling glance.

'Of course, though I must admit I was surprised you suggested it. Not that I didn't wish to come,' she hastened to add, 'but after what you said in your office . . .'

'Unfortunately, I allowed myself to presume too much on that occasion,' he admitted a trifle stiffly. 'However, with the hope you will forgive my momentary weakness, perhaps we can continue as before.'

'Of course,' she murmured.

Once their tour of Murano was completed, they returned to where the launch was moored.

'I suggest we return to Venice for refreshment as it looks like rain is on the way,' Marco commented as he helped her aboard.

Kate glanced up, observing the swiftly-moving clouds.

'Have we time to call in that little café

where we had the accident in your launch? The man was so kind, I'd like to thank him.'

'Most certainly, though I have already called to assure him you were not seriously harmed.'

Just off the Grand Canal they tied up at the same mooring they had used on the previous occasion. They entered the small café which stood back from the water's edge just as the rain began to fall quite heavily.

'Signore, signorina!' the proprietor gushed, rushing forward to greet them. 'I have news for you!' he said excitedly, leading them to a table in a secluded corner of the room.

After Marco had ordered, he reverted to his familiar tongue when Kate lost gist of the conversation. She saw Marco's brows rise enquiringly as he spoke to the proprietor, then noticed the latter's excited response when he nodded in the direction of the canal outside and gestured expressively as he glanced her way. She assumed they discussed the accident and understood the word meaning boat. But when the word, Verdi, was spoken, she noticed Marco frown. Marco then spread his hands resignedly and sighed, causing her curiosity to increase. Perhaps it wasn't the collision they spoke of after all, but Camilla. She needed to clarify the Italian woman's place in his affections for her own peace of mind.

'I've been meaning to ask you about Camilla,' she ventured when the proprietor had left their table. 'Does she spend all her

84

time working on art exhibitions?'

'Not all her time. Organising fashion shows and cocktail parties plays quite a large part, and the odd art exhibition is fitted in when there's time.'

'I wonder where she met Jonathan Webb,' Kate pursued thoughtfully. 'Have you any idea?'

'No, can't help you there. But Camilla loves mixing with the rich and famous, so maybe he fits into that category,' he said with a smile. 'Why do you ask?'

Kate avoided his question and remarked, 'She's still young so I expect she enjoys her return to social life.'

He laughed quietly.

'During her period of mourning she rarely left the house then, quite suddenly, in the past six months, her feet haven't touched the ground.'

'Do you think she'll marry again?'

The laughter faded from his eyes as he said, 'Camilla possesses a temperament which is most impetuous, and also rather . . .'

'Possessive?' Kate ventured a trifle apprehensively.

'What makes you say that, Kathrine?'

'Well, she appears quite possessive where you're concerned,' she declared. 'In fact, I get the distinct impression she resents me being in your company, so I hope it doesn't cause trouble between you.'

It was a moment before he replied.

'I shall be relieved when the time comes for me to hand over my responsibilities,' he said. 'My degree in law came in very useful when she was widowed as her estate gave me many problems, but now everything is almost settled.'

'Oh, I see,' she murmured, barely managing to conceal her relief. 'Then she's fortunate to have the benefit of your advice.'

She was about to ask about the boat which struck the launch when last they were here, but then, with a half smile, Marco reached for her hand across the table.

'Do I detect a hint of my own Latin failing in you, caro?' he asked softly. 'Are you also just a tiny bit jealous?'

'Oh, Marco,' she murmured, her cheeks growing warm, 'of course not.'

'I had hoped you were,' he groaned in mock dismay, his eyes sparkling mischievously, 'just a little.'

She smiled at him, only withdrawing her hand when the proprietor returned to ask if there was anything else they required.

'Grazie, no,' Marco replied pleasantly, thrusting some notes into the man's hand, and to Kate he suggested, 'I do believe the rain has stopped. Perhaps this is a good time to leave.'

'When do you leave tomorrow?' she asked as they reached the launch.

'Mid morning, I expect,' he said as he untied

the painter. 'Georgio will take me to the station and from there we will go our separate ways. Will you miss me?' he added softly as he drew her into the shelter of the wheelhouse.

Realising he was awaiting her reply, she admitted quietly, 'Yes, I expect I shall. I've enjoyed coming out with you today.'

He smiled and started the engine, taking the launch out to reach the wide canal in the direction of the palazzo. As they travelled along, she uttered a small sigh of contentment, knowing she would eagerly await his return.

'You could have dropped me off at the bridge,' she said as they left the boathouse to ascend the steps leading to the palazzo's upper floors. 'I'm sure you must have things to do before you leave tomorrow.'

'Georgio will have the packing finished by now so I am not in a hurry,' he said. 'And there is something I'd like you to have before you go.'

Curious, Kate followed him into the salon overlooking the canal. But, before Marco would enlighten her, he went to pour two glasses of wine.

'I have a small gift for you,' he said as he brought the drinks over, and taking a slim box from his pocket he handed it to her saying, 'I hope this will be a little more permanent than the one I gave to you on your birthday.'

Intrigued, she opened the box and there, beneath a layer of tissue, modelled in fine glass, lay a perfect red rosebud, its delicate stem and single leaf a realistic shade of green.

'Oh, it's really beautiful!' she exclaimed, putting down her bag to lift it carefully from the box. 'It's so lifelike I can almost smell it.'

'Just a little something to remind you of today,' he said in reply.

'Thank you, Marco, I shall treasure it.'

Smiling, he caught her chin in his warm hand, lifting her face to his when he sought her parted lips.

'I shall miss you,' he murmured as he raised his head, then drew away from her as footsteps sounded in the corridor outside.

A cloud of dismay descended upon Kate when she saw the figure in the doorway. After those last precious moments, the unexpected appearance of Camilla caused the surge of happiness she felt to fade.

'Ah, I see I am not the only one to call to wish you farewell, caro,' the woman declared, strolling across the room. 'But, of course, Kathrine being a special friend, that is different.'

Kate noticed the uncertain glance Marco sent her before he invited, 'Are you staying for drinks, Camilla?'

'It was my intention,' she replied, removing Kate's bag from the settee before seating herself in a most elegant pose before she went on to add, 'And I have arranged for my American friend to be brought here. He will not be long arriving. You must meet him again, Kathrine.'

Kate glanced at her watch but she knew it would appear impolite to leave now, before Jonathan got here. When he finally arrived, it took him some minutes to settle down.

'That kid of yours is crazy, Camilla!' he exclaimed breathlessly. 'At the speed that young devil travelled, we must have cut the time by half.'

Camilla laughed shrilly.

'That is how I like to travel. It is more exciting.'

'I don't like to think of him endangering your life, sweetheart,' Jonathan interrupted.

'Or anyone else's!' Marco interjected sharply. 'I've already reprimanded him about another incident.'

'Which incident, Marco?' Camilla inquired.

Marco frowned.

'I think you are already aware to which incident I am referring, Camilla.'

Camilla shrugged.

'No, caro, I have no idea, but I like a man with spirit.'

'Spirit!' Jonathan spluttered. 'It's a great wonder the golden hawk hadn't gotten washed off the bows the way he travels,' he declared, reverting to a steady drawl. 'Damn it, the kid's mad!'

Kate sensed Marco's quick glance in her direction. She was convinced this boat Webb spoke of with its golden crest was the same one which had struck them. And this, no doubt, would be the reason Marco had spoken to its helmsman.

Noticing the rain had started to fall again, Kate suggested it was time for her to leave and accepted Marco's offer to escort her over the bridge. Keeping a careful hold on the little box containing her souvenir she said farewell to the others while Marco went in search of an umbrella.

'I hope we can meet again when Marco returns,' Camilla said pleasantly. 'Perhaps dinner one evening?'

'Yes, perhaps,' Kate murmured, forcing a smile, though she doubted the sincerity behind the invitation.

At the door leading out to the enclosed garden, Marco drew her under the shelter of his umbrella.

'Mind where you tread,' he advised, guiding her carefully between the puddles when she enjoyed the close contact with his body.

As they entered the hallway of her aunt's home he set aside his umbrella, and took her hands.

'Keep Friday evening free, will you, Kathrine?' he asked softly before his lips met hers in a farewell kiss.

Immediately he left, Kate rushed upstairs hoping to catch a glimpse of him on the bridge below. It was as though he had sensed her presence at the window as he looked up, raising his hand to his lips in an affectionate salute. Friday seemed years away.

When he left next day, Kate watched as the launch pulled away from the palazzo, heading for the station with Marco and Georgio aboard. The canal looked distinctly grey, reflecting the cloud-laden sky on its choppy surface. She turned her thoughts away from Marco's leaving to Friday evening, the evening he requested she should keep free.

With a tiny smile of anticipation, she searched for something suitable to wear on such a gloomy day, planning to take a further look at the smaller shops away from the main square. But when she had finished dressing and looked for her little crocheted bag, it was nowhere to be found.

'I must have left it in the cloakroom at the palazzo,' she said when she joined her aunt in the main salon. 'I remember having it with me when we returned from Murano, but not when I came back here.'

'All you carried was the box containing the rose,' the signora reminded her, smiling. 'You were far too happy to care about anything else.'

'Never mind, it will have to stay there until he gets back. It contained nothing of great importance, but I'd hate to lose the bag.'

'It will be quite safe,' the signora assured her, but as Kate was leaving she raised a warning finger. 'I hope that Courtney fellow isn't hanging around. Do be careful, dear.'

Kate smiled.

'Don't worry, I will, though I expect he will have gone by now.'

Even so, the signora's reminder left her with a touch of anxiety so, instead of the quieter alleyways and squares, she chose the well-used thoroughfares only a short distance from Saint Mark's square.

She was nearing Marco's shop which sold the beautiful Venetian ornaments. She paused to look at the dazzling display from the safety of the pavement outside. As her gaze travelled over the items on show, she was suddenly aware of being observed from inside and glanced up to see the face of the assistant, Luigi, whom she'd met on the previous visits.

Now, unlike the earlier occasion, he grinned as he raised his hand in recognition. Giving him a rueful smile, she acknowledged him with a wave, and was just about to continue on her way when she was jerked to a sudden halt and confronted by the leer of triumph on Greg Courtney's face.

'Thought I'd find you alone, eventually,' he said with a mirthless laugh. 'Now your precious Marco's out of Venice we can have that little chat.'

'Take your hands off me!' she cried as she wrenched her arm away.

'I asked you to get me an introduction, you

know, a visit to his palace,' he said, reaching for her again. 'I expect he'll have left you with a key.'

'No, he hasn't,' she shrieked, 'and if he had I wouldn't give it to you.'

'Remember your reputation, Kate. He won't want to know you when he reads the letter I've sent him. Of course, if you have a key, I can easily get it back before he sees it.'

To Kate's immense relief, Luigi appeared in the doorway of the shop.

'Is this man troubling you, Miss Macleod?' he enquired, casting a thunderous look in Greg's direction 'Shall I call the police?'

'Thank you, I don't think that will be necessary,' she managed, stepping away from Greg. 'I think he knows he's wasting his time.'

Greg raised his hands in a protective pose.

'OK, OK, forget the police. I'm going. 'But as he turned away he hissed, 'This is not the end of it, Kate. If you won't play the game my way you can suffer the consequences!' Then he dashed off along the crowded street.

'Would you like to step inside?' Luigi invited, standing back for her to enter the shop. 'I expect he was after your money, but threatening to call the police soon sent him on his *way.*'

Shocked though she was, Kate managed a grateful smile.

'Yes, I expect you're right,' she agreed shakily, 'and I'm grateful for your intervention,

but I don't think he will trouble me again.'
With a short laugh she added, 'Anyway,
perhaps it will be safer if I don't come inside.
Remember last time?'

Leaving Luigi chuckling on the doorstep,
she turned in the opposite direction to the one
Greg had taken. Determined not to allow
herself to be intimidated, she made for the
nearest café, planning to continue her
shopping once she had recovered her
composure. But as she sipped a cup of strong
coffee, her glance continually strayed to the
lace-curtained window. Anyone passing only
slightly resembling Greg caused her to tremble
afresh.

As she watched, it suddenly occurred to her
that Greg had known Marco had left Venice.
How could he have known, unless he had
observed Marco leaving that morning? Or
perhaps Greg and Jonathan Webb were better
acquainted than he was willing to admit, and it
was Webb who had given him the information.

CHAPTER EIGHT

Troubled by her encounter with Greg, Kate
returned home earlier than expected with the
excuse of the weather being too unpredictable.
She wondered about the letter he'd supposedly
sent to Marco, or was it simply an empty

threat, his way of manipulating her to gain entry to the palazzo?

She'd been distressed by the way her employment back home had been terminated, and although her employer had denied her a reason, she'd felt a cloud on her conscience, almost as if she had been accused outright of stealing. Her aunt had believed she was innocent, but what would Marco think if Greg had sent a letter suggesting she was guilty?

The following day, though determined not to allow the worry of Greg to keep her indoors, she experienced a curious sense of relief to see the weather was far from perfect as predicted. Greg always hated being out in the wind and rain, so it was unlikely she would encounter him today.

'I shouldn't go too far. By the look of the sky there's a storm brewing,' her aunt advised. 'According to the weather report, heavy rain and gales are forecast for the next few days.'

'That is exactly why I'm going, to see what all this talk of a storm is about. I've heard about the flooding, and Saint Mark's Square being under water. They say it's quite spectacular.'

Making sure Greg was nowhere in the vicinity, Kate strolled towards the Grand Canal, feeling the force of the wind on her face as she left the narrow street. There she saw boats buffeting noisily against their moorings as their owners strove to make them secure against the roughening waters.

This was a very different scene from the one she had come upon the day of her arrival and, to everyone's concern, the following day was the same. Only the sturdily-built waterbuses and motor launches ploughed their way through the turbulent waters of the Grand Canal and the wide lagoon.

Keeping well away from the narrow streets and the vicinity of Greg's hotel, Kate strolled along the waterside, watching the waves spray over the crowded moorings in Saint Mark's basin. She prayed the stormy outlook would keep Greg indoors. Then, furious with herself for allowing thought of him to intimidate her, she walked on until the rain increased to a steady downpour when she had to retrace her steps. As she hurried back to the house, thoughts of Marco's return lifted her spirits. Only two more days.

Smiling to herself, she jumped over the rapidly forming puddles on the uneven paving of the empty street until she was jerked back to the present by the harsh sound of an engine revving loudly from somewhere near the palazzo. She was just approaching the stone bridge when the echoing roar made her hurry forward in time to see a boat moving at high speed along the narrow canal. Though she couldn't tell who was at the helm, her heart lurched when she caught a glimpse of the emblem on its side. It was a large golden bird.

Filled with concern over the dangerous speed of the boat, she was about to turn in the direction of home when the sound of a terrified voice reached her ears. She paused. There it was again, a high-pitched scream, and another, muffled this time, coming from the direction of the canal. Heedless of the pouring rain, Kate moved quickly in the direction from where the sound came. Arriving at the bridge, she looked over the parapet. There was someone in the canal, clinging desperately to the iron bars of the gate safeguarding the entrance to Marco's boathouse.

With Marco away, she knew it would be a waste of time to call in at the palazzo for help so, seeing no-one close-by, she ran on to the bridge, casting aside her light waterproof coat. Without thought for her own safety, she pulled off her shoes and climbed over the lower end of the parapet to slide down into the swirling, dark water. Staying close to the damp, slimy wall of the palazzo as a safeguard against being struck by a boat, she swam strongly towards the gateway of the boathouse. As she drew near to the terrified form still clinging to the bars, she raised her head to assess the situation and gave a choking gasp of recognition.

With her long black hair moulded wetly to her head, Camilla bobbed up and down in the turbulent water, her screams of terror turning to sobs of relief as Kate came up beside her.

'Don't panic!' Kate directed firmly, grabbing for the iron grille where she attempted to recover her breath. 'Just hang on.'

But Camilla, wide-eyed with fear, let go of the bars and made a grab for Kate, almost pulling her under the water.

'Hold the bars,' Kate shouted, keeping Camilla's head above water with one arm, 'or you'll have us both drowned!'

Thankfully, Camilla obeyed, releasing the strain on Kate as she took further steadying breaths. Remembering the life-saving technique she had been taught during her schooldays, Kate took hold of Camilla and pushed herself away from the canal wall. With a sharp word of instruction, she kept the woman's head above water and swam the short distance to the bridge.

By the time they reached it, someone was calling from the parapet above and waving frantically at a launch that was coming in their direction. Wondering how she was going to get Camilla out of the water, she felt a surge of relief when the boat slackened speed and drew alongside.

It didn't take long for the owner of the water-taxi to haul the spluttering, sobbing Italian woman aboard with the offer to take her home. And, once she had satisfied herself Camilla was to be taken almost to her doorstep, Kate declined the boatman's offer of assistance, assuring him she was quite capable of climbing on to the bridge when she would be almost home.

Reaching for a finger-hold on the wall, she managed to haul herself from the water on to a narrow, stone ledge and glanced across to see the owner of the boat wrap a blanket around Camilla's shivering form. The woman appeared desperate to catch her attention so she held on.

'Don't tell Marco,' Camilla cried through chattering teeth, 'or Signora Rossini, please, Kathrine,' she implored. 'They must not know of this.'

Then her voice faded, drowned by the noise of the boat's engine. Kate almost slipped black into the water as the wake from the boat washed against her, but a man on the parapet called down. With aching muscles, she struggled to get her foot on to the next ledge when, with a grunt of extra effort, the man reached down a little farther and caught hold of her wrist. Once she could support her own weight, it was easy for him to grasp both her hands and help her over the parapet.

Reaching the safety of the bridge, she uttered a shuddering gasp and attempted to express her gratitude to the man who regarded her with puzzled interest. When she managed to explain why she had chosen to climb back on to the bridge rather than take the water-taxi, he appeared relieved, satisfied she would be home and dry in minutes. Draping her coat around her shoulders, he praised the English signorina for her bravery.

Suddenly, aware a number of people were beginning to collect around them, she realised her sodden appearance was causing more interest than she cared for. So, thanking the man once more, she slipped on her shoes and made off in the direction of her aunt's house. Recalling the woman's plea not to mention the incident, she climbed the stairs and made straight for the bathroom. However, before she reached it, her aunt spotted her.

'Good gracious!' she cried in horror. 'You look as though you've been in the canal!'

'I have,' Kate replied, striving to control her chattering teeth, 'and I'm about to run a hot bath and get out of these wet things. I'll explain later.'

'I should have warned you. The paving can be extremely slippery just now. You must be more careful,' the signora fussed as Kate disappeared into the bathroom.

Lying in the hot, scented water, Kate thought again about how Camilla had begged her not to mention the incident to her aunt or Marco. Why make such a request, she wondered, and how had she come to be in the water in the first place? Reflecting on the unglamorous picture Camilla presented as she struggled in the water, Kate knew for certain she could only have got there by accident. Yet, being familiar with her surroundings, it was unlikely she had slipped into the canal dressed in some fashionable creation, particularly as she couldn't swim. Kate was convinced there was something very strange about the incident, and this disturbed her.

Cosily dressed in a tracksuit, she took the cup of steaming hot chocolate Rosa had prepared and sipped it gratefully. Only then did she realise she would be expected to account for her soaking but, after Camilla had begged her not to reveal the truth, how was she to explain?

'Now you can tell me what happened,' her aunt began as she refilled her cup. 'I could hardly believe my eyes when you came in. Thank goodness you're a strong swimmer, but it must have been difficult to get out.'

Kate searched her mind for an explanation.

'A man saw me from the bridge,' she began, 'and he helped me out. You see, someone had fallen in the water. I couldn't ignore her.'

'You mean, you've saved someone's life?' the signora exclaimed, sitting bolt upright in her chair. 'Was it a child? Where is she now?'

'Don't worry, she's quite safe,' Kate assured her, and rushed on evasively. 'I expect it's an everyday occurrence here—slippery paving, a careless step. I often fell in the river at home when I was a child.'

The signora's eyes narrowed.

'Kate, I suspect you are hiding something.'

101

she pressed. 'Who was it?'

Kate sighed and looked away.

'Actually, it was Camilla,' she admitted quietly, 'but please don't say anything as she didn't want you or Marco to know.'

The signora gasped and leaned towards her.

'Camilla!' she exclaimed, but Kate merely shook her head. 'But why ask you not to say anything? What could be her reason?'

'I haven't the faintest idea,' she said and went on to relate what had happened in the canal. 'Of course, by telling you, I've betrayed her trust,' she ended with a sigh, 'but promise me you won't say anything to Marco.'

'If that is what you wish,' she agreed, 'but I hardly think she had the right to ask. After all, you probably saved her life.'

'Oh, I'm sure the boat that came along would have picked her up, but what puzzles me is how she came to be there in the first place.'

'Yes, it's very strange. Was her launch anywhere near? Could she have fallen from it?'

'No, but just before I spotted Camilla, a boat went away under the bridge at a terrific speed, and if the emblem on hers is a gold bird, then I'm sure this one had the same thing on its side.'

'Did you see who was at the helm? I never did trust that man of hers.'

'Actually, I believe I saw two people, men, I

think, both wearing wetsuits, but I didn't recognise either of them.'

'Two? I wonder, could one have been Georgio?'

The signora thought for a moment then discarded the idea.

'No, I don't suppose he owns a wetsuit.'

Kate shook her head.

'I really couldn't say, but in any case it would have been most unlikely he'd have left Camilla in the water.'

'You're right, he's too much of a gentleman. Perhaps Marco can enlighten us.'

'Only if he brings the matter up,' Kate put in firmly, 'otherwise, I won't mention it. After all, it really isn't any concern of ours. As it's not a matter of life or death, I'll keep it to myself.'

'It almost was, both for Camilla and for you!' the signora countered crossly just as the telephone rang.

'It's for you, Kate,' she announced moments later.

'It's not Greg, is it?'

The signora shook her head and put her hand over the mouthpiece.

'No, but speak of the devil, it's Camilla!'

Kate experienced a twinge of apprehension as she took the receiver.

'Are you all right, Camilla?' she enquired and couldn't fail to hear the heartrending sobs that came over the line.

'You won't tell Marco, will you?' Camilla gasped.

'If that is what you want,' Kate agreed, 'but I'm afraid Signora Rossini had to know as I could hardly expect her not to notice my appearance.'

'Please, I beg you, ask her not to tell Marco.'

Kate's responding sigh of impatience was quickly cut short when Camilla continued, 'Greg Courtney—he makes trouble for you?'

'Greg! What has he got to do with it?' Kate demanded.

'He seeks revenge,' Camilla replied. 'He makes trouble for you. I warn you because you saved my life.'

'Otherwise, you wouldn't have bothered,' Kate put in icily, and when Camilla protested she cut her short. 'Don't you worry. Greg Courtney doesn't frighten me!'

She then replaced the receiver.

'What was all that about?' her aunt asked when Kate returned to her seat. 'You sounded extremely agitated.'

'I was! That stupid woman has been listening to Greg and his ridiculous threats, but I won't allow myself to be intimidated!'

'Do you suppose there's any truth in it? I mean, if he's likely to cause you trouble, I'll call the police.'

'No, I'm ignoring the whole thing,' she responded firmly. 'Whatever he threatens, I'm not lying about the accident merely to save his skin!'

After her exhausting experience in the canal, Kate decided to follow her aunt's example and take a short rest before tea. She was lying on the bed with her book opened at the page where she'd left it the previous day when there was a tap on the door of her room and Rosa peeped in.

'I am very worried,' Rosa began, 'and I don't want to disturb the signora as she is sleeping now.'

Kate beckoned Rosa into the room. The girl pointed towards the window.

'You can hear something, signorina? I believe someone is calling from near the palazzo. I think someone is ill.'

'Oh, no, not again!' Kate groaned.

Even so, she rose immediately and went to the window, straining her ears for a sound. Then, there it was, the weak cry of what sounded like a male voice but she couldn't distinguish what the words were. Struggling into thin cotton trousers and a T-shirt, she called Rosa over.

'Will you come with me? I can't tell where the voice is coming from, nor can I understand what he's saying.'

Outside, on the bridge, Kate paused, straining her ears as she tried to decide where the distressed cries came from. Rosa had gone ahead to the door of the palazzo garden, but soon signalled to say it was locked.

'I think it is coming from where the boat must go,' Rosa said, pointing in the direction of the heavy grille at the entrance to the boathouse. 'It's calling for help in Italian. Maybe it is Georgio.'

'I think he's away,' she said, but thought it worthwhile to call his name to which there came a wavering response.

'Si, si, it is Georgio,' Rosa confirmed excitedly.

'Ask him where he is, what is wrong, and can we get in?' Kate instructed, and heard Rosa convey her request in the man's own language.

'We must go to the main entrance,' Rosa translated after a few minutes' wait. 'This door is unlocked, and he is falling on the floor.'

'But how do we get to the entrance from here, Rosa?'

'A boat! We must have a boat. This door is flooded.'

Kate grabbed her hand.

'Come on,' she said briskly. 'We can get a water-taxi round the corner, but I'm afraid you'll have to speak for me and explain that we'll pay later.'

At first they had a negative response from the boat owner until Rosa explained the reason for their short journey. Then, albeit reluctantly, he helped them into his craft and soon they were on the Grand Canal, mooring as close as it was possible to the palazzo's main entrance.

'Rosa, ask him to wait,' Kate directed, splashing over the flooded steps to reach the heavy main door.

With Rosa beside her, they made their way into the building, arriving in the cool courtyard where she called Georgio's name again. Recalling the direction of the passage leading to the boathouse, she hurried along as Georgia's voice grew clearer. And there, halfway down the flight of steps, they found him, struggling to drag himself up.

'There you are,' Kate said gently, her professional manner coming to the fore. 'Now don't worry, we'll soon have you more comfortable,' she continued, observing the man's shocked state. 'Translate for me, will you, Rosa? And do stay calm. I'm just going to check him over before he moves any farther. The position of his right leg doesn't look too good to me.'

Kate made a brief examination of the state of Georgio's health. The wound on his head was still oozing blood, and by what she could detect, he had been rendered unconscious by his fall. The position of his leg really worried her. Only a broken limb could lie in such a twisted way.

'He has just returned from Padua,' Rosa translated, 'and he was concerned about the boathouse in the flood.'

'I see,' Kate broke in. 'Well, he requires

hospital treatment so will you go back and ask my aunt if she knows the name of Georgio's doctor? Tell her we require an ambulance. Also, ask her for money to pay the boatman.'

CHAPTER NINE

Kate stifled a sigh of relief when the doctor arrived. She had covered Georgio's shaking form with the blankets Rosa had found, and with one of her aunt's clean towels against the wound on his head and a cushion tucked beneath it, she had managed to make him more comfortable.

As the doctor slid a needle into a vein in Georgio's arm he praised her efforts to keep his patient in a stable condition until the extent of his injuries became known. Rosa had been asked to await the medical team and bring them into the building, and it wasn't too long before they arrived to manoeuvre Georgio on to the special stretcher and carry him off to the ambulance boat.

'I think I'd better take charge of the keys after we've locked up,' Kate said. 'Signora Rossini will know what to do.'

Thankfully, their boatman was still waiting when they went out by the main entrance and locked the door. He took them back into the narrow canal where they struggled to disembark on the flooded sidewalk. Rosa paid him the required amount.

'One way or another, it's been quite a day!' she said once safely back in her aunt's house. 'Thank goodness Rosa heard poor Georgio.'

'Rosa believes he must have fallen on the steps but she couldn't quite make out what he was saying. I'll telephone the hospital later to enquire.'

'Marco will get a shock when he returns to find Georgio in hospital,' Kate remarked. 'And if he knew about the Camilla incident as well, I can't imagine what he would say.'

'If it hadn't been for you and Rosa, they both could be dead by now.'

'Oh, I doubt that, somebody would have heard them,' Kate responded with a modest shrug, 'although I must confess, I quite enjoyed putting my nursing skills into practice again.'

'Yes, Marco was most relieved to know you had rendered first aid.'

'You mean you've spoken to him?' Kate queried. 'When was that?'

'I have the number of his mobile phone, so I thought it only right to let him know Georgio is in safe hands.'

Later that afternoon, Kate received a phone call and the signora was delighted when Kate related the message.

'It was Marco,' Kate announced happily. 'He's coming back earlier than he originally intended and wants to take me out to dinner after he has visited the hospital this evening.'

'Oh, I'm so pleased for you, dear,' Aunt Margaret said happily. 'I'm sure everything will be all right between you now.'

'Perhaps his impression of me is not as bad as I'd imagined,' she said with optimistic cheerfulness, 'though he did say there were things we should discuss.'

'Then let us hope it is not in connection with what happened in the canal this afternoon. I'm worried, Kate. That devious creature is up to something, I'm sure, and I don't like it.'

'If you mean Camilla,' Kate replied, 'she's the least of my worries.'

But even as she brushed aside her aunt's concern, deep down, the reason Camilla had warned her about Greg continued to bother her. She wondered if Camilla had been in conversation with him and, if so, what had they discussed. Even more important, had Greg carried out his threat to reveal to Marco the reason Kate was no longer employed?

However, when Marco called later that day to announce his return, all her worries over Camilla and Greg were completely dispelled.

'Can you be ready in fifteen minutes, Kathrine?' he asked, and she had difficulty keeping the note of eagerness from her voice when she agreed.

'I have visited the hospital and had a word

110

with the doctor,' he continued. 'Evidently Georgio has suffered a compound fracture, also a great deal of bruising to his ribs. However, I was unable to speak with him as he was still under the anaesthetic.'

'I suspected it was a bad break when I discovered him, though he's in the best place possible,' she ended comfortingly.

'Thanks to you,' he said, and she could detect a smile in his voice. 'I shall telephone the hospital later, meanwhile I will hire a boat to take us to our little waterside café.'

'I shall look forward to that,' she murmured, replacing the receiver.

When the doorbell rang a short time later, she didn't use the intercom or wait for Rosa, but went down to open the door to Marco herself.

'How long have you been back?' she asked as he took her hand to lead her in the direction of the canal.

'Only seconds before I last spoke with you,' he replied with a smile. 'I haven't yet checked for business messages, or looked around the place. I just showered and changed, and hurried over here to take you to dinner.'

'I'm flattered,' she murmured.

'I asked for a table in a secluded corner so that we can talk in peace,' he told her, squeezing her hand. 'And by not taking my own boat, no-one will know we are there.'

It didn't take long for the hired water-taxi to

find its way to the little café. She noticed the proprietor glancing expectantly from the doorway, and on seeing them disembark he rushed over the paving to greet them. With a huge smile, he led them to the far end of the long room where he drew back a beaded curtain to reveal a cosy alcove. The table was covered in spotless white linen and in the centre stood a slim vase holding a single red rose.

'Now I have you to myself,' Marco began as the proprietor withdrew with their order. 'Tell me what has been happening during my absence.'

'Well, you know about Georgio's accident,' she managed to respond, concealing the matter of Camilla. 'Otherwise, little else happened worth mentioning. How about you? Was your business trip successful?'

'I think so,' he said slowly. 'I now have Camilla's financial affairs in order and no further responsibility in that direction. In addition, I have acquired three beautiful paintings of Carlo's for which Camilla had little regard. They will make a perfect display at the exhibition.'

'Camilla?' she queried with a slight frown. 'Considering she is arranging your exhibition, I assumed she would appreciate art.'

Marco leaned forward, brows raised.

'I regret to say Camilla doesn't appreciate Carlo's work, only enjoys the fame and attention which goes with it. But I want to see you smile again so let us forget everything else. We are here to celebrate. To begin, we should celebrate just being together, and then, well, who knows?'

Just then, the proprietor brushed through the curtain to place an ice bucket beside their table, and once he had the bottle of champagne expertly uncorked, he filled the two tall glasses.

'To us,' Marco said, raising his glass as he went on to add, 'I have missed you so, Kathrine,' and before she could respond he continued, 'During the time I was away you were constantly in my thoughts.'

'Was I really?' she murmured, happiness rising within her.

'Yes, constantly. Did you miss me?'

'Yes, I did,' she began, pausing as their first course arrived and she plunged into a more familiar topic. 'Of course, it's been raining hard most of the time, and we've had extremely strong winds.'

'Which is another reason I came back earlier than intended. I didn't want to find the whole place awash, and I must inspect the door leading to the boathouse. Although it doesn't hold back the water during a very strong tide, it does keep out the rubbish.'

At once, her thoughts flew back to her experience in the canal that afternoon and she shuddered.

'But I haven't brought you here to discuss flooding, Kathrine. I wish to know more about you.'

'I think you already know most things,' she said a trifle uneasily. 'I'm just a very ordinary person.'

'Hardly,' he said with a smile. 'I've seen you grow from a very pretty schoolgirl into a beautiful young woman who is far from ordinary.'

Her eyes widened, then she smiled as she realised what he meant.

'You're referring to the photographs my aunt keeps in her album.'

'Signora Rossini is always so proud of you. She often showed them to me, and I do believe I was a little in love with you then,' he ended reflectively as he took up his glass.

'Merely a schoolboy crush, I'm sure,' she supplied with a nervous laugh.

'My dear Kathrine, I most certainly was not a schoolboy. Had you not realised, I am at least ten years older than you?'

'Now you're teasing,' she said. 'No-one falls in love with a photograph.'

'Maybe I didn't realise it at the time, but during the last few days I have become extremely aware of what has been tormenting me. You see, Kathrine, I feel I have known you for longer than the short time you have been in Venice, and long enough for me to want to know your feelings.'

'My feelings, Marco?' she queried hesitantly. 'Do you mean . . .'

'Yes, your feelings for me,' he replied, taking her hand once more.

For a moment she was silent. She wanted to blurt out just how much she loved him, tell him he meant everything to her, but something held her back.

'I like you very much,' she whispered.

'Enough to marry me?' he asked softly as his fingers entwined with hers.

'Marry you!' she exclaimed in a hushed voiced. 'Are you serious?'

'Never more so. This was my reason for a celebration.'

'But you hardly know me,' she began breathlessly.

'Quite long enough to know you are kind and gentle, and sincere. You made me aware of that when I was a little overbearing with you once before. Now I find you possess many other qualities.'

Kate swallowed hard. Sincere! Marco didn't know everything. She couldn't possibly give him an answer, not now, with Greg and the problem of the summons hanging over her, in addition to the mystery concerning Camilla. What reply could she possibly give?

Kate spent a very restless night. Of course she wanted to be Marco's wife, more than anything else, but she couldn't possibly accept. She'd agreed that she could very happily live in

Venice, but still couldn't bring herself to reply to his proposal. He hadn't pressed her further, offering her a little more time to think it over.

'I assume your evening didn't turn out as well as you expected,' Signora Rossini commented the following day when she saw Kate's rather troubled expression. 'I thought you and Marco were good friends once more.'

'Oh, yes, we are,' Kate replied. 'In fact, he proposed to me last night.'

'Oh, my dear, I'm so pleased for you. I suspected he was in love with you, remember? You do love Marco?'

'You know I do,' Kate replied, 'but I can't agree to marry him until I've got the problem of Greg and that summons off my mind. Also, there's something nagging me regarding Camilla and her warning about Greg, and insisting Marco shouldn't know other escapade in the canal.'

'Darling, do remember you are not at fault in any way, and whatever Greg or Camilla choose to do is no concern of yours. Let them solve their own problems,' the signora advised kindly, 'and put them out of your mind.'

'Thanks,' Kate said warmly, 'I needed that pep talk. Somehow, Greg has made me feel like a criminal and I just wish he would own up.'

'Why not deal with that matter when, or if, it arises,' the signora suggested wisely. 'Personally, I think he's bluffing, though I'm sure Marco can advise you. After all, he has studied law.'

'I promised to ring Marco this morning, but before I agree to marry him I've decided to tell him the truth. I don't want to hide anything from him.'

'An ideal way to start a marriage,' the signora said approvingly. 'But what about the Camilla incident. Doesn't that count?'

'Yes, I suppose you're right,' Kate agreed thoughtfully then, recalling something Marco had said the previous evening, asked, 'By the way, do you know the connection between Camilla and the paintings?'

'Well, Camilla hurt Marco terribly. You see, she likes to live her life as though there's no tomorrow, and to repay her debts she sold some valuable paintings of Carlo's which originally had been intended for Marco. I believe she sold them to raise money for her trips around Europe.'

'Last night Marco said he had acquired three paintings during the time he was away,' Kate put in. 'He appeared highly delighted about it.'

'Oh, that is good news!' the signora exclaimed joyfully. 'I expect it is part of the collection I've just mentioned.'

'I gather from what he said, Camilla doesn't appreciate art so I suppose she wouldn't mind parting with them.'

'You suppose correctly. Marco must have

contacted every art dealer in the country in an effort to get them back. Now, don't you think it is time you rang Marco to enquire after Georgio's progress?'

Kate got her feet just as the telephone rang. The signora indicated for Kate to answer it.

'I was just about to ring you to ask about Georgio, I expect he will be conscious by now,' Kate began happily the moment she heard Marco's voice. 'And there's something I would like to discuss with you, assuming it is convenient for me to come over this morning.'

'So, you have something to confess?' he responded shortly, his tone bitter, making her wonder what he already knew.

'I don't want there to be any misunderstanding between us.'

'Misunderstanding!' he exclaimed. 'I consider that an understatement.'

'I'll come over,' she said hurriedly, and, replacing the receiver, turned an anxious face to her aunt to ask, 'You haven't said anything about the summons, have you?'

'Of course not, dear. Why do you ask?'

'Marco sounded very annoyed. I'd better get over there right away.'

CHAPTER TEN

It was Marco himself who called her in, and she hesitated as she saw him standing at the top of the wide staircase, his expression grim. He gave a curt gesture for her to join him.

'Come into the study,' he directed coolly, marching ahead.

When she reached it, he was standing with his back to the window.

'Is something wrong?' she asked, rushing on to add, 'If it's anything to do with Greg Courtney and the accident, I can explain. In fact, that is what I want to speak to you about.'

He raised his brows and queried, 'Accident?' as he went to seat himself behind his desk and beckoned her to the chair opposite. 'Yes, tell me about this accident.'

She was a little uncertain of where to begin.

'Do you recall the occasion when I was mistakenly thought to have been in Greg Courtney's hotel room?' she began at last.

'Mistakenly or not, I do,' he replied.

'I was there only a few minutes,' she insisted, 'just long enough to read a letter from his solicitor regarding a forthcoming summons.'

Noting a sudden spark of interest in his expression, she hesitated. Obviously, this was something he hadn't expected. Frowning, he gestured for her to go on.

'Perhaps I should explain how the accident happened,' she offered, and plunged into the full story, including details of her own injuries and the fact Greg had put the blame on her, saying she was driving when making his original statement. 'And now he expects me to continue to lie for him,' she ended with a despondent sigh.

Marco sat back in his chair, his expression thoughtful as he warned, 'It would amount to perjury, Kathrine.'

'I know, which is why I will not do it, whatever he threatens.'

He nodded, but when he remained silent she went on.

'I couldn't give an answer to your marriage proposal, not with this hanging over me, at least, not until I'd spoken to you about it.'

Her voice trailed off when Marco made no response. But she continued.

'Does it make such a difference? I mean, I have explained, so I hope you don't think I'm at fault.'

He gave a mirthless laugh and rose to his feet.

'My dear Kathrine!' he exclaimed with an expressive lift of his shoulders. 'What you have just told me has no connection with my problem here! Somehow, I have become a victim of my own foolishness,' he declared, his tone bitter. 'Come with me and observe the result.'

Curious as to what could possibly be wrong, she hurried behind Marco along the corridor leading towards the room containing his valuable works of art. Whatever it was, it had disturbed him deeply, and it seemed he thought her to be somehow involved. At the door of the room, he paused.

'This is what I returned home to find,' he told her grimly as he pushed it open. 'I wonder if you can also explain this!'

For a second Kate couldn't understand his anger until she moved farther into the room and saw the wall which had once been filled with beautiful works of art. Now there were two empty spaces on the lower row, and three more on the one above. Five of Marco's most valued pictures had disappeared, their empty frames cast aside on the floor below.

'Your pictures!' she gasped and turned to meet his hard stare. 'But surely you don't think I had anything to do with it?'

He gestured towards the ornate table in the corner upon which, to her amazement, she saw the little crocheted bag Rosa had made for her.

'Yours, I believe?' he said, extending his arm to prevent her retrieving it.

'Yes, but I didn't leave it in here,' she cried. 'It was either in the cloakroom, or the sitting-room. I didn't miss it until after you left.'

She looked up to find Marco's expression

121

had softened a little.

'I rather thought you hadn't,' he said more gently. 'It is too obvious. But someone placed it there to incriminate you, so don't touch anything.'

'But who would want to incriminate me?'

'That is exactly what I intend to find out!' he told her, but before he could continue, his housekeeper appeared in the doorway to call his attention.

Feeling utterly distraught, Kate gazed in dismay on the pile of empty frames as she waited for Marco to return. Then, suddenly, a dreadful thought occurred to her and her heart sank. Could this be Greg's way of taking his revenge? He knew Marco was away, but how could he have entered the palazzo?

When Marco came back she looked up to meet his steely gaze when he demanded, 'Why didn't you tell me you met Courtney whilst I was away?'

'I didn't meet him,' she denied furiously. 'He happened to be on the same street!'

'So, it was him,' he said with a bitter smile. 'Luigi described our, er, robber, perfectly. It was only by chance my housekeeper met Luigi this morning and, thank God, she is of a curious nature, otherwise I should not have known.'

'There is nothing to know!' she cried. 'I hardly spoke to Greg.'

'But he threatened you. Luigi heard him,

122

and you were very upset,' he stated, reaching for her. 'Did he persuade you to let him into the palazzo and tell him where my pictures are kept? After all, I believe you are in possession of Georgio's keys.'

'No, Marco, no,' she denied wildly. 'I wouldn't have told him that! In any case, my aunt has the keys!'

Retaining his hold on her, Marco continued, 'So, if he didn't coerce you into helping him, why were you so nervous? Kathrine, you must tell me all you know before I call in the police.'

'He wanted an introduction to the palazzo, but I didn't allow him to intimidate me. How could you even think I would!' she cried. 'But I can't prove my innocence. You'll have to accept my word.'

He uttered a harsh sigh and spread his hands in a helpless gesture.

'I do, but I wish you had been frank with me before I left,' he said heavily. 'Now you are threatened, my paintings stolen, and there's a connection somewhere, I'm certain.'

Deeply hurt, Kate couldn't help but feel he was accusing her of being involved, and she spun away from him.

'I don't know anything about your damned paintings!' she cried as she sped towards the staircase. 'Just leave me out of it!'

'Kathrine, come back!' she heard as she ran down the steps. 'Please, Kathrine, come back!' he repeated, but she rushed on heedless.

123

By the time she reached the door to her aunt's home, her anger was beginning to subside and uncertainty was creeping in. Was Marco accusing her of assisting the thief, or was his only concern that someone was trying to place the blame on her? She was certain that that someone was Greg. Hadn't Camilla warned her, and who else would wish to incriminate her?

Confident Greg was the culprit she decided to confront him right away, and it was as she hurried in the direction of his hotel that another thought struck her. Was Greg the only one to blame, or had Camilla assisted him? Also, what reason was there for Camilla being in the canal? Was there a connection between that incident and the missing paintings?

At the hotel reception she asked to see Greg but was dismayed to learn he had checked out earlier in the day. Her spirit of determination began to ebb as she left the building to walk disconsolately along the narrow street. But she had barely gone more than a few yards when she heard her name and glanced back to see Marco about to enter the hotel, accompanied by two men in uniform.

'Kathrine!' he called sharply. 'What on earth are you doing here?'

'Merely hoping to prove my innocence,' she returned, adding sarcastically, 'though I expect you assumed I'd come to warn him!'

'Don't be ridiculous!' he snapped. 'You are

not under suspicion.'

'I'd begun to doubt that!' she retaliated. 'But we've both made a wasted journey. He's already left!'

She heard Marco's muffled curse, then he hailed her once more.

'I'll see you later. I want to know how the devil you and Camilla came to be in the canal!'

'Why don't you ask her?' Kate shot back and saw the policemen direct him towards the water's edge.

'I intend to!' he returned before moving quickly out of sight in the direction of the waiting launch.

There was now nothing left to do but go home, she decided dismally as she retraced her steps. Yet, when she reached the house she found her aunt in a very agitated state.

'Where on earth have you been?' the signora demanded crossly. 'Marco telephoned more than half an hour ago, expecting you to be here.'

'So much has happened today, you would never believe it!'

'Yes, I would,' her aunt replied. 'Marco told me all about it when he rang. Now he's gone off to find Courtney so, hopefully, it will all be sorted out.'

'I know, I've just seen him, but I'm afraid we were both unlucky. Greg's already checked out of his hotel.'

'You went to his hotel? Oh, Kate, that

wasn't very wise!'

'I wanted to challenge him about the theft, but I was too late,' she explained, and on a sudden thought asked, 'By the way, how did Marco find out I'd been in the canal?'

'I told him,' the signora admitted defiantly. 'As soon as he told me they had discovered entry to the palazzo had been gained by way of the boathouse, I was convinced that Camilla had something to do with it. I'm sorry to break a confidence, but I felt he ought to know.'

With a sad shake of her head, Kate agreed.

'It really doesn't matter any more. I'm tired of hearing about Camilla, and paintings, also the fact I seem to be involved. It's just too much!'

Signora Rossini's brows lifted in surprise.

'Really, Kate,' she said gently, 'this is not like you. Marco doesn't consider you are at fault, you know. He's more concerned with who has tried to involve you, and he was horrified when he heard about you risking your life in the canal.'

'I would hardly have described him as horrified or concerned this morning!' Kate exclaimed indignantly.

'Yes, he admitted he had upset you. He will want to make amends.'

'I'd rather he didn't bother,' Kate began. 'He's so arrogant! I hate him!'

'He believes passionately in fair play, but arrogant, certainly not!' the signora admonished. 'He'll stand by you, my dear, because he loves you.'

* * *

It was in the early evening when Marco called. Kate wasn't prepared for his visit and quickly rose from the settee, seeking an excuse to escape.

'Please stay, Kathrine, I have a great deal to tell you,' he insisted.

'I'm not in the least interested in anything you have to say,' she responded bitterly, turning away.

'But before I continue,' he persisted, 'I want you to believe I hold you in no way responsible for what has happened.'

'That wasn't the impression I had earlier!' she shot back angrily. 'In fact, I almost expected to be arrested by those policemen you had with you!'

'Obviously, I must have expressed myself badly and I hope you will forgive me if I gave that impression.'

'It really doesn't matter, one way or the other,' she shrugged.

'Oh, yes, it does!' he declared passionately, advancing towards her. 'Before you condemn me, you will listen to what I have to say.'

'No, Marco,' she retorted. 'There's nothing more to say.'

'Kathrine, I have asked you to be my wife,'

127

he reminded her more gently. 'Doesn't that give an indication of my true feelings towards you?'

The appeal in his eyes began to melt her anger, and with a long, wavering sigh she shook her head and said brokenly, 'I'm so confused, I don't know what to believe.'

'Believe me, Kathrine,' he murmured. 'I'll always love and protect you.'

'Oh, Marco, I want to, but with this hanging over me how can I . . .'

She spread her hands in a helpless gesture as the signora came into the room. Marco indicated for her to stay, and, placing an arm round Kate's shoulders, he led her over to the settee.

'I have made a great deal of progress since I last spoke with you,' he said, seating himself beside her. 'After you saw me at the hotel I went immediately to the airport.'

'Why the airport?'

'Because that was where I hoped to find Courtney, and I was right. He was waiting for his flight back to London.'

'You saw him!' she cried. 'What did he say?'

Marco looked at her with laughter in his eyes.

'Kathrine, if you continue to interrupt I shall use devious means to silence you,' he threatened, then went on to say, 'I wish you could have seen his expression when the police arrested him. He was absolutely astounded!

And, can you believe it, he actually had the paintings with him, simply rolled up in a plastic bag!'

'But you got them back?' she asked anxiously.

'Yes, I did, though at first he wouldn't admit to taking them. He told me Camilla had given them to him, and he had presumed they belonged to her.'

'Can they be restored?'

'I expect so as they were removed with reasonable care though, unfortunately, it will delay the exhibition,' he told her. 'However, here comes the interesting part. Guess who was travelling with him?'

'Who? Please, Marco, don't keep me in suspense.'

'Our American friend, Webb, who soon lost his accent in the scuffle. Of course, Webb denied knowing Courtney. He got quite nasty. But when more police arrived he soon backed down. According to the police,' he went on, 'Webb has been involved in art theft all over Europe, and used Greg in the process, and now I understand they were responsible for a theft from your previous employer.'

Kate's eyes narrowed.

'How did you know about that?' she asked, with a glance in her aunt's direction.

'You were going to tell him about that yourself,' the signora reminded her, 'so there was no point in delaying.'

Marco smiled.

'You have no need to worry, Kathrine. I didn't consider you at fault. After you rushed away from me earlier, Signora Rossini and I had a little chat, and it was then I learned about the dreadful time you have had concerning the accident and your loss of employment. You have suffered all this unnecessarily as, if I had known before, I could have advised you about what steps to take.'

'I realise that now. I was sure I'd met Webb before, and when both he and Courtney turned up here it seemed more than just a coincidence.'

'Indeed it was, and they both tried to implicate you in the theft. Of course, I realised Webb was a professional thief and Courtney merely a weak character who was easily manipulated. This being so, Courtney quickly confessed to how the theft had been committed.'

'Did you discover what part Camilla played in all this?' Signora Rossini queried with a shrewd glance in her niece's direction.

'Indeed, I did,' he said gravely. 'I left a very subdued Camilla after we had spoken about the trouble she has caused, and this time she had the decency to appear contrite. She tells me she was on the point of coming to me with her confession. After what you did, Kathrine, she actually felt guilty. Knowing you would risk your life for her after she had helped Webb and Courtney with their plans to discredit you made her realise what a fool she had been. But in future she must take responsibility for her own recklessness. I've done everything Carlo expected of me so I suggested she leave Venice.'

He broke off and turned to Kate, taking her hand as he went on.

'Actually, I found her only too willing to comply.'

'What puzzles me is, how did Camilla come to be in the water in the first place?' Kate said.

'It seems that Courtney and Webb used her launch and she had acted as lookout for when they came out with the goods. But in their hurry to get away she fell into the water.'

'Fortunately for Camilla, Kate spotted her shortly afterwards,' the signora put in.

'She tells me it was all Courtney's and Webb's doing,' Marco said. 'Evidently they wore wet suits to enter the palazzo by swimming under the boathouse grille and breaking the bolt on the inner door while she waited in her launch. According to her, Webb took over the wheel and pulled away so quickly she fell overboard.'

'Her launch?' Kate queried, recalling how she'd caught a glimpse of a boat speeding away just before she had heard Camilla's cries for help.

'Yes, her boat,' Marco confirmed, 'and not the first time she has caused trouble with it.

Remember, near our little restaurant? However, on this occasion, Webb and Courtney contrived to use her launch purely for their own convenience. Georgio was fully conscious when the police and I visited this afternoon and he told us he'd found the inner boathouse door was damaged and blamed the pressure of the floodwater, until he was knocked down the steps by the escaping thieves. Of course, when I returned nothing appeared to have been disturbed, that is, until this morning when I unlocked the room where my paintings are kept.'

'And you immediately thought I was the culprit,' she reminded him.

'Of course not!' he exclaimed with a sigh of exasperation. 'But I was concerned Courtney might have pressed you into telling him where the paintings were, though I know you wouldn't have been a willing partner.'

'I suppose I should at least be grateful for that!' she rejoined.

'Ah, yes, but do remember, you had shown an interest in who would be left in charge of the palazzo whilst I was away. You knew where I kept the key and, as you are now aware, Courtney had been overheard threatening you. Oh, Kathrine, you must understand, I was so furious it rocked my judgment, and if I gave the wrong impression I'm extremely sorry.'

Meeting the appeal in his eyes, Kate couldn't help but smile and, taking this as a sign of forgiveness, Marco cupped her face in his warm hands and kissed her. A little surprised by this show of affection, she drew away and glanced towards the chair opposite, but the signora was no longer there. Marco chuckled.

'Yes, we are alone, and now the time has come for you to give me your answer,' he said softly as he drew her close. 'I love you so much and, more than anything, I want you to be my wife.'

'So you do trust me?' she whispered, looking up into his eyes.

'Completely, darling,' he murmured against her cheek, 'and I will never allow anyone to come between us,' he continued before capturing her lips once more.

'I must go home next week,' she reminded him as they drew apart. 'My ticket expires, and my parents, they ought to know everything.'

He raised a dark brow.

'Know? Does that mean your answer is "yes"?'

'Yes, Marco,' she replied on a deep sigh, 'but I'd like to return and be married in Venice.'

'Then I shall accompany you back home,' he declared. 'I cannot bear being parted from you ever again.'

133

We hope you have enjoyed this Large Print book. Other Chivers Press or Thorndike Press Large Print books are available at your library or directly from the publishers.

For more information about current and forthcoming titles, please call or write, without obligation, to:

Chivers Large Print
published by BBC Audiobooks Ltd
St James House, The Square
Lower Bristol Road
Bath BA2 3BH
UK
email: bbcaudiobooks@bbc.co.uk
www.bbcaudiobooks.co.uk

OR

Thorndike Press
295 Kennedy Memorial Drive
Waterville
Maine 04901
USA
www.gale.com/thorndike
www.gale.com/wheeler

All our Large Print titles are designed for easy reading, and all our books are made to last.

**Welcome to the world
of Sydney Harbour Hospital**

**(or *SHH*... for short—
because secrets never stay hidden for long!)**

Looking out over cosmopolitan Sydney Harbour, Australia's premier teaching hospital is a hive of round-the-clock activity—with a *very* active hospital grapevine.

With the most renowned (and gorgeous!) doctors in Sydney working side by side, professional and sensual tensions run sky-high—there's *always* plenty of romantic rumours to gossip about...

Who's been kissing who in the on-call room? What's going on between legendary heart surgeon Finn Kennedy and tough-talking A&E doctor Evie Lockheart? And what's wrong with Finn?

Find out in this enthralling new eight-book continuity from Medical Romance™—indulge yourself with eight helpings of romance, emotion and gripping medical drama!

Sydney Harbour Hospital
***From saving lives to sizzling seduction,
these doctors are the very best!***

Dear Reader

How much fun was this?! Being part of an eight-book series set in gorgeous Sydney, Australia, and working with seven other fabulous Aussie authors was an absolute delight. It made me long for my days working in a big hospital, even though the doctors weren't nearly as gorgeous as the ones you'll meet in this series, but their stories resonated with me. Big hospitals are like a country town—everyone knows everyone else *and* everyone else's business—and 'SHH' is no different.

I especially loved the Lockheart sisters: eldest sister Evie, who has gone against her father's wishes to become a doctor and has had to prove herself in the hospital which was established by her great-grandfather; middle sister Bella, who not only has 'middle sister' syndrome but also a serious medical condition; and Lexi, the youngest, whose extroverted personality hides a tragic secret.

The sisters share an extremely close bond due to circumstances, and to be able to see their story develop over the course of the series, and in particular in Melanie's book and now mine, was fantastic.

Bella longs for lots of things—to be healthy, to be loved, and to be more like her extroverted, confident, gorgeous sisters—but she's worried she might not live long enough to achieve any of her dreams. Despite her situation she manages to stay positive, considerate and generous, and I love that about her. She deserves to have her dreams come true, and charming orthopaedic surgeon Charlie Maxwell is just the man she needs to help her.

I have really enjoyed getting to know these girls and their men, and I hope you enjoy their stories too.

Love

SYDNEY HARBOUR HOSPITAL: HOSPITAL: BELLA'S WISHLIST

BY
EMILY FORBES

First published in Great Britain 2012
by Mills & Boon, an imprint of Harlequin (UK) Limited.
Large Print edition 2012
Harlequin (UK) Limited, Eton House,
18-24 Paradise Road, Richmond, Surrey TW9 1SR

© Harlequin Books S.A. 2012

Special thanks and acknowledgement are given
to Emily Forbes for her contribution to the
Sydney Harbour Hospital series

ISBN: 978 0 263 22488 7

Recent titles by Emily Forbes:

GEORGIE'S BIG GREEK WEDDING?
BREAKING HER NO-DATES RULE
NAVY OFFICER TO FAMILY MAN
DR DROP-DEAD-GORGEOUS
THE PLAYBOY FIREFIGHTER'S PROPOSAL

**These books are also available
in eBook format
from www.millsandboon.co.uk**

Dedication:

To Marion, Alison, Amy, Fiona,
Melanie, Fi and Carol.

Thank you for making this such a wonderful
experience. It was an absolute pleasure
working with you all!

And to Lucy and Flo.
Thank you both for all your hard work
in making this series
something we can all be proud of.

Sydney Harbour Hospital

Sexy surgeons, dedicated doctors,
scandalous secrets, on-call dramas…

Welcome to the world of Sydney Harbour Hospital
(or *SHH…* for short—
because secrets never stay hidden for long!)

New nurse Lily got caught up in the hotbed of hospital gossip in
SYDNEY HARBOUR HOSPITAL: LILY'S SCANDAL
by Marion Lennox

And gorgeous paediatrician Teo came to single mum Zoe's rescue in
SYDNEY HARBOUR HOSPITAL: ZOE'S BABY
by Alison Roberts

Then sexy Sicilian playboy Luca finally met his match in
SYDNEY HARBOUR HOSPITAL: LUCA'S BAD GIRL
by Amy Andrews

And Hayley opened Tom's eyes to love in
SYDNEY HARBOUR HOSPITAL: TOM'S REDEMPTION
by Fiona Lowe

Last month heiress Lexi learned to put the past behind her…
SYDNEY HARBOUR HOSPITAL: LEXI'S SECRET
by Melanie Milburne

This month adventurer Charlie helps shy Bella fulfil her dreams—
and find love on the way in
SYDNEY HARBOUR HOSPITAL: BELLA'S WISHLIST
by Emily Forbes

There are two more books to come in this fantastic series.

SYDNEY HARBOUR HOSPITAL: MARCO'S TEMPTATION
by Fiona McArthur

SYDNEY HARBOUR HOSPITAL: AVA'S RE-AWAKENING
by Carol Marinelli

And not forgetting *Sydney Harbour Hospital's* legendary heart
surgeon Finn Kennedy. This brooding maverick keeps his women
on hospital rotation… But can new doc Evie Lockheart unlock the
secrets to his guarded heart? Find out in this enthralling new eight-
book continuity from Mills & Boon® Medical Romance™.

A collection impossible to resist!

These books are also available in ebook format
from www.millsandboon.co.uk

PROLOGUE

'LEXI, please, can't you do this for me?' Bella Lockheart begged her younger sister.

Bella was feeling dreadful. Her chest was hurting and every breath she took was a struggle. Her temperature was escalating with every passing minute and it felt as though her forehead was on fire. She wanted to be upstairs, in bed, not sitting at one end of her father's massive dining room table that comfortably seated eighteen people. She wanted to close her eyes and sleep. The only reason she'd agreed to meet with her sisters was because she wanted the chance to try to persuade Lexi to do this one thing for her.

Lexi was sitting at the head of the table with Bella on her left and their older sister Evie on her right. Evie had joined them at Lexi's invitation to begin planning what Lexi described as 'Sydney's society wedding of the decade' and, knowing

Lexi and her talent for planning events, her wedding to cardiothoracic surgeon Sam Bailey would be one of the most spectacular events Sydney had witnessed for some time. That was unsurprising really—Lexi had plenty of experience as she was employed by her father's multi-million-dollar empire to run the events side of his company, and Lexi generally got what she wanted. Bella had some doubts about whether Sam was as keen on the idea of a huge wedding as Lexi was but if she'd learnt anything about Sam since he'd proposed to her sister it was that he wouldn't sweat the small stuff, and if an enormous wedding made Lexi happy, that's what she would get. Their father would never quibble either; nothing was ever too much trouble, expense or fuss for Lexi. Richard loved an extravaganza as much as Lexi did.

Bella knew the only way to get Lexi to move quickly on the wedding was to play the only card she had. 'I want to see you get married and the longer you wait the less chance I'll have of being there. Please.'

They all knew the odds of Bella seeing her

next birthday weren't good but Bella had *never* played this card before. Not with her father, who had pretty much ignored her for her entire life, or with her mother, who couldn't cope and had replaced her family with bottles of gin, or with her sisters, who had always been there to support and protect her. But she figured if there ever was a time to play this card, it was now.

As Bella watched Lexi, waiting for her response, she was aware that Evie had stopped flicking through the pile of bridal magazines and was watching them both. The highly polished wood surface of the antique table reflected their images. The golden highlights in Evie's brown hair shone in the surface of the table and Lexi's platinum-blonde hair glowed in the reflection, while the dark auburn of Bella's curly locks was absorbed into the wood, making her seem dimmer in comparison. A sigh escaped Bella's lips. Seeing herself as a duller reflection of her sisters was nothing new. She'd had twenty-six years to get used to the idea that she wasn't as beautiful, intelligent or amusing as her two sisters, although she hoped that her kind heart went some way towards redeeming her character.

Not that it seemed to count for anything as far as her parents were concerned. She'd given up trying to mend those relationships, although she was blowed if she would give up on her sisters. They were the most important people in her world and she did not intend to miss out on seeing her younger sister get married. She *had* to convince Lexi to set a date for her wedding and make it soon. She'd missed out on an awful lot of things in her relatively short life and there was no way she was going to sit back and miss out on this. Lexi had to listen to her.

'You only need a month and a day to register. You could be married before Christmas,' she insisted.

'I need time,' Lexi replied.

Time. The one thing Bella didn't have. She knew that. Lexi knew it too, so why wouldn't she agree?

'Time for what?' Bella countered. 'I can't see why you'd want to wait. If I had the chance to get married, I'd grab it.'

All three of them knew what a romantic Bella

was. Her favourite pastime was watching romantic movies, comedies, dramas, anything, as long as it had a happy ending. It was looking increasingly unlikely that she would get her own happy ending so she had to enjoy other people's. She adored weddings, she'd been glued to the television for the most recent British Royal wedding and avidly followed the lives of modern-day princesses in the magazines. But her own sister's happy ending was bound to be so much better than anything she could watch on television. Surely Lexi couldn't deny her this?

'I want time to find the perfect dress,' Lexi said.

'I'll design you the perfect dress.' Normally Bella would offer to make it too, but she knew she'd never have time to design and make a wedding dress, not if she wanted the wedding to take place this year. In a parallel universe her dream was to be a fashion designer and to see her sister walk down the aisle in something she'd created would be the icing on the cake for a romantic like her. But she'd have to settle for designing the dress and have someone else make it. Their father would probably fly Lexi to Hong Kong or even Paris to get it made. Money was no object. Richard Lockheart was phenomenally wealthy and Lexi was the apple of his eye. Everybody knew that.

'Look,' Bella said as she opened the sketch book that was lying on the table in front of her. Her sketch book was never far from her side. She turned some pages and then spun the book to face Lexi. 'I've already started.' The large page was covered with half a dozen wedding dresses—a halterneck, a strapless version, some with full skirts, some in figure-skimming satin. 'You just need to tell me which bits you like and I promise you'll be the most beautiful bride but, please, don't wait too long. You *know* time is running out for me, Sam told you that. If you won't listen to me, would you at least listen to him?' Bella paused to catch her breath. She could feel her chest tightening and could hear herself wheezing. 'What do you think, Evie? You agree with me, don't you?'

'I think you have a valid point but it is Lexi and Sam's decision. It's their wedding.' Bella would have argued if she'd had the breath to spare but the end of Evie's answer was partially drowned out by a coughing fit. Bella's slim frame shook with each spasm.

Lexi stood up. 'I'll get you a glass of water.'

'It's all right,' Bella replied as the coughs subsided and she caught her breath, 'I can get it.' She pushed her chair back from the table and stood. She looked at Evie and dipped her head slightly towards Lexi, silently imploring Evie to intercede on her behalf. She knew Evie would understand the signal. Having spent so much of their life relying on each other, all three sisters could read each other instinctively.

'Perhaps you should talk it over with Sam,' Bella heard Evie suggest as she went to the kitchen to pour herself a glass of water and mix up her salt replacement solution. She was feeling quite feverish now and she knew she was in danger of dehydrating more rapidly than usual if she was running a temperature.

Evie waited until Bella had time to reach the kitchen and be out of earshot. As so often happened, her younger sisters deferred to her to solve any difference of opinion between them. At five years older than Bella and seven years older than Lexi she had taken over mothering duties at the tender age of nine when the girls' mother had walked out and left them with their father, to return only sporadically over the ensuing years. There had been a succession of nannies, with varying degrees of success, and Evie had adopted the role of mother and still maintained it twenty-two years later. Evie never minded the responsibility but she did wonder why she needed to act as referee in this case. Why was Lexi so resistant to Bella's request?

'What's the problem, Lex? You know Bella's right. She might not be around in six months. Why do you want to wait?'

Lexi's deep blue eyes shimmered with unshed tears. She fidgeted with Bella's sketch book, which lay on the table in front of her, absent-mindedly doodling on the clean pages. 'I can't think like that. I can't stand the thought of Bella not being here.'

'That's why I think you should consider getting married sooner rather than later.'

'But what if we set a date that's soon and Bella gets sick again? She could be in hospital on the day of the wedding. Or what if she's in surgery? If I wait until Bella is okay, we'll all get a happy ending.'

'But Bella might not get her happy ending. You know that, don't you?' Evie said gently. 'If you wait, Bella might not be there anyway. She's only asking you for one thing.'

Lexi was shaking her head. 'But if I give in then that's like admitting I think she's not going to make it. I don't want to think about her dying. I can't.'

Evie knew Lexi hated the idea of death. She'd been through one traumatic loss already in her life, when she'd terminated a pregnancy, and that made this situation more difficult for her. But she couldn't let her sister bury her head in the sand. Evie had to get her to face reality. 'Please, just agree to talk to Sam about it. If you set a date and you need to change it to accommodate Bella, is that such a big deal? It's certainly not impossible.' Sam knew what Bella's chances were better than anyone, Evie thought. As Bella's specialist and Lexi's fiancé, maybe he would have more success in persuading Lexi.

Before Lexi had a chance to agree or disagree, they were interrupted by the sound of breaking glass coming from the kitchen, followed by a loud thud as something heavy hit the floor. Then there was silence.

'Bella?' Evie and Lexi leapt from their chairs and ran to the kitchen. Broken glass was strewn over the marble bench tops but Bella was no-where to be seen. Evie raced around the island bench and found Bella collapsed on the tiles sur-rounded by the remnants of the glass cupboard.

'Bella!' Evie knelt beside her sister, oblivious to the shards of glass that littered the floor. To her relief she could see that Bella was conscious and breathing. 'What happened? Are you hurt?'

Bella's grey eyes were enormous in her pale face. 'Dizzy.' Her words were laboured. 'Cramp.' She was obviously having difficulty with her breathing. 'I grabbed the shelf when I fell. Sorry.'

'Don't worry about the glasses,' Evie said as

she brushed Bella's auburn curls from her face. Her skin was flushed and her forehead was hot. Feverish.

Bella's powdered drink mixture that she used for salt replacement sat on the bench. Evie picked up Bella's wrist and took her pulse, counting the seconds. Her pulse was rapid and Bella's skin under her fingers was dry and lacking its normal elasticity.

Evie ran through Bella's symptoms in her head. A high temperature, dizziness, cramping, rapid pulse rate. 'You're dehydrated,' she said. 'Why didn't you tell us you weren't feeling well?'

Why hadn't she noticed something? Evie accused herself. *She was a doctor, for goodness' sake.*

She knew she'd been distracted by the tension between Lexi and Bella but she still should have known something was wrong. Bella's behaviour should have alerted her. She wasn't normally so insistent or stubborn.

But that didn't explain why she hadn't told them she was feeling unwell. Evie could only assume it was because she didn't want to make a fuss. That was typical of Bella. She'd been unwell more frequently than usual over the past few months and Evie knew she would be trying to pretend everything was normal. But they all knew it wasn't. They all knew Bella's health was going downhill and Evie was furious with herself for not noticing the signs tonight. But there was no time to berate herself now. They needed to get Bella treated, she needed to be in hospital.

'Lexi, ring Sam and tell him to meet us at the hospital,' Evie instructed. 'I'll call an ambulance and then see if you can get a drink into Bella. She needs fluids.'

CHAPTER ONE

BELLA lay on the stretcher in the rear of the ambulance. She was vaguely aware of her surroundings but the activity felt like it was going on around her, independent of her, even though she knew it all related to her. The emergency lights were flashing, it was dark outside and the lights were reflecting back into the interior of the ambulance, bouncing off the walls. The siren was silent, the traffic a constant background noise. Evie was with her in the ambulance, she could hear her talking with the paramedic. Bella could feel the pressure of the oxygen mask on her face, the grip of the oximeter on her finger, the sting of the IV drip in her elbow. She saw Evie take out her phone and heard her leaving a message for their father.

She was hot and sweaty, flushed with a fever and tired, so tired. She wondered what it would be like just to close her eyes and drift off. To never wake again. But she wasn't ready. There were still things she wanted to do and things she wanted to see.

She felt the ambulance come to a halt and the flashing red and blue lights were replaced by harsh fluorescent strip lighting. She knew where they were—in the emergency drop-off zone at Sydney Harbour Hospital. This was where she had spent countless days and nights over the past twenty-six years. It was the closest hospital to the Lockheart family home in the north shore suburb of Mosman and the cardiothoracic ward had become as familiar to Bella as her own bedroom.

But her connection to the hospital went beyond that of a patient. Her great-grandfather had been one of the original founders of the hospital and it was also where Evie worked. Bella couldn't fault the medical care she received here, she just wished she hadn't had to spend so much of her life within these walls.

The rear doors swung open and Bella felt the stretcher moving as she was pulled from the ambulance. A familiar face loomed over her. Sam

Bailey, the hospital's newest cardiothoracic surgeon and next big thing, was smiling down at her.

'There you are,' he said. 'I've been stalking the ambulances, waiting for you.'

Sam was her new specialist, but again the connection didn't end there. He was engaged to Lexi, which also made him her future brother-in-law.

Bella tried to smile then realised it wasn't worth the effort as the oxygen mask was hiding her face and she was sure her smile would look more like a grimace. Sam squeezed her hand before he began talking to Evie and the paramedics, getting an update on her condition. Bella lay silently and concentrated on breathing in lungfuls of oxygen. She wasn't required to contribute. She wasn't required to do anything except keep breathing. 'I've notified Cardiothoracics, we'll take her straight up there,' Sam was saying, and Bella closed her eyes against the glare of the fluorescent lights as they began to wheel her inside.

'Evie? Is everything okay?'

Bella heard a familiar voice. She recognised it but her brain was sluggish and she was unable to put a face to the voice. If she opened her eyes she'd solve the mystery but that was too much effort.

'Charlie!'

Evie's reply jogged her memory and Bella was glad she'd kept her eyes closed.

Dr Charlie Maxwell was one of Evie's closest friends and definitely one of her cutest! Bella idolised him. But she kept her eyes closed, not wanting him to see her like this. She pretended that if she couldn't see him, he wouldn't be able to see her.

Charlie was too gorgeous for his own good and she knew she wasn't the only one who thought so. He had a reputation as a charmer and he'd cut a swathe through the female nurses and doctors at Sydney Harbour Hospital and most probably further afield too. Bella had long worshipped him from afar, knowing he'd never look twice at her, certain he saw her just as his friend's little sister. This wasn't a fairy-tale where the handsome prince would suddenly fall in love with the plain girl and sweep her off her feet. This was real life and the safest thing for her to do was to keep her eyes closed and wait for him to go away. That way there was less chance of her embarrassing herself.

'Is everything all right?' he repeated.

'No, not really. It's Bella.'

That was the last thing Bella heard before the paramedics pushed her into the hospital and Evie's voice faded.

Stay with me, Bella wanted to say. She didn't want to be alone even though she knew Evie wouldn't be far behind her.

Bella? Charlie took a second look at the figure on the stretcher. Her face was obscured by the oxygen mask but her hair was distinctive. It could only be Bella, but he hadn't recognised her at first. She had the same curly, dark auburn hair, the same pale, almost translucent skin, but she was thin, painfully thin. What had happened to her?

Charlie knew Bella had a rough time with her cystic fibrosis. She'd had a higher than average number of hospital admissions, but he'd never seen her looking as sick as she looked now.

'What's going on?'

'She's got a high temperature and she's badly dehydrated. I suspect she has another chest infection,' Evie replied.

'Is there anything I can do?' He knew it was unlikely but he wanted to at least offer his help.

Evie shook her head and he could see tears in her eyes. He and Evie had been friends for almost ten years and she was normally so strong, so resilient. Things must be grim.

'You'd better catch up with her but call me if there's anything I can do.' He leant down and gave Evie a quick kiss on the cheek. 'I'll drop into the ward in the morning.'

He watched Evie as she hurried after Bella's stretcher and wished he could offer more than just support. He viewed all three of the Lockheart sisters as his surrogate family. He knew they had a lack of family support and he knew how much of the burden of worry Evie carried on her slim shoulders. He would do what he could to help but he wished there was something more proactive that he could do for Bella too. But he was an orthopaedic surgeon. He was not what she needed.

* * *

Evie caught up to Sam and Bella as they waited for the lift. The next half-hour was frantic as Sam ordered a battery of tests and examined Bella. Lexi had driven to the hospital and she joined Evie on the cardiothoracic ward to wait. Together they tried to stay out of Sam's way. Evie had to remind herself she was Bella's sister now, not her doctor.

Sam appeared from Bella's room and motioned for them to join him. 'I'm admitting Bella. She has a temp of thirty-nine point five, which I suspect is the result of another chest infection, and she's lost three kilograms since her last admission. She was supposed to be putting on weight but her BMI is down to seventeen.'

Evie knew Bella was thin. Too thin. Her body mass index should be at least nineteen—although this would still only put her at the bottom end of normal. Evie knew it was difficult for Bella to put on weight, all cystic fibrosis sufferers had the same problem, but Bella should weigh five or six kilograms more than she currently did. Being underweight made it more difficult to fight infection and increased her chances of ending up back in hospital. Which was exactly what had happened.

'Is your father coming in?' Sam asked.

Evie shrugged. Sam's guess was as good as anyone's. 'I've just tried to get in touch with him again. I've left two messages but I don't know where he is.'

She kept one eye on Bella, wondering how she would react to the news that her father was uncontactable. Bella watched her, her grey eyes huge and pensive, but she didn't look surprised. Evie supposed the news didn't surprise any of them. 'Lexi, do you have any other way of contacting him?' Lexi worked with their father so it was possible she would know where to find him.

Lexi shook her head. 'No, he was going out to dinner but it was private, not business related, so I don't know any more details.'

Evie sighed. If Richard was out with one of his female 'acquaintances' it was highly unlikely that he'd answer his phone. It was also highly unlikely that he'd even make it home tonight, and if he did Evie wondered whether he'd even notice that Bella, and possibly Lexi, weren't in their beds.

'Do you think we need to try to find him?' she asked. Was Sam telling them it was important for Richard to get into the hospital tonight or did they have some time up their sleeves?

Sam was shaking his head and Evie breathed a sigh of relief. He couldn't think it was that urgent. 'I just want to try to get Bella stabilised tonight,' he said. 'I'll start a course of IV antibiotics and get her rehydrated. We'll have to see how that goes but this is now her third admission this year. To be honest, things are heading downhill, but she'll make it through the night. I'm sure your father will turn up eventually.'

Until then Evie would stay by Bella's side. Even when Richard decided to join them Evie knew that she and Lexi would be Bella's main support team. She wished things were different, for Bella's sake, but their father and Bella had always had a difficult relationship, he'd never coped very well with his second daughter or her illness.

Evie's own relationship with her father had been tainted by the departure of their mother. Something Evie held her father partially responsible for. She knew her mother had made her own choices but she felt that he could have been more supportive, offered more assistance, made more of an effort to convince her to stay. If he had, the bulk of the responsibility of raising her younger siblings wouldn't have fallen to Evie and she would have had a very different childhood.

But the Lockheart family dynamics weren't going to change overnight and once again Evie opted to set up a folding bed in Bella's room. She sent Lexi home with Sam but she wasn't going to leave Bella alone. She hoped Sam was right, she hoped Bella would make it through the night, but what if he was wrong? Doctors had been wrong before. She knew that better than anybody.

Bella had been awake since the crack of dawn, woken by the nurse who'd come in to take her six-o'clock obs, although in reality she felt as though she'd been awake most of the night. She always slept badly in hospital. Struggling for every breath ruined a good sleep, not to mention two-hourly obs and the fact she was always cold.

Evie had been by her side all night and she'd waited until Lexi arrived before disappearing in search of coffee while promising to be back in time for Sam's early-morning consult.

Evie and Lexi were the two constants in Bella's life. The two people she knew she would always be able to rely on. She knew she was lucky to have them and she'd given up waiting for her parents to give her the same support. But it didn't stop her wishing that things were different. She didn't like to be so dependent on her sisters but it was the way it had always been. She knew her illness was a strain on everybody but she also knew she wouldn't cope without the love and support of her siblings. She wondered sometimes how they managed, especially Evie, who traded looking after Bella for looking after all her other patients at the hospital. Bella knew Evie had a shift in Emergency today but she had no idea how her sister would carry out such a demanding job after spending the night in a chair by her bed. She hoped Evie didn't get any complicated cases.

'I brought something to brighten your day,' Evie said when she returned, carrying a tray of coffee and hot chocolate for her sisters. Bella felt her eyes widen in surprise; Evie wasn't talking about the drinks.

'Charlie Maxwell,' Lexi said in greeting. 'I'd recognise that bald head anywhere.'

Charlie Maxwell was in her room! Bella knew she was staring and she could hear the 'beep beep' of the heart-rate monitor attached to her chest escalate as her autonomic nervous system responded to his presence. Thank goodness he didn't seem to notice. He wasn't looking at her, his attention focussed on Lexi. Bella was used to that. People always noticed Lexi and Evie before they noticed her, and even though she wished, on the odd occasion, that someone would notice her first, today she was pleased to be ignored as it gave her time to try to get her nerves under control.

'Morning, Lexi,' Charlie said with a grin. 'And for your information, I'm not bald,' he protested. 'I do this on purpose. It stops the women from being jealous of my golden locks.'

'You'd have to be the only bloke I know who voluntarily shaves his head,' Lexi retorted, before Evie interrupted them.

'Bella, you remember Charlie, don't you?' she asked as she handed Bella a hot chocolate.

Who could forget him? Bella thought. She knew she never would, not in a million years. He looked as fit, healthy and fabulous as always. Charlie had been a professional surfer in a past life and he certainly had the body of an athlete. Muscular, tanned and perfectly proportioned, he was wearing a white shirt and Bella could see the definition of his biceps and pectoral muscles through the thin fabric. She swallowed hard as she tried to get her mouth to work but she was short of breath and her mouth was dry and parched. Unable to form any words, she nodded instead.

'*Ciao*, Bella,' Charlie said.

He always greeted her in the same way and it never failed to make her feel special, even though she didn't flatter herself that she was the only one on the receiving end of his charm. But therein lay even more of his appeal. He was one of the few people who didn't treat her any differently because of her medical condition. He was a serial flirt and he gave her the same attention he gave to every woman who crossed his path, and to Bella, who was used to either being shielded or ignored, Charlie's attention was a rare delight.

He winked at her and her heart rate jumped again. She felt herself blush and cursed her fair skin.

'How are you feeling?' he asked.

'I've had better days,' she said, finally managing to get some words out. But it wasn't the cystic fibrosis making her short of breath, it was Charlie. She was always shy around anyone other than family and even though Charlie behaved like family he was so damn sexy she'd never managed to overcome her self-consciousness around him, especially when other people were within earshot. One on one she was more comfortable but with other ears around she always worried about making a fool of herself.

He was gorgeous and she always felt so plain by comparison. His facial features combined so perfectly together she'd never really noticed that he shaved his head. Of course she'd noticed he was bald but she'd never wondered about the reality behind it, she was too busy being mesmerised by his other physical attributes—his chocolate-brown eyes that she felt she could melt into, his smooth, tanned skin, which provided the perfect foil for straight, white teeth, even his small, neat ears all combined into an appealing package. But his best feature was his mouth. She could visualise him with sun-bleached surfie hair but it was irrelevant really because her attention was constantly drawn to his lips. They were plump and delicious, full but not hard like a collagen-injected pout, they were juicy and soft, almost too soft for such a masculine face. He was smiling at her, a gorgeous smile, full and open and honest. You'd have to be dead not to be affected by his smile and while she wasn't feeling anywhere near one hundred per cent healthy, she wasn't dead yet.

'So Evie tells me,' Charlie replied, 'but if there's anything you need, just ask me. I know how to make things happen around here.'

He winked at her again and Bella didn't doubt for one minute that Charlie could get whatever he wanted both inside the hospital and out. She knew his reputation as a charmer, she'd heard the nurses talk about him during her numerous admissions, and she knew they competed for his affections and attentions. The combination of his wicked sense of humour, his infectious smile, his gentle nature and his hardened muscles had the female staff members regularly flustered, and Bella herself was no exception.

As far as she knew, only Evie seemed immune to Charlie's charm. Their ten-year friendship had only ever been platonic and for that Bella was grateful. It meant she was free to adore him without feeling as if she was invading her sister's territory. She knew that from the day Evie had first met Charlie she'd thought of him as the older brother she wished she'd had. But Bella's thoughts towards Charlie were far from familial—although she'd never be brave enough to flirt with him, she knew she wasn't experienced enough to handle Charlie Maxwell. So she just nodded dumbly in reply. She'd lost the capacity to speak again, completely tongue-tied at the thought of Charlie doing things for her. Fortunately Sam's arrival saved her from needing to answer. He was followed by a nurse and a couple of interns and suddenly her room was overflowing with people.

A ninth person came into the room and Bella saw Evie's double-take. It was their father.

Bella had assumed Evie had gotten in touch with him during the night, or vice versa, but looking at Evie's expression now it was obvious she'd heard nothing back and hadn't been expecting him.

He looked tired and drawn. Bella wished she could pretend he'd lost sleep worrying about her, his middle daughter, but she knew it was far more likely to be a result of a late night of a different kind. She waited for her father to push through the crowd gathered at the foot of her bed but of course he didn't. He remained standing just inside the doorway, separate and apart from his family. She sighed, wishing for the thousandth time that things were different. At least he was here, which was more than Bella could say for her mother. She nodded in greeting and then proceeded to ignore him as her sisters took up positions on the bed on either side of her. She was tired of always being the one who reached out to make a connection with her father.

Evie took her hand and Bella relaxed, knowing her sisters would try to protect her from harm. Bella saw Sam acknowledge Richard's arrival with a nod of his own before he began his consult. He checked Bella's vital signs, checked her obs, listened to her chest and generally prodded and poked while she tried to pretend she wasn't surrounded by people. The procedure was familiar to her but that didn't make it any less embarrassing. Once he'd finished he spoke to Bella as though they were the only two in the room.

'You've lost weight since I last examined you, that's not what we were hoping for, your admissions are getting more frequent and your lung function tests are down.' Sam was ticking things off on his fingers as he recited the list.

'Is there any good news?' Bella asked hopefully.

'One positive note is that you've made some improvement overnight. You've rehydrated and your temperature has come down but it's still higher than I'd like. You're showing some resistance to the antibiotics and I've had to increase the dosage to try to get your chest infection under control. Individually all these things are not so concerning but combined it means I need to re-assess your management.' He paused briefly and Bella knew what he would say next. 'It's time for the next stage.'

Bella couldn't speak. This wasn't unexpected but she didn't know what to say. Sam was watching her, waiting for her to acknowledge his words, and she thought she nodded in response but she couldn't be sure.

Sam looked away from her now, turning to the members of her family, stopping briefly at each and every one as he spoke. 'I know we've talked about this before but the time has come. Bella needs a lung transplant now. She is already on the active transplant list but I have revised her status. This will move her up the list and means she will get the next pair of suitable lungs.'

Bella tightened her grip on Evie's hand. This was really happening. During her last hospital admission Sam had told her she would need a transplant eventually. That was the way things went with cystic fibrosis. But eventually had become now. Her lungs were officially failing.

Out of the corner of her eye she saw Richard collapse into a chair as though his legs would no longer support him. His response surprised her. Her father was a man of action, he always had a solution for everything, a way to deal with everything—except when it came to her and her mother—but he never normally showed any sign of weakness. Was he actually concerned for her? Bella knew there was nothing he could do for her now but she couldn't ever recall seeing him flummoxed. Was he concerned or was he confused?

'What do we do while we wait?' Lexi's voice was unexpectedly loud in her ear and Bella jumped.

'In the meantime, we start the pre-op processes. Physical tests, including blood work and organ function tests, as well as psych assessments,' Sam replied.

'What does the surgery involve?' Richard asked, and his question answered Bella's own. His tone said this was a question from a man who wanted information and clarification, not a question from a concerned father.

'Obviously it is major surgery. Bella will be several hours in Theatre. It can take up to twelve hours. She will be placed on a heart bypass machine while both lungs are transplanted via an incision across the bottom of the diaphragm, then she will be transferred to ICU for at least twenty-four hours and then back to the cardiothoracic surgical ward.'

'What are the survival rates?' As was his style her father was keeping any emotion out of the equation. He preferred to deal with the facts and figures.

'The figures are good. Currently eighty-five per cent of people undergoing bilateral, sequential lung transplants in Australia survive one year and sixty per cent are still alive after five years.'

Bella heard a sharp intake of breath. For a moment she thought she'd made the sound but then she realised it had come from Lexi.

Bella knew the odds. She'd lived and breathed them since her last admission. She knew the statistics were good, for the short term at least, but she also knew that to those who hadn't spent countless hours doing the research she'd done, the odds didn't sound that fantastic.

'These stats are not just for CF sufferers,' Sam clarified. 'They're for everybody and Bella has age on her side. Although she will still have cystic fibrosis, it won't be in her lungs.' Sam looked directly at Bella. 'If your lungs are functioning properly, you should notice a far improved quality of life. You'll have more energy, you should gain weight and you'll be able to be more active.'

'What do you mean, she'll still have CF?' Richard was frowning.

'Bella's lungs will be clear but she will still have CF in her pancreas, sweat glands and reproductive tract. She will still need her enzyme-replacement medication and she will start a course of anti-rejection medication. The transplant is not a cure for the disease, it just eliminates the disease from her lungs, and will hopefully extend her life.' Sam turned to face her. 'Bella, do you have any questions?'

She still hadn't uttered a word.

'How long do I have?'

'A month, maybe two.' Sam's voice was deep and soft but his words were clear and distinct in the absolute silence of the room.

It was already November. Would she see another Christmas?

'What choice do I have?'

Her question put an immediate and definite end to the silence. Lexi started to cry and Evie started to reason with Bella. They both knew her choices were limited.

Bella held up one hand, asking Evie to wait. 'It was just a question,' she said. 'I didn't say I won't have a transplant, I just wanted to hear if I have any other options.'

'Of course you have a choice,' Sam said, 'it's your body. You can choose to have a transplant if we find a suitable donor or you can choose not to. But you don't have any other options.' He spoke to her as though they were alone in the room. 'It's a big decision and I know how daunting this can be but ultimately I wouldn't expect you to find it a hard decision to make. The consequences of your decision are self-evident. You're free to talk to the psychologists and the transplant team in more detail, you can ask them anything you want or need to know, but you don't have a lot of time to decide. Your lungs are failing. Without a transplant you're on borrowed time.'

Borrowed time. She knew that but it made it more important than ever that she get things sorted. There were things she needed to do. She had to prioritise. She needed to think. She closed her eyes. As she'd hoped, Sam took that as a sign to usher everyone out of the room.

'Okay,' he said, 'I need to run a couple more tests and Bella needs to rest. You can come back later.'

Bella thought Lexi was going to argue but she saw her look at Sam before she said anything. Sam gave a slight shake of his head and Lexi stayed quiet. The medical team was leaving the room and Lexi and Evie kissed Bella before they followed. Charlie and Sam were the last ones remaining. Bella looked from one to the other. Charlie was wedged in next to the bathroom doorhandle, he would have to wait until everyone else had left before he'd be able to get out. She needed to ask a favour and if she was running out of time she needed to do it soon. It looked as if Charlie or Sam were her only options. Not that they were bad options. This was a topic she couldn't discuss with her sisters; she'd tried already and failed, but by the same token she didn't think it was something to discuss with Sam either.

Bella needed a sounding board. Charlie had offered his help and even though she knew this wasn't exactly what he'd pictured, perhaps he wouldn't mind. After all, this concerned Evie and he knew her better than most.

Bella hadn't seen Charlie for some time. He had been a frequent visitor to the Lockheart home but since Evie had moved out into an apartment there was no reason for Charlie to drop by. But she knew from experience that Charlie was a good listener and he could be relied upon for level-headed advice. She and Charlie had a history of heart-to-hearts, albeit a very short one, and perhaps he could help her again.

Besides, she was running out of time and options. He would have to do.

'Charlie, could I talk to you for a second?' she

asked. She knew he saw himself as family, maybe he could do this for her.

Bella saw Evie glance back over her shoulder as she left the room. She'd be wondering what on earth Bella needed to talk to Charlie about, wondering why she wasn't talking to her, but Bella knew this was one thing Evie couldn't help her with.

CHAPTER TWO

EVIE hesitated when she heard Bella ask Charlie to stay. She wondered what that was all about but she didn't stop. She had to catch her father before he disappeared again. There were things they needed to talk about.

'Richard,' she called out to him. She hadn't called him 'Dad' since she'd started working at the Harbour Hospital. Evie's paternal great-grandfather had been instrumental in establishing the hospital and Richard was one of its biggest benefactors. Evie hadn't wanted to be accused of nepotism when she'd joined the staff. Although the Lockheart surname was a clear indication that there was a relationship there, she hadn't wanted everyone to know just how close the relationship was.

He turned and waited for her to catch up.

'Where have you been?' Evie asked. She was

furious that she'd heard nothing from him all morning. 'Why didn't you return my messages?' She must have left him half a dozen in total.

'I tried. Your mobile is switched off.'

Evie knew there would be no apology. She always switched her phone off at work and Richard knew that. He could have guessed she'd be at the hospital, he could have contacted her through other avenues. 'You could have paged me.'

Never one to back down he said, 'I spoke to Lexi and came straight here. Tell me, how do we fix this? What can I do?'

'You can't buy lungs,' she replied, knowing that Richard's preferred way of dealing with things was just to throw large sums of money at a problem until it went away. That wasn't going to work this time. 'We just have to wait.'

'What is Sam doing about this?'

'There's nothing he can do other than push Bella up the list, which he has done. It's all dependent on having a suitable donor and convincing Bella to go ahead with the surgery once compatible lungs are found. All we can do is support her through this.' Her little sister was in dire

straits and while Evie had known this day was in-
evitable it didn't make it any less heartbreaking.

She hoped Richard was listening. She hoped,
for once, he could be there to support his daughter. She hoped he realised he might never get
another shot at this. But she and Lexi would be
there for Bella even if her parents weren't. Which
brought her to the next item on her mental check-
list.

'Will you tell Miranda?' Evie asked.

Evie had started calling her mother by her first
name when she was fifteen, when she had finally
admitted that her mother preferred her bottle of
gin to her daughters. Miranda's contact with her
offspring was sporadic, associated with brief periods of sobriety mostly, although there had been
plenty of times when the girls had seen Miranda
far from sober. But despite this Evie felt Miranda
needed to know what was happening with her
second daughter and she thought it was Richard's
job to inform her.

Richard's expression told Evie all she needed to
know but she was not going to let him out of this
task. 'You need to tell her. Whether she can un-

derstand what's going on is not your problem, but she has to be told. I need to get back to work. I'll see you back here later.' Evie's final words were not a question. Someone needed to tell Richard what was required and she was happy to do that. But she'd have to wait and see if he listened.

Bella looked exhausted. She was waiflike, a pale shadow of a figure against the white hospital sheets. She was sitting up in bed and the only exception to her pallor was her auburn curls, which were vibrantly bright against the pillows that were plumped around her. Looking at her, Charlie thought she could pass for eighteen years old but he knew she was in her mid-twenties. She'd been seventeen when they'd first met, almost ten years ago, when he'd gone back to med school and found himself in Evie's class, and that would make her twenty-six now.

He waited until Bella's room had emptied itself of all the other occupants before he dragged a chair closer to the bed and sat. 'What can I do for you?' he asked. When he'd offered his help he hadn't expected there would be anything he could do, but his offer had been made in good faith and if Bella needed assistance he would do his best to give it to her.

'I need an unbiased pair of ears.'

Charlie frowned. Bella wasn't maintaining eye contact. Instead, she was fidgeting with the bed covers, repeatedly pleating them in her fingers before smoothing them out. He wondered what was bothering her. 'Is this about the transplant?'

'Sort of,' she replied.

'You *are* planning on going ahead with it?'

'Yes.' Bella nodded and her auburn curls bounced. 'But I don't want to talk to you about the actual operation or anything medical. I'm worried about Evie.' She looked up at him then but her fingers continued to fiddle with the bed sheets.

'Evie?' He'd expected that she wanted to discuss the transplant. He had expected to advise her to talk to Sam. Charlie was an orthopaedic surgeon. Lung transplants were Sam's area of expertise, not his. 'I don't understand.'

'You heard Sam, I'm on borrowed time. I'm not

ready to give up yet but there's no guarantee that a suitable donor will be found in time.'

Her breathing was laboured and when she paused to catch her breath he could hear a faint wheeze. She had an oxygen tube resting on her top lip and out of habit he checked the flow and her oxygen sats on the monitor to make sure she was getting an adequate supply. The flow was fine so he returned his attention to Bella.

'If I'm running out of time,' she was saying, 'I want to make sure my sisters are okay.'

His frowned deepened. 'Sam has just told you that your last hope is to find a suitable donor for new lungs and you're worried about your sisters?' Charlie was amazed. If he were in the same situation he doubted he'd be able to think about anything except whether he was going to live or die.

Bella shrugged. 'There's nothing I can do about finding a donor but making sure Evie is okay might be something I can have some influence over.'

'What's wrong with her?' He hadn't noticed anything amiss but, to be honest, he hadn't seen a lot of Evie lately.

'I know this whole donor thing is stressing Evie out. She feels responsible for me. She always has ever since our mother walked out on us. But, really, this situation isn't unexpected, we all knew this day would come. But Evie doesn't seem to be coping as well as I would have thought.'

Bella stopped, interrupted by a coughing fit, and Charlie could only watch as her slight frame shuddered with each spasm. She had asked him to stay behind. There must be something she needed. 'What did you want me to do?' he asked as he poured some water into a glass for her and waited while she sipped it.

'Thanks,' she said as she moistened her throat before she continued to speak in a voice that was just louder than a whisper. 'She seems on edge, which isn't like her, and she's been like that for a little while. Something is bothering her but she won't tell me what it is. Have you noticed anything?'

'I haven't seen that much of her lately,' he admitted. But if Bella was right and Evie was troubled, he was pretty sure he knew what the problem was. The sisters were extraordinarily close and he could just imagine how much this situation was tearing Evie apart. 'I imagine she's just worried about you and doesn't want to burden you with her concerns.' He wished he felt like he was doing a better job of comforting Bella but he didn't think he'd be improving her spirits with this clumsy attempt at reassurance.

'I think it's something unrelated to me,' Bella admitted.

'Like what?'

'I don't know. Sometimes it's as though she has the weight of the world on her shoulders and you know what she's like, she doesn't like to burden people with her troubles. A couple of the nurses were talking about Evie and they mentioned Finn Kennedy. I wondered if something had happened between them, something that would upset her. Have you heard anything?'

Bella's earlier nervousness had disappeared. She'd stopped fidgeting and Charlie wondered whether he'd only imagined her to be on edge. He shook his head. 'I've heard nothing. There's been the usual gossip about the staff and usual complaints about the doctors' egos, but I've heard nothing about Evie specifically.'

'Will you promise me that if anything happens to me, you'll look out for her?' Bella asked. 'She needs somebody to take care of her and she's so independent, which makes it tough. At least she might let you close.'

Charlie nodded. 'I promise I'll make sure she's okay.' He could do that. He wished he could tell Bella that she'd be able to keep an eye on Evie herself but they both knew that might not be the case. They both knew what the reality was.

He could hear Bella wheezing as she breathed and he knew she needed to rest. He should leave and let her recover but he needed to know that everything was under control first. 'Is anything else bothering you?' he asked.

'Well, I also want to see Lexi happily married to Sam but I don't think you can help me there.' Bella smiled and Charlie caught a glimpse of humour despite her circumstances.

'Why wouldn't they get married?' he asked.

Bella shook her head. 'I'm sure they will but I want to be there when they do. Lexi wants time to organise a huge circus, and I know it's her wedding…' She smiled. 'Their wedding,' she corrected, 'but I wish she'd agree to hurry things up. I don't want to miss out.'

Her smile had gone and the tension had returned to her shoulders. She had the bed sheet bunched up tight in her right hand and her knuckles were white with the effort. Maybe it had been stress he'd been witnessing all along.

Charlie wished again that there was something he could do to reassure her. 'You need to be positive. You have to believe you will get a second chance.' He knew his words were hopelessly inadequate but he was out of his depth.

'All right, I'll go along with your fairy-tale for now,' Bella replied. 'Let's say a donor is found in time, before Lexi and Sam have a chance to get married. What if something happens to me during the surgery? That's a risk too. Sam is my surgeon. How do you think that will affect their relationship? I know the idea of me dying terrifies Lexi but if they're already married they'll have to get past it, but if they're not…' Bella paused and shrugged her bony shoulders. 'I don't want to be responsible for something happening and coming between them.'

'How can what happens in surgery be your responsibility?'

'It's my decision to have the surgery and the other alternative if something goes wrong is for it to be Sam's responsibility. If I don't have the surgery then that pressure is removed.'

'If you don't have the surgery, you'll die.' Charlie knew he was being blunt but he also knew Bella understood the facts. 'It's Sam's job to make sure nothing happens to you. He's a surgeon, that goes with the territory.'

'Don't get me wrong. If a donor is found, I will have the transplant, but I'd just prefer it if Lexi and Sam were married first. Does that make sense?'

Charlie nodded. In some strange roundabout way it did make perfect sense. He could understand her logic. 'I assume you've spoken to Lexi about this?'

She nodded. 'But Lexi has a tendency to get her own way and she wants it all to be perfect. In Lexi's mind the wedding will happen when I've had a transplant and life is going on for everyone just as it should. She won't consider the possibility that I might not make it. She won't admit that waiting might mean she doesn't get perfection. She thinks if she ignores the facts, it'll all go away. She thinks wishing it will make it so. I don't want to make a fuss but it's a big deal to me.'

'What about having someone else perform the surgery? Someone other than Sam?'

'Like who?' Bella asked. 'Evie told me Sam is one of the best. If I'm going to have a lung transplant, I want the best odds I can get.'

Charlie thought about Bella's options. Finn Kennedy, Head of Surgery at Sydney Harbour Hospital, was one of the best cardiac surgeons in Australia but he wasn't a heart-lung specialist. If Charlie had needed heart surgery, he'd happily choose Finn to operate on him, but if he needed a lung transplant his money would be on Sam.

'I guess Sam is your man,' he agreed. 'But if Lexi isn't listening, why don't you talk to Sam? See if you can get him to persuade Lexi to speed things up. Get him to explain the urgency to her.'

Bella nodded. 'That makes sense. I wanted

Lexi to talk to Sam about it but I don't think she will. Maybe I should approach it from the other angle, from Sam's side.'

Charlie watched as Bella's fist relaxed and her fingers uncurled, releasing the bed sheet. Perhaps his advice had been more effective than he'd anticipated. Could he leave her to rest? 'So you'll talk to Sam?'

'I guess.'

'Shall I come back tomorrow, check up on you?'

'You don't need to do that.'

'Why not? I can be your conscience, make sure you've spoken to Sam. And once you've got your sisters' lives sorted out, I'm interested to know what you want for you.'

'Me?' Her tone suggested she hadn't given any thought to herself and Charlie was astonished by her undemanding, unselfish attitude.

'Yes. What do *you* want?'

She frowned as if she'd never given any consideration to her own desires and her grey eyes darkened. 'Nothing.'

* * *

How could she want nothing? Charlie wondered as he left the cardiothoracic ward. Everyone wanted something. But he supposed the only thing she wanted might be unattainable. Bella's life was in someone else's hands. Actually, it was in someone else's body. Bella's chance at life would come at the expense of someone else's. Was it better then *not* to think about it? Was it better not to put that longing into words?

And what was he doing, offering to come back tomorrow? Offering to be her conscience? Why was he getting involved?

Normally he would steer clear of any sort of involvement. He'd learnt that lesson a long time ago. He yearned for freedom and in his experience that didn't come from involvement with others. But the Lockheart sisters were different. He'd learnt *that* a long time ago too. Almost ten years ago.

Besides, it was too late to ask himself whether he should get involved. He already was. Ever since he'd first met Evie and she'd dragged him into her world and rescued him from the depths of darkness, the Lockheart sisters had become part of his life. They'd been good for him at a time when he'd been disheartened about life and his future. Evie had helped him through that period, and her situation with her parents and with Bella's illness had made his troubles seem less significant.

Now it was his turn to repay that debt. It was his turn to support the girls and he would do what he could to make sure all three of them got through this time with their spirits and hearts intact.

Bella was Evie's little sister. He would help in any way he could. He would be involved but in a practical sense only. This was one woman who was safe from his advances. Not because she was unattractive, far from it, her auburn hair, pale skin and grey eyes were a mesmerising combination, but Bella was Evie's little sister, which meant she was practically family and she was definitely off limits. But he could offer support, he knew they would need it, and that would be the extent of his involvement. She was Evie's little sister and he would be wise to remember that.

With his involvement sorted in his mind, he

headed for the bank of elevators to take him up to the orthopaedic wards and was surprised to find Evie waiting in the corridor. He thought everyone would have been long gone.

'Were you waiting for me?' he asked.

Evie shook her head. 'No. I just finished talking to Richard.'

Charlie waited. He knew Evie and her father had a volatile relationship. Sometimes things went smoothly, other times not so much. He wondered how things were at the moment. 'How did that go?'

'No different from the usual,' Evie sighed. 'Bella needs his support, she needs support from all of us right now, and I don't know if any of them understand how serious this is. Richard certainly doesn't seem to grasp just how difficult it is to find suitable donors, Lexi doesn't want to think about the consequences if there is no donor, and don't get me started on my mother.'

'So that leaves you to try to hold it all together?'

'I guess so.'

The burden of Bella's illness had always fallen on Evie and it looked as though that was still the case. Sam was obviously some support but Evie's immediate family sounded as though they were all still in denial, assuming her mother even knew what was going on. He wondered if he'd been right. Was the stress upsetting Evie? Even so, Charlie knew Evie would always be there to support Bella. Maybe Bella was right—if something was bothering Evie, perhaps it was another issue.

'Walk with me?' he invited. 'I need another coffee.'

She was silent as they walked back to the doctors' lounge. He kept quiet too, thinking that if he waited she might tell him what else was on her mind, but she didn't break the silence. He shrugged as he spooned coffee into the machine. He'd never pretended to understand women. Perhaps there wasn't anything else bothering her.

Evie watched as Charlie fiddled with the coffee machine. The doctors' lounge in this ward had a proper coffee machine and the hospital's best coffee. Technically neither of them should be using it as it had been purchased by the cardiothoracic unit for their doctors, but Evie knew Charlie would get away with it, just like he got away with most things, and she wasn't about to argue.

She was silent as the machine gurgled to life. She knew Charlie was watching her, waiting for her to say something, but she didn't know what else to say. She didn't know what she could do.

'It'll be okay, Evie.'

Did he know what she was thinking?

'You don't know that,' she retorted.

'You're right, I don't, but it's all we can hope for. We have to stay positive. Bella needs that from all of us,' he said as the coffee dripped into the cups.

'What did she want to speak to you about?'

'She needed to get some things off her chest.'

'Why didn't she talk to me?' she asked, hating the petulant tone she heard in her voice, but she couldn't help it. For as long as she could remember she'd been Bella's confidante and protector. What made Bella think she couldn't come to her now?

'I think she just needed to talk to someone

who isn't quite as invested emotionally in her as you are.'

. 'But she's always confided in me.'

Not always, he thought. But Evie didn't need to hear that now.

'Don't worry, she's okay.' Charlie's deep brown eyes were sombre as he stepped towards her and wrapped his arms around her, hugging her against his chest. 'The best thing you can do for her right now is just be there. Just like you've always been. She needs you.'

Evie closed her eyes and leant against Charlie's solid chest as she let out a long breath. It felt good to have a hug with no hidden agenda, a straightforward, comforting hug from a friend. It felt good to let someone else worry about her for a change.

'I'm consulting today. Call me if there's anything you need,' he said. 'Anything. I'm here for you, okay?'

His words vibrated in his chest and into Evie but she was also aware of the air in the room moving and she knew someone else had entered the lounge. She opened her eyes and her gaze settled on the last person she expected to see. The last person she wanted to see.

Finn Kennedy.

The last time she'd been in somebody's arms they'd been his. He stood in the doorway, rigid and forbidding, with his usual unfathomable expression on his face. His gaze was locked on her as she was held in Charlie's embrace. He didn't speak and he didn't move. Heat flooded through her, unbidden, unwanted, unplanned, as he watched her with his piercing blue eyes.

Evie stepped back, breaking Charlie's hold on her. 'I'd better go. I need to hit the showers and get downstairs.' She picked up her coffee and stirred milk and sugar into it, resolutely keeping her gaze focussed on her drink.

'I'll see you later,' Charlie said.

She looked up at him as he spoke. The doorway was empty. She and Charlie were alone again.

It was probably just as well, she thought with a sigh. She didn't have the time or the energy to deal with Finn Kennedy, esteemed cardiac surgeon, Head of Surgery and her most recent lover. Although that term was probably too generous.

They'd shared one fiery sexual interlude but she couldn't call it lovemaking. It had been steamy, fierce and passionate but without tenderness. It had been raw, impulsive and gratifying but it could not be repeated.

She did *not* have time to think about Finn Kennedy. She needed to stay in control and, where Finn was concerned, she'd already demonstrated an extreme lack of self-control.

She thanked Charlie and kissed his cheek before she left to get on with her day, hoping and praying for it to improve. She showered in Bella's bathroom and changed into surgical scrubs. She hadn't thought to ask Lexi to lend her some clean clothes and there was no way she'd fit into any of Bella's things, even if Lexi had packed some choices other than pyjamas. At five feet nine inches, Evie was four inches taller than Bella and about two dress sizes bigger. While no one would call Evie plump, Bella was as thin as a whippet because of the cystic fibrosis.

She kissed Bella goodbye and headed for the lift to go to A and E. She yawned as she waited.

She was halfway through the yawn when the lift doors slid open to reveal one occupant.

Finn.

Obviously she hadn't been wishing hard enough for her day to improve.

All it took was one glance, no more than a second long, before her heart was racing in her chest. Her lips were dry and her face burned under the scrutiny of his gaze. She couldn't let him see how he affected her.

She turned her back to push the button for the ground floor only to find it had already been pressed. No other buttons were lit. Which meant Finn was riding all the way down with her.

'Late night?' Finn's deep, husky voice made her jump. She hadn't expected him to speak to her. The way he'd looked at her earlier with his disapproving, ice-cold blue eyes she would have bet he'd ignore her. What was it about him? When she wanted him to talk he refused to open up to her yet when she wanted to be left in peace and quiet he had to engage her in conversation. He was so infuriating.

'Yes.' She turned to face him as she answered

and saw him look her up and down. She knew he would notice what she was wearing.

'I take it you couldn't make it home?'

Yep, he'd noticed, and she knew what he was implying. She was tempted to let him think he was right but she was too tired to play games.

She glared at him. She was tired and worried. She'd let him take the brunt of her bad mood.

'I spent the night in the cardiothoracic ward. Bella is in hospital again. She was admitted last night.' She was happy if her comment made him feel bad. Why should she be the only one who worried about other people's feelings?

He reached out a hand and took half a step towards her before he thought better of it. She could literally see him change his mind. His hand dropped to his side and his tone softened. 'Evie, I'm sorry, I didn't know. Is there anything I can do?'

Don't be nice to me. I don't know how to handle it if you're nice. She was terrified she'd burst into tears in the lift. In front of Finn. 'There's nothing you can do unless you're a miracle worker. She needs a pair of new lungs.' She was snappy and defensive. It was the only way to ensure she didn't crumble.

'I doubt even the Lockheart name can get lungs to order.' His tone was cool now, his blue eyes appraising. 'I meant, is there anything I can do for you?'

'What could you possibly do?'

'I could organise for someone to cover your shift so you could be with Bella.'

Great, Finn hands you an olive branch and you set it on fire before you give it back. That's just great. Well done, Evie.

She would love to take him up on his offer but she couldn't back down now. It wasn't in her nature and she certainly wasn't about to give Finn the satisfaction of having the last word. 'There's nothing I can do for her,' she said. Evie expected Bella to sleep for most of the day and Lexi was going to stay with her. 'I'd rather be busy down here,' she added as the lift doors opened and she stepped out into the emergency department. Work would ensure her mind was occupied. Staying busy was the best way to keep her mind off Bella's situation. And off Finn.

CHAPTER THREE

IT WAS amazing what a difference twenty-four hours and a hefty dose of no-nonsense antibiotics made. After a full day and two nights in hospital Bella was feeling a lot more positive and Sam was pleased with her progress too. She'd broached the topic of hurrying the wedding along with him and he'd seemed amenable to the idea. Now Bella just had her fingers crossed that he could convince Lexi it was a good idea.

Thinking of weddings, Bella's fingers itched to continue sketching. If her plan was to succeed she needed to build Lexi's excitement and feed her imagination about how beautiful this wedding could be. She needed Lexi to be so excited she couldn't wait to get married and would agree to do it soon. She needed to get some more ideas down on paper but her sketch book wasn't there. Lexi hadn't considered it a priority when she'd thrown belongings together the other night and Bella had been too concerned about other things yesterday to miss it. Lexi was bringing it into the hospital this morning but until she arrived Bella would have to make do with scraps of paper.

She was halfway through sketching a sleeveless figure-hugging satin gown with a plunging back when Lexi appeared, carrying a large tote bag.

'Morning,' she said as she dumped the bag onto Bella's bed before kissing her cheek. 'Sam says things are looking up?'

Bella nodded. 'I'm definitely feeling better today.'

Lexi unzipped the tote bag and began to haul things out of it. 'I've brought the things you asked for. There's plenty to keep you occupied if you get bored,' she said as she deposited Bella's laptop and a stack of DVDs on the bedside cupboard.

'Did you bring my big sketch book and coloured pencils?'

'Yes,' Lexi said as she retrieved the items and put them on the table over the bed. 'Is Charlie coming in to see you today?'

Bella frowned. 'I think so,' she said cautiously. 'Why?' He'd told her he would call in but why was Lexi asking?

'I thought you might need this,' Lexi said as she pulled a wisp of red fabric from the bag. She shook it out and Bella recognised the skimpy red negligee Lexi had bought for her the last time she'd been in hospital. 'It took me ages to find it. Why was it in the back of your wardrobe? You're supposed to wear it.'

Bella looked at the minuscule slip. It was so not her style and she had no intention of wearing it, which was why she'd shoved it to the back of her cupboard.

'I'm not going to wear it in hospital,' she protested. She had no plans to wear it at all, not in hospital or anywhere else. 'You know how cold I always feel in here.' She floated her old excuse past Lexi. Because she was so thin she did feel the cold and she used that as a reason to wear thick winter pyjamas that hid her figure. She couldn't imagine why Lexi would ever think she'd wear something as tiny as that red negligee.

'I knew you'd say that so I brought you this to

wear over the top.' Lexi pulled out a little black, cropped bed jacket. Or something Bella assumed was a bed jacket. It wasn't much bigger than the negligee but it did have sleeves and a fluffy, furry collar, but even so Bella knew it still wouldn't leave much to the imagination. She'd feel like a model in a lingerie catalogue. Lexi might be comfortable in that situation but she certainly wouldn't be.

'I'm in hospital, Lex, not in an adult movie!'

'Come on, Bella,' Lexi pleaded. 'One of the hottest doctors in the hospital is coming to visit and you're in daggy old flannelette PJs. If ever there's a time for some glamour, it's now. You can't wear what you had on yesterday.'

Bella felt her eyebrows shoot up and almost disappear into her hairline. Lexi expected her to wear this in front of Charlie!

She wished she had the confidence to wear something like that. Just once. She knew Lexi had a dozen items just like this one in her own wardrobe. She'd bought herself one too when she'd purchased this for Bella, and Lexi made sure she wore them. But Bella wasn't Lexi. She didn't have her confidence, or her figure, and she couldn't imagine she'd ever feel comfortable in something that revealing.

Bella was shaking her head in protest but Lexi was used to getting her own way and she hadn't given up yet. 'Won't you at least try it on? Look how cute this jacket is.' She held it up against her. The black was a dramatic contrast to her platinum blonde hair and Bella knew the colour would work well against her own auburn curls. Lexi held the negligee and jacket out to her. 'Why don't you go into the bathroom and try it on?'

Bella could tell from Lexi's expression that she wasn't going to let this rest. The quickest way to get some peace and quiet was to give in. She'd try it on and then change straight back into her pyjamas.

She slipped the oxygen tubing over her head and unhooked the IV drip to carry it with her. She sighed. Getting changed wasn't simply a matter of swapping clothes. All the paraphernalia attached to her made the task that much more complicated. She grabbed the clothes and stepped into the bathroom, wondering why she always gave in and Lexi never did. Once again she was letting Lexi get her way while Lexi refused to budge an inch over the wedding date. Bella knew it wasn't quite the same thing but, still, it wouldn't kill Lexi to give in for once.

She hung her pyjamas on a hook behind the door and wriggled into the negligee. The bodice was firm and she had to tug it down over her head. It had built-in support that pushed her breasts together and created the illusion of a cleavage before the silk skimmed her ribs and flared out slightly over her hips. The silk was cool against her skin and as she turned around to try to see the view from the rear the silk swished around her hips and the sound of it made her feel like an actress in one of the 1950s movies she loved so much. But the negligee left very little to the imagination. She felt extremely exposed. She slid her arms into the jacket and tied it together at her throat. It gave her a little bit of cover but not nearly enough. She stuck her head out of the bathroom to catch Lexi's attention. She had no intention of stepping back into her room dressed like this. She waited until she'd caught Lexi's eye before opening the door a little wider.

Her sister looked her up and down. 'It looks gorgeous. Do you like it?'

'It feels fantastic,' Bella admitted. She loved the feel of the silk against her skin but it was far too revealing an outfit for her. 'But I couldn't possibly wear it in here.'

'Not even the jacket?' Lexi asked.

The jacket was rather fun but Bella knew it would look ridiculous over her pyjamas. Maybe she could wear it over a singlet top but she'd still have old pyjama pants on. She shook her head, she had nothing to wear it with, and then she closed the door and swapped glamour for comfort.

She handed the garments to Lexi as she emerged from the bathroom.

'I'm not taking them home,' Lexi said, 'I'll just leave them on the bed in case you change your mind.' Slightly mollified, Lexi laid them across the foot of Bella's bed before she left, promising to come back later in the afternoon.

Bella's morning tea had been delivered but

as she ate she couldn't stop thinking about the red negligee. And about how different she was from her sister. Although perhaps their taste in men wasn't so dissimilar, she thought. She had to agree with Lexi, Charlie was hot. But that was where the similarities ended. Bella would be mortified if anyone saw her in that outfit whereas Lexi would lap up the attention. Lexi would have worn the negligee and flicked her platinum locks and flirted up a storm with an attractive man, while Bella would retreat into the safety of her androgynous pyjamas. She reached for the negligee and picked it up, letting the silky fabric run through her fingers before she stroked the soft collar of the jacket. Perhaps she could redesign this into something she might wear. Something a little less flamboyant, a little less showgirl, a little more restrained.

She had one last mouthful of chocolate ice cream and a final bite of the chocolate muffin before she pushed the morning tea tray to one side to start drawing. She looked at the wedding-dress sketch she'd begun on the scrap of paper and ideas based around the little jacket began

popping into her mind. She started sketching another wedding dress, pretending it was something she might one day wear but knowing she
was kidding herself. It would never be her. She'd
spent so much time in and out of hospital in her
short life that she'd never even had a proper boyfriend. When she'd been well enough to go to
school she'd always been so far behind in her
work that her time had been spent trying to catch
up. Making matters more complicated was her
mild dyslexia, which had made schoolwork even
harder. She could have decided not to bother and
concentrated on boys and having a good time
instead but it wasn't in her nature to give up so
she'd struggled on. Besides, it wasn't like the
boys had ever been interested in her anyway, not
when her gorgeous younger sister had always
been nearby.

The only time Bella had ever come close to
having a romantic experience had been on a
camp run by the cystic fibrosis foundation. That
was where she'd had her first, and only, kiss and
she didn't kid herself it had been because the
boy hadn't been able to resist her. It had hap-

pened because it was a teenage camp and most of them had been in the same boat, looking for normal teenage experiences. With her history, walking down the aisle as a bride wasn't something that was likely to happen in her future. She was resigned to being the spinster sister. Lexi was already engaged and even though Evie wasn't showing any signs of settling down yet, Bella knew it would only be a matter of time. Whereas, for her... She sighed, but, she supposed, being unmarried was probably better than being dead. Probably.

She needed to be positive. That's what Charlie had told her. She looked again at the red negligee as she thought about Charlie. She wondered what he would make of it. He'd probably seen more than his fair share of gorgeous, scantily clad women and she wondered how she would compare. Unfavourably, she imagined.

She thought back to their conversation yesterday. She'd amazed herself that she'd actually been able to get the words out, she'd been terribly nervous and had had difficulty stopping herself from fidgeting obsessively, but in the end she'd managed to have a one-on-one conversation with Charlie. It was no small coincidence that the last time she'd had a personal conversation with someone who wasn't related to her or who wasn't her doctor had also been with Charlie. She doubted he even remembered that night, the night of her high-school graduation ball, or more accurately the night she'd missed her high-school ball, but Charlie had made her night considerably better and even if he might have forgotten all about it, she knew she never would. She didn't find it easy to open up to people but Charlie was a good listener. He was always so relaxed and that seemed to relax her. Still not enough to completely eradicate her nerves, but it was a start.

Charlie had wanted to know what she'd wanted. 'Nothing,' she'd said. But that wasn't quite true. There were a lot of things she wanted. Well, not things exactly, experiences would be a better term for it. Because of the cystic fibrosis she'd missed out on so many things her sisters had done and if she could, she'd love a chance to try some of those things for herself.

She wanted to go on a proper date.

She wanted to be held in the arms of a gorgeous man and twirled around the dance floor.

She wanted to wear a fabulous dress with a full skirt that floated around her and a plunging neckline before she had terrible scars.

She wanted to stand under a starry sky and be kissed senseless.

She wanted to stay up all night and watch the sun rise over the ocean.

She wanted to lie on a picnic rug with her head in her boyfriend's lap and eat strawberries and drink champagne.

She wanted to be able to say, 'They're playing our song.'

She wanted someone to look at her as though she was the most desirable woman he'd ever seen.

She wanted to fall in love.

Bella laughed at herself. She couldn't go back in time and she was so unaccustomed to looking forward that she couldn't imagine getting a chance to do any of those things. There were way too many variables.

First she'd have to have the opportunity to meet someone, then she'd have to be brave enough to engage them in conversation, then she'd have to wait and hope for them to ask her out. She wished she could be a bit more like Lexi. Lexi wouldn't wait to be asked out. Lexi never needed to wait.

Bella wished she was confident enough to flirt and chat but even if she was, who would she flirt with? Who was she going to meet in here? Charlie was coming but there was no way she could flirt with him. Even assuming she knew how to flirt, he would wonder what on earth had gotten into her. It was all she could do to have a normal conversation, she'd have to be crazy to push herself any further. She wished she didn't find Charlie quite so attractive. She might be able to flirt with someone she didn't have a crush on, but what was the point in that? She wouldn't want to date anyone she didn't fancy. But did that mean she would date Charlie? She knew she would in a flash and just thinking about it made her blush. It was a ridiculous idea. She couldn't imagine him asking her out any more than she could imagine flirting with him.

'*Ciao*, Bella, you're looking brighter today.'

The sound of his voice made her jump. She'd

been a million miles away and for a moment she wondered if she'd imagined him and his familiar greeting, but when she looked up she found him smiling at her and her heart skipped a beat.

He was wearing short-sleeved blue scrubs and had obviously just come from Theatre. His forearms were tanned and muscular but tapered nicely into narrower wrists and the long, slender fingers she always associated with surgeon's hands.

Bella took a deep breath as she willed herself to stay calm. *You've known him for years, he's just a man.*

But he was so gorgeous, was it any wonder she got all flustered? He was standing in front of her, looking hot and sexy, while she was in bed, looking frumpy and pale. They were at opposite ends of the spectrum as far as sex appeal went. Perhaps she should have left the negligee on. It might have been better than her ancient pyjama pants.

The two of them were such a contrast it almost made her laugh out loud. It was ridiculous to even imagine he'd ever ask her out.

Somehow she found her voice. 'I'm feeling much better,' she answered. 'Whatever cocktail Sam has put me on seems to be working.' She knew she had more colour in her cheeks but it wasn't because she was feeling better, it was because she'd been daydreaming about Charlie, and now that he was standing in front of her she felt her cheeks redden further.

Charlie stepped closer and brought the smell of sunshine with him, which overpowered the antiseptic smell of the hospital. Bella took a deep breath and savoured his scent as she tried to commit it to memory.

'Have you had a chance to speak to Sam about the wedding?' he asked.

She nodded.

His brown eyes watched her intently. 'How did that go?'

She smiled, remembering how nervous Sam had seemed. 'He said he'd do his best but I could tell he didn't like his chances. You'd think someone who's feted as being a top-class surgeon would be afraid of nothing, but I think Lexi is calling the shots.'

Charlie burst out laughing. The sound of happiness filled the room and made Bella smile even wider.

'He did say he'll file their notice of intent to marry. They need to have that lodged a month and one day before they can legally tie the knot.'

'That's a start at least,' Charlie said as he reached out his hand and ran a finger lazily around the edge of her almost empty bowl. He slid his finger into his mouth and Bella's eyes were riveted to the sight of it disappearing between his delicious lips as he licked it clean. He raised one eyebrow. 'Chocolate ice cream for morning tea? That's an interesting diet.'

'Don't you know? A high-fat diet is recommended for cystic fibrosis sufferers.'

'Is that right?' His brown eyes caught the light and the tiny flecks of gold in his irises reflected the light back at her.

She nodded. 'There has to be an upside every now and again, and eating dessert at any time of the day or night is one of them.' Never mind the assortment of tablets lined up on her shelf. Pancreatic enzyme replacement tablets, vitamin capsules and salt replacement tablets marched along the wall in an orderly row, ready and waiting to be taken regularly, but fortunately Charlie hadn't noticed them. His attention had moved on from the ice cream to her sketch book, which was lying open on the table.

'What have you been up to?' he asked.

She glanced down at her sketch book, surprised to see the pages covered with drawings.

A full-skirted wedding dress with a fur-trimmed fitted jacket took up most of one page and beside it she'd drawn a pair of intertwined rings. She remembered starting the dress but she didn't recall filling in the rest of the pages. Luckily she could pass the dress off as Lexi's wedding dress but the other sketches had nothing to do with Lexi. While she'd been daydreaming her hand had been transferring her thoughts to the paper. There was a sunrise warming an ocean and casting light onto a sandy beach. She could see footprints in the sand and in the corner of the page, where the footprints stopped, she could see the tasselled fringing of a picnic rug.

In the centre of the other page she'd drawn a

pale green silk dress, its neckline similar to that of the negligee but with a full skirt. She'd drawn the skirt so that it was billowing out as if it was spinning to the music made by the notes she'd surrounded it with. She must have continued doodling absent-mindedly and stars, strawberries and music notes were scattered over the page, surrounding the green dress.

Around the edge of this page, framing it in a border, were lips—plump, juicy, soft lips, coloured in shades of pink and red. She blushed as she saw the frame she'd made, a frame of Charlie's lips. But it was too late to close the book, too late to hide her thoughts. Charlie had spun the book around, looking more closely at the pictures.

'Your drawings are really good.'

Please, please, don't let him recognise the lips.

'Is this for Lexi?' he asked, pointing to the wedding dress.

'Mmm,' Bella replied.

'And is this the bridesmaid's dress?'

She shook her head. 'No.'

Could she tell him? Talking about other people

was easy, that came much more naturally to her; talking about herself was harder, much harder. But she'd managed to talk to him yesterday. It was silly to be so nervous.

She looked at her sketches. If she wanted any of those things to happen she would have to force herself to bury the introvert within her. Shy, re-tiring wallflowers didn't get any of those things she wanted, experience had taught her that al-ready. She was twenty-six years old, she'd known Charlie for ever, it was time to start being a little more extroverted.

She took a deep mental breath. 'That's the dress I want to wear to go dancing.'

'Who are you going dancing with?'

She could hear the note of surprise in his voice.

'No one,' she replied. 'I was daydreaming. These are things I'd like to do when I get out of here.'

'You've drawn a "to do" list?' he asked.

Bella shrugged. 'I think in pictures, not words,' she explained. Even before she'd been diagnosed with dyslexia she'd always thought in pictures and found drawing a much easier way of expressing herself. 'And it's not exactly a "to do" list, more a wishlist.'

'So, dancing?'

Bella nodded and Charlie pointed to the next picture.

'I want to stand on the beach and see the sun rise,' she told him. She held her breath as she waited for him to point to the next picture. *Please don't ask about the stars in the sky.* She didn't have the words to explain that she wanted to be properly and thoroughly kissed by someone who knew what they were doing. She relaxed when he pointed to the footprints in the sand that led from the sunrise to the picnic blanket.

'I want to go on a picnic.'

'A picnic?' He was frowning. 'Surely you've been on a picnic?'

'A proper picnic,' she said.

'What on earth is a "proper picnic"?' he asked with a smile which made Bella's heart rate kick up a notch.

'You know, like the ones in movies where there is such an enormous amount of food you wonder how they've managed to fit it all into the basket

let alone carry it across the field. Just two people, in a world of their own, no one else around,
just peace and quiet.'

'Let me guess.' Charlie laughed. 'The champagne has stayed cold, the salad isn't soggy and
the ants aren't trying to share your meal.'

'Laugh if you must, but someday I am going
to enjoy a proper, perfect picnic.'

'So you're going to be at Lexi's wedding, watch
the sunrise, go on a perfect picnic and dance
under the stars?' he said as he turned the page,
obviously looking for more pictures. 'Where're
the rest?'

'That's it.'

'That's not much. You could knock that all over
in one weekend.'

'You might be able to. I'm not sure if I'd have
the stamina.'

'So what's this for?' Charlie treated her to a
wicked grin as his hand dipped down towards the
end of her bed and disappeared behind the table
holding the remnants of morning tea. When he
lifted his hand back up the red negligee dangled
from his index finger. The table positioned across

her bed had hidden the negligee from sight and Bella had forgotten it was lying in full view.

Bella blushed furiously. 'Nothing. Lexi was supposed to take it home for me.'

'Pity. I was hoping it had something to do with your list.' The negligee looked particularly minuscule and flimsy hanging from Charlie's finger and Bella couldn't help but recall that this was the same finger that had sampled her ice cream and been licked clean by those luscious lips.

'Like what?' Bella asked, half terrified and half excited to hear what his answer might be.

'It looks like something you might wear for a long lazy weekend in bed...' he paused ever so slightly '...with company. Drinking champagne by moonlight and getting up only to cook scrambled eggs at midday before getting back between the sheets.'

The picture Charlie painted was enough to make her blush. She'd never had a weekend like that, although it sounded as though Charlie was speaking from experience. He was folding the negligee as he waited for her answer and his hands looked strong and masculine tangled up in the flimsy fabric. The sight took any words right out of Bella's head. All she could do was shake her head in reply.

'So that's really it, that's your entire wishlist? What about something more challenging?' Charlie asked.

'Like what?'

'I don't know. Learning a musical instrument, running a marathon, learning another language, all those things other people always talk about doing one day.'

'I'm not sure I'm going to have time to do those sorts of things.'

Charlie frowned. 'Why not?'

'They're all long-term goals,' Bella said.

'What's wrong with that?'

'Nothing.' There was nothing at all wrong with it for other people. 'It's just I've never really thought long-term.'

'Oh.' She could see him connecting the dots.

'I've never got into the habit of long-term goals,' she explained. While things had improved considerably in the past twenty years, cystic fibrosis sufferers still didn't have a long life expectancy.

'But if you're going to have a transplant, surely now's the time to set some long-term goals. There must be something big you want to do?'

'I've learnt not to set unrealistic goals,' she told him. 'Every time I started something that was going to require a large investment of time the wheels would fall off and I'd get sick and never finish anything. I barely even finished high school because I missed so much time. I haven't expanded the list for after surgery because I've never thought long term, I wouldn't know where to start. My goals have always had to be achievable in the short term.' She looked up at him. 'Do *you* have a plan for your future?'

'Most definitely,' he replied.

'So how did you work it out?'

'Trial and error mainly. It's a work in progress.'

'If you thought you only had a few years left, would you be doing anything differently?'

That was an interesting question but not one he wanted to examine too closely. His current goals centred around his medical career. Medicine had served him well, it had given him another option when his life had gone pear-shaped, but if he hadn't had to plan for a long life, if he'd been living on limited time, would he have tried harder to recover a lost passion? A lost love?

Who was he kidding? He could have tried to resurrect those dreams but he never would have succeeded. He shook his head. Those dreams hadn't died, they'd been killed off and he hadn't had a chance to resurrect them.

'I guess I wish some things could have been different,' he answered, 'but they were out of my control. Things happen for a reason. One door closes, another one opens.'

'I'm just worried about doors closing at the moment,' Bella said. 'If I get through the surgery I can make a new list but I thought I'd start with the ones I've missed.'

'Fair enough, but I still think you should put a couple down for post-surgery. Something to look forward to, instead of back. There must be something.'

She didn't answer immediately and Charlie wondered if perhaps she had really never dared to dream of a future. Was there really nothing she wanted? He didn't think he'd ever met anyone as selfless as Bella. She had her head down again, drawing more pictures on her sketch pad. He watched as her hand flew across the page covering it with tiny high-heeled shoes that reminded him of Cinderella. Then, as suddenly as she had started sketching, she stopped and looked up at him.

'Fashion design,' she said, her voice whisper quiet.

'Fashion design?'

She nodded. 'That's my dream. To study fashion design.'

'Why aren't you already doing it?'

'I have to submit a written application.' She also had to submit six examples of her work but that part was easy. She had hundreds of sketches and finished designs to choose from.

'And?'

'I haven't been able to get the written part done.' Because of her dyslexia she'd never been a competent reader or writer and she'd gravitated towards the practical courses like art and design where she could rely on her drawing skills. The idea of writing a submission to a college, one that would determine whether or not she secured a place in their course, terrified her.

'What does the written part involve?'

'I have to explain why I want to do the course, what I hope to get out of it and why I should be accepted.'

'That doesn't sound too bad.'

She couldn't begin to imagine where to start. 'I can draw anything but I'm not good with words.' She wasn't about to admit her struggles to Charlie. She wasn't ready to have that conversation with him.

'I'll help you but you'll have to add it to your wishlist. It's already November—applications for next year will close soon if they haven't already.'

'Next year?'

Charlie was nodding. 'This is perfect. It'll give you something to look forward to. You tell me what this course means to you and I'll write the application letter for you,' he said as his pager began beeping. He took it from his pocket and checked it before adding, 'I'll come back tomorrow and we'll get started.'

He gave her a quick wink and was gone before

she could protest. Before she could tell him she couldn't possibly go to college. It wasn't just the submission—how would she manage the written aspect of a serious course?

She picked up the negligee from where he'd dropped it on her bed. She stroked it while she imagined wearing it, imagined wearing it while Charlie's finger slid underneath the strap and pulled it from her shoulder. She imagined him bending his head and pressing his lips to the bare skin over her collarbone. She could almost feel the heat of his soft lips searing her skin.

She opened her eyes and shoved the negligee into one of the drawers beside her bed. That could stay buried along with her fantasies about studying fashion design and her fantasies about Charlie. None of those things needed to see the light of day again.

CHAPTER FOUR

BELLA felt as though she spent the best part of the next day with one eye on the door, waiting for Charlie. Lexi visited, Evie visited, Sam came on his rounds and pronounced her almost ready for discharge again, but Charlie didn't appear.

She didn't want to think about how much she'd been looking forward to seeing him. How often she'd checked the time during the day and as the hours advanced thought he must have forgotten about her. How she'd deliberately changed out of her daggy pyjamas into a slightly more respectable T-shirt and leggings. How she'd made sure the red negligee was still safely stowed out of sight in one of the bedside drawers.

It was late in the afternoon and Evie was visiting for a second time when Bella heard a new set of footsteps approaching. For a moment she let herself hope it was Charlie but she could hear that the steps were slightly uneven and whoever was walking towards her room was wearing high-heeled shoes.

An older version of Lexi tottered into her room. This woman had the same platinum blonde hair and the same bright blue eyes but Bella knew the similarities were only skin deep. This was her mother.

As usual she was immaculately dressed all in black. She had tucked her skinny black pants into high-heeled black patent leather boots and she wore a long black cardigan over a black top. A stranger could be forgiven for thinking Miranda was on her way to a funeral but this was her colour of choice broken up only by her blonde hair and masses of silver jewellery. Her make-up had also been perfectly applied. But underneath the make-up Bella could see the tell-tale redness of Miranda's nose. It wasn't red from crying, it was red from alcohol, and her eyes had a familiar glazed appearance. But otherwise her presentation was flawless.

Even when she's been drinking she's better groomed than I am, Bella thought. She and Evie exchanged a glance. *What is she doing here?* But before either of them had a chance to speak, Miranda broke the silence.

'Bella! My baby!' She leant over to kiss Bella and almost lost her balance. She reached out one hand and steadied herself on the bed. Bella's nose wrinkled under the smell of gin.

'Mum. What are you doing here?'

'I came to see you, of course.'

'I've been in hospital for three days and you're only coming in now?' As usual it was plainly obvious to Bella that she was not high on the list of her mother's priorities.

'Three days! I only just found out. Why didn't someone tell me sooner?'

'Richard has been trying to contact you,' Evie told her.

'Well, he didn't try very hard.' Miranda pouted.

'He's left several messages.'

'Why didn't *you* ring me?' Miranda asked Evie. 'Do you know how much it hurts to think that my own daughters wouldn't contact me?'

Typical, Bella thought. It was always about what was happening in Miranda's world. She had no great regard for anything other than her appearance and her alcohol supply. Her daughters came a poor third behind her wardrobe and her alcohol addiction. Bella wanted to ask her if she knew how much she'd hurt her daughters. How much her abandonment of them as young children had hurt, how much her selfishness and drinking continued to hurt. But Bella didn't want to create a scene, she always did her utmost to avoid scenes, although that was hard to manage whenever her mother was around.

'We agreed that Richard would contact you,' Evie replied. 'Don't tell me you haven't got his messages. If you've been in no state to answer the phone or listen to your messages, that's no one's fault but your own. There's no need for all of us to be running around after you. Bella needs us now. We've been here for her as much as possible.'

Bella didn't know how Evie stayed strong. Bella wanted to stand up for herself but she wanted her mother to love her even more, and because of that she very rarely took a stand.

Miranda did her best to appear affronted. She

drew herself up to her full height of five feet
six inches but her heels gave her the extra two
inches, which brought her almost up to Evie's
height. 'I beg your pardon. I had one pre-dinner
drink, you know how much I hate hospitals.'

Bella knew that even if her mother did detest
hospitals, which she thought was unlikely, one
pre-dinner dinner drink would still have pre-
ceded several more and dinner would be forgotten in favour of another glass of gin.

Did their mother have any idea how much
her daughters wished she loved them enough to
fight her demons? Bella knew Evie had long ago
given up praying for that day but Bella hadn't.
But there was no point in arguing about it. She
wasn't going to change the facts. But she was exhausted and her mother's visit was making her
emotional. She wondered if she had the strength
to ask her mother to leave. Before one of them
said something they might regret.

'Perhaps you should go, then, if hospitals disagree with you so much,' Evie said, coming to
Bella's rescue once more.

'I have as much right as you to be here.'

'Actually, you don't,' Evie said. 'Bella needs to rest and as a doctor at this hospital I can ask you to leave. This is not about you. Bella needs positive support. If you can't give her that then you should leave. You need to take responsibility for your actions. Bella doesn't need to listen to your complaints. She doesn't need you to try to make her feel guilty about being in hospital. It's not as if she wants to be here. I'll walk downstairs with you and organise a taxi to take you home.' Evie turned to Bella. 'Will you be all right on your own for a bit?'

Bella nodded. 'I am tired. Perhaps you could come back one morning,' she said to her mother, unable not to make a peace offering, as Evie took a slightly bewildered Miranda gently but firmly by the elbow and steered her towards the door.

Evie kept hold of Miranda partly to make sure she came with her but also partly to prevent her from stumbling. While Miranda was so neatly presented Evie could pretend everything was fine. The girls knew that their mother's fastidiousness with regard to her appearance was all part of her deception but they held onto the hope that while she retained her sense of vanity maybe there was a chance she would one day seek the help she desperately needed. While she knew Miranda's disease wasn't something she could control or be responsible for, Evie wasn't sure that everyone else would see it from her point of view and she didn't want the hospital staff to see her mother in this state. Did that make her complicit in Miranda's problem? Did that make her an accessory to Miranda's addiction? She knew it probably did but she wasn't going to stop and think about it. Not now. She didn't want to be mean but she didn't have the energy to deal with her mother's issues today and she knew Bella didn't need the drama either. She would make sure her mother got safely out of there.

As she reached the doorway she saw Charlie approaching and saw him rapidly assess the situation. But she didn't worry. Other than her immediate family Charlie knew Miranda's history better than anyone. Evie and Charlie had shared many confidences during their final university years but Evie knew Charlie would be discreet, just as she always was with his personal history.

'Is everything okay?'

'Yes,' Evie answered, but she kept walking. She didn't want to stop and give Miranda an opportunity to create a scene. She knew very well just how likely that was. 'Are you on your way to see Bella?' She waited for Charlie to nod. 'Can you stay for a bit?' she asked. She didn't want Bella to be alone. Miranda's impromptu visits were always disturbing and she knew Bella would replay the conversation and stress over it. She needed company and Charlie would be a good distraction.

'Sure.' He knew what was needed.

Charlie continued walking and knocked briefly on Bella's door as he entered her room. She was sitting up in bed. She was still pale but the oxygen tubing had been removed from under her nose and for the first time since she'd been admitted Charlie could see her whole face without obstruction.

'*Ciao*, Bella. Is this a bad time?' he asked. 'I brought chocolate,' he said as he showed her the paper carry bag he held.

Bella's smile lit up her face. 'As far as I'm concerned, there's never a bad time for chocolate.'

Suddenly Charlie didn't notice how pale she was, or how thin—all he noticed was how her grey eyes sparkled and how the shape of her face changed. For someone of such a slight build she had a round face, but when she smiled her face became heart shaped and she looked less like a teenager and more like a woman. She was beautiful.

He'd always thought of Bella as the quiet one, the unobtrusive one. He'd never thought of her as being the pretty one. Tall, slim, glamorous Lexi with her platinum blonde hair and extroverted personality was hard to miss and Evie with her positive, confident attitude and easy smile was always in the midst of whatever was going on. Thinking of them like that, he supposed it wasn't surprising that Bella could slip through the cracks between her sisters and go unnoticed, that she would become lost amongst the dominant characters of her siblings.

But when he looked at her now it was as though he was seeing her properly for the first time. Her grey eyes were luminous, an unusual cool contrast to the fiery colour of her hair, and her skin was slightly flushed now, giving her a healthy glow. Her unusual colouring had always made her interesting to look at but he couldn't believe he'd never noticed her classic beauty.

He shook his head, trying to clear his mind as he handed her the bag of sweet things and pulled a chair up to the bed. Her bed was covered with pencils and sketch books but the red negligee was nowhere to be seen.

Her laptop was on the overbed table and she pushed it to one side before she emptied the contents of the bag, depositing them beside the computer. Chocolate muffins, chocolate cheesecake, caramel slice and chocolate bars covered the surface. 'What would you like?' Bella asked.

'You choose first, it's your treat,' he replied as he searched in the bag for spoons for the cheesecake. Bella was still smiling and he realised that for the first time she didn't seem self-conscious around him. Her smile seemed natural today; perhaps that was why she looked so different. He was amazed she didn't seem more rattled by her mother's visit considering the state she was in but he supposed she was used to it. 'So things haven't improved for Miranda?' he asked.

'No. But I've learnt there's nothing I can do that will change things there,' she said.

He saw her straighten her skinny shoulders, preparing herself. He was finding her more and more admirable. For someone who looked so frail and young and delicate she was showing a remarkable amount of spirit. He liked that about her. The fact she wasn't going to give up.

'My mother has never made any secret of the fact that I have been nothing but a problem. I spent years trying to atone for it but nothing I do has ever made any difference so now I try to ignore her barbs. Although at times I admit it's difficult. But I certainly don't want to dwell on her tonight. She doesn't spend any time worrying about me. I'm going to return the favour.'

The Lockheart sisters were lucky to have each other, he thought; they certainly didn't get a lot of love and attention from their parents. No wonder they were so close. He may not have had the same privileged lifestyle that the girls had had, in fact his family had struggled financially, but he'd never suffered from a lack of love and attention. His family was close, and even though more money would have made a difference to their daily lives, it wouldn't have changed their relationships. Money could never replace love.

Bella reached out and took one of the spoons from his hand as he sat mutely contemplating their differences. 'I suggest we eat chocolate and talk about something else,' she said as she reached for the bottles of tablets, shaking some enzyme-replacement pills into her hand before selecting several, which she swallowed with a mouthful of water.

He tried to stop staring but he was finding it difficult. He didn't want to freak her out but he couldn't think of anything to say and it took him a moment to even remember why he was there. 'Let's talk about your course application. I came to help you submit it.'

Bella looked startled, her grey eyes wide. 'I appreciate your offer but you don't have to help me, you know.'

'Are you going to do it without my help?'

Bella shook her head and her auburn curls bounced around her shoulders. 'No.'

'Did you want me to come back tomorrow instead?'

'Sam thinks I'll be able to go home tomorrow. I'll get Lexi to help me then.'

'No, you won't,' he argued.

'How do you know?'

'If you were going to let Lexi help you, you would have done this ages ago. I've done all the research, we have chocolate, let's get to work.' He'd promised Evie he'd keep an eye on Bella. She needed distracting. Otherwise, despite her protests, he knew she'd dwell on her mother's issues. Working on her application would provide a perfect distraction.

'You've done all the research?'

He nodded. He liked to be prepared in everything he did. He didn't like surprises. In his experience surprises were never a good thing. 'I had a look at it in some more detail last night. It shouldn't take too long to get it together.'

'You looked at it last night?' Bella raised an eyebrow. 'Didn't you have a date?'

Last night had been Wednesday, traditionally a big night with half-price drinks at Pete's Bar, the local watering hole for hospital staff. Normally Charlie would have been at Pete's. It was always a good place to hook up with an attractive woman, there were plenty of them at the hospital and plenty of them frequented Pete's for drinks at the end of a shift. But he had promised to help Bella and he'd been keen to see her reaction when he arrived prepared. Besides, pretty nurses would be at Pete's again the next time he called in.

'Not officially.' He changed the subject, bringing them back to the reason he was there. 'Did you know the cut-off for applications is next week? Have you got samples of your work to send in?'

Bella nodded. 'The practical aspect of things I'm prepared for, it's just the written application that terrifies me. Words aren't my thing.'

Charlie grinned. It felt good to be doing something like this. He enjoyed finding solutions to problems and that was something he loved about medicine too. 'That's why I'm here. Can you log onto the college website?'

Bella opened her laptop and ran her finger over the mouse pad, bringing the computer back to life. She'd forgotten she'd been watching a DVD earlier and before she could minimise the screen the movie reappeared and Charlie immediately recognised it. Normally she'd be embarrassed if someone discovered her watching the romantic comedies she adored but she'd decided that after the episode with the red negligee she wouldn't waste time being embarrassed. Besides, he already knew her deepest, darkest secrets and if he could accept her alcoholic mother, surely he'd accept her penchant for light cinema.

'Good movie,' he said as he sat down.

Bella felt absurdly pleased that he hadn't criticised her taste in movies. She smiled. 'You've seen it?'

'*Pretty Woman*? Of course. Hasn't everyone?' he said. 'If I remember correctly, it's a modern version of the classic fairy-tale. The rich, handsome hero arrives in his chauffeured limousine, climbs the fire escape to the heroine's tower with a rose between his teeth and rescues her from her tortured life. That sounds suspiciously like Snow White, or maybe Sleeping Beauty, don't you think?'

'Careful. You're having a go at one of my favourite movies,' Bella retorted as she closed the program and logged onto the internet. 'I like to think there's more to it than that. Vivienne wants someone who can see past her outer shell, someone who can see the woman underneath.' Bella knew she identified with the character of Vivienne, probably more than was good for her. 'Edward needs someone to make him see the joy in the little things, to make him see that there's more to life than making money. They need each other. That's what I love. There's nothing wrong with a happy ending, is there?'

'No, not at all. I'm only teasing. I meant it when I said it was good, I just didn't know people still watched it.'

'Go ahead, make fun of my taste in movies, but I'm not the only one who loves it.'

He laughed at the expression on her face and the sound of his laugh and the way his brown eyes crinkled at the corners made her forget all about being cross. She could sit there all day and watch him laughing. He looked so comfortable, completely at ease, happy and relaxed. She couldn't remember feeling like that for a long time. Perhaps if she could spend more time in his company some of his joie de vivre would rub off on her.

'Has that website loaded yet?' he asked once he'd finished laughing at her expense.

She turned her attention back to her laptop, pleased to have something to focus on, something to distract herself from those fanciful thoughts.

'Why are you doing this for me?' she asked as she waited for the website to load. Once she was in she followed the links to the page she needed. She knew how to navigate her way around the site; she visited it regularly. She'd just never been brave enough to take the next step of applying online.

'You'll thank me when you've recovered from your op and you've got all those years stretching ahead of you.' He was still grinning at her and she forced herself to concentrate on what he was saying. She knew she was too easily mesmerised by his smile, by his perfect pink lips. 'You'll need something to do. Even Vivienne in *Pretty Woman* has a job. Not that I'm recommending you follow in her footsteps, I think fashion design is a better fit for you.'

There he went again, making jokes at her expense. 'I never realised you were such a comedian,' she said.

'I'm doing this because I want to help. You asked me to keep an eye on Evie and she asked me to do the same for you,' he admitted. 'This is a way I can be useful at the same time.'

That made sense. Charlie was here because Evie had asked him to come.

Bella wanted to be upset that he hadn't come for her sake but if this was the only way of getting him to visit, she wasn't going to complain. She was used to people doing things for Evie, just like she was used to Lexi always getting her own way. It was just how things worked around her sisters.

'But I don't mind, I can think of worse things to be than the Lockheart sisters' unofficial guardian,' Charlie added, and he sounded so sincere that, once again, Bella found her irritation disappearing immediately. She couldn't have stayed annoyed with him even if she'd wanted to.

He lifted the laptop off the table and set it on the edge of the bed. 'Now, you need to tell me all the reasons why you're desperate to do this course, what your goals are and why you should be considered as an applicant. Then I'll make you sound so fantastic they won't be able to refuse you entry.'

And, over the course of the next hour, that's exactly what he did. By the end of it Bella didn't recognise herself as the girl who'd barely graduated from high school and struggled to read. Instead she sounded accomplished and talented and Charlie had made it sound as though the college would be lucky to have her. 'Okay, that box is ticked,' he said as he saved the file. 'Once you get home you'll need to choose which examples of your work you want to submit and get everything into the college by the end of next week. What else do we need to organise?'

'I think you've done more than enough,' Bella

said gratefully. 'I really appreciate your help but I'm okay. I'll be home tomorrow and then I just have to wait and hope that things don't deteriorate too much more before I get new lungs.'

'What about your wishlist?'

'That was just me being silly. It's not important.' She tried to stifle a yawn, knowing that Charlie would leave if he thought she was tired, but she was unsuccessful.

'Okay,' he said, 'we'll save that discussion for another day.' He stood and gathered up the remnants of their chocolate feast. 'Get some rest. I'll see you again soon.'

Bella didn't know when. She wanted to remind him she'd be going home tomorrow but she didn't want it to sound as though she was begging him to come and see her before she left. Why was it so hard to know what the right thing to say or do was? She'd made good progress over the past couple of days, she could actually talk to Charlie without blushing furiously or stammering, but she still continued to second-guess herself. Why couldn't she be more confident? Why couldn't she be more exuberant? Why couldn't she be more like her sisters?

CHAPTER FIVE

IT WAS late afternoon and Bella had not long woken up from an afternoon nap when she heard the intercom at the front gate buzzing. She wandered into the kitchen, wondering where Rosa was. The succession of nannies the girls had grown up with had long ago been replaced by a succession of housekeepers, but the kitchen was empty, Rosa was nowhere to be seen. The buzzing continued. Bella crossed the room to the intercom. Rosa had left a note on the bench, letting Bella know she'd popped out to the shops, and on the intercom screen Bella could see a courier waiting at the bottom of the driveway. She pressed the button to open the gates and met him at the front door.

'I have a registered letter for Miss Lockheart.'

'Alexis Lockheart?' Bella asked, assuming it

was for Lexi, who, as far as she knew, was out of the house. 'Does she have to sign for it?'

The courier checked his records. 'Miss Arabella Lockheart, it says, but anyone can sign.'

Registered mail for *her*? Bella frowned and signed the digital receipt, wondering what it could possibly be. The courier handed her a small envelope. It was thick, glossy cream; it could only be an invitation. The only things Bella ever got invited to were Lockheart Foundation events and she'd never received a formal invitation for those. Her hands were shaking as she closed the front door and slit open the envelope and pulled out the contents.

Dr Charles Maxwell
Requests the pleasure of the company of
Miss Arabella Lockheart
On Saturday 17 November
For dinner and dancing
On board the MV Endeavour 2000
Please be ready to depart at 6 p.m.
Dress: After Five

RSVP: None required. Dr Maxwell will not accept any excuses!

The invitation *was* for her.

Bella sank onto a chair in the front hallway and read it again just to make sure. Charlie was inviting her out. *Her.*

She couldn't possibly go. Could she? A list of excuses ran through her head. She could think of plenty.

She read the invitation a third time. Then re-read the RSVP. Charlie would not accept any excuses. What was she going to do?

At a few minutes after six on Saturday evening Bella eased herself into the soft, puffy comfort of the leather seats and tried to think of something clever or witty to say. *Quick, think of something, anything, before Charlie gets into the car. Before he realises I'm a dud date.*

But Charlie was already getting into the limousine. His subtle, spicy scent combined with the smell of leather and wood polish and made it impossible for her to think.

She was ridiculously nervous. Her heart was racing in her chest and her palms were clammy. She had thought about trying to get out of the date, not because she didn't want to go but because she didn't want to be disappointed. She knew her expectations of the evening would far surpass anything Charlie could have imagined. But when Lexi had arrived home the other day to find her still sitting by the front door, clutching the invitation in her hand, she had quickly put her 'event coordinator' hat on and organised Bella. Lexi wouldn't hear of her passing up this invitation and Bella had let herself be carried away by Lexi's excitement. To be honest, she'd been glad to let Lexi make the decision for her but now here she was, in a limousine, with Charlie, and no matter how many times she tried to tell herself that this wasn't a real date, that Charlie was just being nice, it didn't work. She still held out the hope that this would be the date she'd always dreamed of.

It was almost a fantasy come to life except for the fact that Charlie hadn't greeted her with a kiss. That should have reminded her this wasn't a real date. At least, not in a romantic sense. That should have settled her nerves but as she looked across to where Charlie sat in his dark navy suit, looking more handsome than she'd ever thought possible, her nervousness kicked up a notch. The cut of his suit was perfect, the back was double-vented, which accommodated Charlie's muscular frame and gave him room to move, and his plain white shirt had French cuffs which he'd fastened with silver cufflinks. She knew most people wouldn't notice little details like that but fashion had been her obsession for as long as she could remember. As she looked at Charlie sitting alongside her, she wondered whether she was becoming just a little bit more obsessed with him than was healthy. He was truly gorgeous.

'Can I pour you a glass of champagne?' His question broke into her thoughts.

She wasn't accustomed to drinking, after seeing its effect on her mother she tended to avoid it, but surely a taste of champagne couldn't hurt? Perhaps it would take the edge off her nervousness. She needed to relax if she was going to fully enjoy the evening.

'Are you still taking antibiotics?' Charlie asked when she didn't reply immediately. 'Would you rather something soft to drink?'

Bella hadn't even considered the medication she was taking. Perhaps it wasn't a good idea? But she felt like celebrating, tonight was a big deal for her. 'Would a small glass be all right, do you think?'

'I think so. I promise to keep a close eye on you and administer first aid if necessary,' he replied with a grin as he rotated the champagne bottle and removed the cork with a satisfying 'pop'.

Bella watched as he poured champagne into flutes. He handed her one before gently clinking their glasses together in a toast.

'Here's to a fun evening. And to you. You look beautiful.'

Had he just told her she was beautiful? She couldn't believe her ears. 'I do?' She swallowed hard, trying to dislodge the lump in her throat so she could speak clearly. If she sipped her champagne now, she knew she'd choke on it.

Charlie nodded. 'It's a big improvement on flannel pyjamas.' He laughed.

Bella's cheeks reddened. Once again he'd managed to make her blush. Being embarrassed seemed to be becoming a permanent state around Charlie. 'It's bad manners to laugh at your own jokes,' she managed to mutter.

'My apologies,' he said, looking anything but apologetic. 'But what happened to the green dress?'

She sipped her champagne and felt the tiny bubbles fizz in the back of her throat. For the life of her Bella couldn't remember what she was wearing. She looked down at her dress and saw silver sequins and white chiffon. Not a trace of green in sight. That's right, she'd borrowed a dress of Lexi's. 'The green dress?'

'The one in your sketch book.'

'That was just a design, I didn't have time to make it!' She'd only just had enough time to take Lexi's dress in at the seams and it was still a little big in the bust, but Lexi had fixed that with a padded bra. It was a beautiful dress, a bodice of silver sequins that would shimmer in the lights and a skirt of white chiffon that was made for dancing, but it definitely wasn't green. 'I need a bit more notice if you expect me to whip something up,' she added as the champagne loosened her tongue.

'I'll remember that next time.' Charlie smiled at her and Bella's heart did a funny flip and collided with her stomach.

She had no idea whether it was the effect of his smile or the champagne or his words that caused her insides to take up gymnastics. *Next time?* She didn't even understand what was happening this time.

'Where are we going tonight?' she asked, barely managing to get another sentence out.

'We will be cruising Sydney Harbour in style,' he replied. 'Dinner and dancing under the stars. I'm sorry it's not a picnic on the beach but I wasn't sure if that was wise given you've just come out of hospital. I thought we could save that for another time.'

There he went again, talking about the next time almost as though he really did have plans to see her again. She couldn't let it go again. 'Why would there be another time?'

'Bella! I'm gravely offended,' he joked, clutching a hand to his chest. 'Most girls wait till the end of the date before deciding they don't want to see me again.'

Bella laughed at his expression and she could feel herself relax. She knew it was his intention to put her at ease. 'Sorry, that's not what I meant. I'm just not sure why you're taking me out tonight, let alone why you might want to do it again.'

'I promised to help you with your wishlist and this cruise had all the things I know you love. Music, dancing, a starry sky and plenty of food.'

It's a pity she suffered from seasickness but she didn't tell Charlie that. She didn't want to hurt his feelings. He was being so sweet. 'You're right, it does sound perfect,' she replied.

She'd had the perfect excuse to get out of the evening, she did get terribly seasick, but he'd said on the invitation he wouldn't accept excuses and she wasn't about to give up what might be her only chance to have a night like this.

'Have you been on this cruise before?' she asked, hoping his answer would be no. She wanted the experience to be a first for both of

them. But he was already nodding. It had been
a silly question. She knew his reputation. He'd
probably done this trip a dozen times, each with a
different girl. She felt deflated but his next words
cheered her up.

'Once before. The ortho department's Christmas
party was on board last year.'

That wasn't so bad, that would have been a totally different experience to tonight. He wouldn't
have been dining at a table for two that night, she
assumed. Although with Charlie she suspected
anything was possible.

The limousine came to a stop and through the
glass partition Bella saw the driver get out of his
seat. Charlie let himself out and came around the
vehicle and waited for her as the driver held her
door open. She climbed out as elegantly as she
could in her unfamiliar high heels, and when her
legs felt a little unsteady she blamed her strappy,
silver stilettos and not the champagne.

The driver had delivered them straight to the
gangplank of the MV *Endeavour* and Bella
looked up at it amazed. It was sleek and white
and ultra-modern. She wasn't sure what she'd

been expecting but this was very slick. And enormous. It towered above them—she could count three decks rising above the water, and dozens of passengers were making their way on board.

Charlie took her hand as they joined the queue. His hand was warm and strong and secure and she was grateful not only for the emotional support but for the physical support as well. She could just see herself stumbling up the gangplank and making a spectacle of herself.

They made their way to the second deck where a waiter led them to a table beside the window on the starboard side. The dining room stretched the width of the yacht and the windows wrapped right around it. They would get glorious views of the harbour through sunset and into the evening, Bella realised as she sat down while the waiter held her chair for her.

Even seated she still felt a little light-headed and it wasn't until her entrée had been served and she had some food in her stomach that she was able to think clearly. At least, she blamed her hunger for her poor concentration, although it had as much to do with Charlie sitting opposite her.

She couldn't quite get used to the sight and she was finding it hard to tear her eyes away from him long enough to look down at her plate or to enjoy the view of the harbour that was passing before them. She had no idea what they spoke about as she ate her prawn dumplings but she knew most of the conversation revolved around her. When their main courses arrived she tried to distract Charlie from the multitude of tablets she needed to take by asking him about himself.

'I think it's time you told me something about you. I've known you for years through Evie but I don't actually know anything about your life, whereas I feel you know everything about me.'

'Even what you wear to bed,' he teased in reply.

Bella felt herself blushing again. 'See, it's only fair that you tell me something about yourself now.'

'Okay, but if I bore you, you only have yourself to blame.' He paused momentarily as he took some vegetables from a bowl in the centre of the table and added them to the beef fillet on his plate. 'Let's see, I'm the youngest of three siblings, an older brother and an older sister. We grew up in Wollongong, south of Sydney, my dad was a professional fisherman, mum is a nurse. I was a little bit wild as a kid. The Gong has some of the best surf beaches in the country and my mates and I spent just about every afternoon after school in the ocean. That's where I learnt to surf.'

Bella closed her eyes and imagined spending lazy afternoons lying on a warm beach or diving through the waves.

'Am I boring you already?' Charlie laughed.

She opened her eyes and smiled at him. She was happy in his company and happy to listen to him share some of his past with her. It made her feel special. 'No, I'm just imagining what it would have been like to be so lucky. I would have loved to have had that freedom.'

'I was given a long leash partly because of the community we lived in and partly by circumstances,' he told her.

'What do you mean?'

'My father had an accident at work when I was fifteen. He was out at sea, chasing a large school of fish, when a big storm hit. The crane on the fishing boat was damaged and fell onto

Dad, fracturing his spine. That was the end of his days as a fisherman. He's in a wheelchair now. You might say I didn't cope very well at the time,' he said with a wry smile. 'Mum was understandably caught up in Dad's needs and I was angry, thinking I'd lost the father I knew. That's when I went a little bit wild. As long as I was home before dark no one minded where I was. I think it was easier if they didn't have to worry about me too. I had always surfed, most of the local kids did, and after Dad's accident I spent more time in the water than out of it. It was an escape. I went looking for freedom. I couldn't stand being cooped up in the house. I think seeing my father confined to a wheelchair, seeing him lose his freedom, made me hungry to make sure I had my own and I found that in surfing.'

'And later did they start to worry about where you were or did you run wild for the rest of your teenage years?' Bella wondered if she and Charlie had something in common after all. Were they both products of emotionally absent parents?

'Eventually things settled down at home, the dad I knew was still there, just physically different. We repaired our relationship. Dad accepted his situation more quickly than I did, he was amazing really. Mum too. Once I learnt to deal with the changes we were okay. Mum got a routine established and I was still allowed a lot of freedom but mum and dad needed to know where I was. By then I was quite a good surfer and I loved it. I think Mum was happy for me to be down at the beach as it meant I burnt off a lot of energy, although I'm not sure they were quite so happy when I won the junior world title and announced I was deferring university to join the professional surfing tour.' He gave her a half-smile and a slight shrug. 'But they didn't try to talk me out of it, just persuaded me to keep my options open. Dad had never had a chance to go to uni, fishing was the only thing he knew, and when that was taken away from him he really pushed the value of getting a good education. He saw it as a form of insurance.'

'So you had your parents' blessing to goof off and travel the world with your surfboard?'

'I did.' He grinned at her then, his smile open and honest. She couldn't see a trace of hurt or disappointment in his dark brown eyes, he looked as though he didn't have a care in the world. But Bella couldn't help but wonder what he'd gone through when his own accident had ended his surfing career, ended the freedom he obviously craved. But their heart-to-heart conversations had always been about her life and she felt it would be too intrusive on her part to ask him how he coped without surfing.

She chose to stay on safer, neutral ground. 'I'm still jealous. I've never travelled anywhere. I feel as though I spent my childhood indoors.'

Charlie was frowning. 'You've never been any-where? I know Evie went on ski trips and didn't she have a trip to Europe when she finished school? Didn't you do those things too?'

She shook her head, sending her auburn curls dancing around her shoulders. 'Evie and Lexi got to do a lot of things that I never did. Not that I blame them. It wasn't as if it was their fault but it would have been nice to have been at my high-school graduation ball instead of in hospital or to have been sent to Paris when I finished school, but some things are just not meant to be.'

'Didn't I come and see you on the night of your grad ball?

Bella nodded and a warm glow suffused her, spreading from her heart through her body. *He remembered.* That had been the first time she'd ever spoken to Charlie alone. The first time she'd opened up to him, but she couldn't believe he remembered. That was the night she had become infatuated by Charlie.

She had been eighteen at the time and Charlie, at twenty-five, had seemed so mature. He'd travelled the world and was studying medicine. Because she'd taken two years longer than most to finish school, the boys she'd known had all been younger than her and in comparison to Charlie they'd seemed immature and silly. Charlie had entertained her with stories about his fellow students and their university pranks and Bella had thought how wonderful it all sounded compared to the drudgery of school. For the first time she'd found herself comfortable talking to someone who wasn't family. In Charlie's company she was able to relax and he'd managed to make her forget all about the graduation ball. Her adoration of him had started that evening and it had never stopped.

'You brought me flowers and chocolate,' she said. She didn't admit she still had the chocolate wrappers and the pressed flowers in a box in her wardrobe. In a box that contained very few keepsakes from her youth but ones that were precious nonetheless.

He grinned. 'I knew the way to a woman's heart even back then.'

Especially this one, she thought.

'You've earned your reputation as a charmer, that's for sure, but I still don't know how you happened to be there that night.'

'Evie and I were meant to be studying for our end-of-year exams but Evie was stressing because while you and Lexi should have been going to the ball together, Lexi was going and you were in hospital. Evie wanted to be in two places at once. She wanted to be with you both but that was clearly impossible. I figured we weren't going to get any studying done so I might as well come to the rescue. I couldn't help Lexi get ready so I volunteered to keep you company instead.'

'That doesn't seem fair.'

'On whom?'

'On you. Getting stuck with the hospital visit instead of the fun.'

'It was fine,' he said with a smile that took the sting out of his words. She wanted it to be better than fine. 'According to you, it wasn't fair that you were missing out on your high-school grad ball so keeping you company seemed like a small sacrifice.'

Bella winced. 'Did I complain an awful lot?'

'Actually, you didn't, even though, in my opinion, you would have been entitled to. You seemed to accept it as par for the course. You couldn't have behaved too terribly. I'm still here, eight years later.'

Yes, he was, but once again it had nothing to do with her and everything to do with his relationship with Evie. He'd promised Evie he'd look after her and Bella knew that was the real reason he'd agreed to help her with her list. That was the real reason they were here tonight.

'But I didn't realise,' he was saying, 'that along with missing your high-school graduation ball you never went on a ski trip or a school camp either.'

'I did get to go on one camp when I was about fifteen,' she admitted, 'but only because it was run by the cystic fibrosis association and Dad felt it would be okay. A whole bunch of us went away for a weekend and it wasn't too bad. Actually, it was quite good to be with other kids who were all going through the same issues but then the camps were stopped because there seemed to be an increase in the number of hospitalisations after the camps and the medicos were worried about cross-infection between the kids.'

'I can imagine what it was like, a camp full of teenagers with raging hormones. It's no wonder kids got sick!' Charlie laughed.

'I know.' Bella knew exactly why kids caught infections. After experiencing her first, and only, proper kiss on that camp she was one of the ones who had ended up in hospital. 'The trouble was we couldn't afford to be sharing germs around so that was the end of that.'

'Well, that's why I'm here. I'm going to make

sure you get to try all those things you missed out on.'

'I think it's a bit late for school ski trips and my high-school graduation,' she said.

'Maybe,' he agreed. 'But will you invite me to your college graduation ceremony when you finish fashion design?'

Bella didn't imagine for a minute that Charlie was serious but she was touched that he asked. She smiled, 'Yes. I will.'

'Great. Now finish your dessert so I can take you dancing.'

Bella realised then that the band was moving from dinner music into dance music. 'Aren't you going to finish yours?'

When Charlie shook his head Bella finished her dark chocolate mousse, minus a spoonful which she gave to Charlie to taste, and then polished off most of his Eton mess before she let him take her from the table.

He took her hand and led her past the dance floor and out onto the large open-air deck on the bow of the yacht. The music followed them.

'Why are we out here?'

'Wasn't dancing under the stars one of the things on your wishlist?' Charlie asked.

Actually, she wanted to be thoroughly and properly kissed under the stars but no way was she going to tell him that! 'Yes, yes, it was,' she said as she stepped into his arms. She closed her eyes and let the music flow over her as she blocked out the thought of other people on the deck watching them. She didn't care, she wasn't going to think about them, she was going to savour the moment, the feel of Charlie's hand on her back, his breath on her skin. This was nearly as good as being kissed and she was determined to enjoy every second and commit the sensation to memory.

Charlie's embrace was warm and solid, making her feel as light as air on her high heels. The skirt of her dress swirled around her calves, just as she'd pictured it, the evening air was warm and the music was the perfect tempo. Bella closed her eyes and relaxed and pretended the night was never-ending as Charlie guided her around the deck. He was a graceful dancer. He danced like he walked, fluid of movement and light of foot.

Bella supposed his graceful movement was a legacy of his surfing days—he would have needed good balance and smooth changes of direction—and she gave herself over to his lead as the songs blurred into one another.

'Look, the Opera House.' His voice was soft in her ear.

She opened her eyes as the yacht cruised past the Opera House. The white sails, backlit by the city lights, glowed against the evening sky. Even though she could see the Opera House from her own bedroom window, seeing the famous roof from within Charlie's arms made her feel as though she was seeing its beauty for the first time.

'It's magnificent, isn't it?' he said.

And it was. But it was poignant too because it reminded her they were now on their way back to Darling Harbour, and the night was almost over.

As if the band was in sync with her thoughts the music ended and the guests inside applauded. 'It sounds as though that's the end of our dancing,' Charlie said. 'Come.' He kept hold of her hand as they made their way back to the table.

'We have time for one last drink before our evening ends.'

The champagne was on ice and Charlie poured the last of it into their glasses as the dance floor cleared. 'So,' he asked, 'as far as dates go, did tonight meet with your approval or is now the point in time when you tell me you never want to see me again?'

She looked across the table at him. 'It was one of the best dates I've ever had,' she said honestly. She couldn't possibly tell him this was her first proper date. Not unless she wanted to confirm she was a total failure in the romance stakes. 'But to be honest, I haven't a lot to compare it to.'

Charlie laughed. 'Careful, woman, you're doing serious damage to my ego tonight. I was hoping to take home the prize for best night ever because it was fabulous, not because of a lack of competition.'

'We haven't all got as many notches in the bedpost as you reportedly have.'

'None of them serious, though,' Charlie told her.

'How come? What's been wrong with them?'

She was genuinely curious and she knew a small part of her wanted to know in case the pitfalls were easily avoided.

'Some of them have been lovely but I've always measured my relationships against my passion for surfing.'

'What does that mean?'

'When I was surfing, if I wouldn't choose to spend time with a girl instead of hitting the waves, I decided I wasn't serious about her and that relationship never lasted long. I didn't see the point. If she wasn't special enough to make me give up an early-morning surf then she wasn't for me. Even when I couldn't surf, I still had that mindset. If I'm being honest, I probably thought even more about it. Surfing was a passion, the sense of freedom, the danger, the escape. A girl had to be something special to rival surfing. And when I couldn't surf any more I had to find a new passion and I found it in medicine, not relationships.'

'I can see how you could have a passion for medicine but it can't be similar to surfing in terms of freedom, surely?'

'You'd be surprised. Being in the operating theatre is a lot like being in the zone when you're
surfing. I have to be in control because, if I lose
it, things go wrong. But at least I am in control.
I had to make split-second decisions while I was
surfing and I have to do that when I'm operating
too, but they are my choices. Everything that happens is up to me and that's a kind of freedom.'

'Does the same apply to your relationships—do
you like to have total control, a sense you can get
out of it whenever you choose?' It didn't take a
rocket scientist to deduce that Charlie still craved
freedom and making sure he didn't restrict himself by getting tied down in a serious relationship
would ensure that. Even so, Bella was surprised
to hear herself actually ask the question. The
champagne must have loosened her tongue, she
thought, she'd never normally be so forthright.
Did she imagine a very slight hesitation before
Charlie shook his head?

'Don't get me wrong. I haven't always been the
one to end relationships. Sometimes the girl has
done it first.'

That surprised her too. 'Why?' she asked.

'Usually because of my hours. Some of them have felt as though they haven't been my priority. They've been right, but...' he shrugged '...I never promised them my undivided attention. I still haven't found a girl whom I'd choose before surfing or my work.'

She raised her glass to her lips and looked over the rim at him. Her eyes were huge and it seemed to take her a second or two to focus on him. He wondered briefly if she'd had too much to drink before he dismissed the notion as ridiculous. She'd only had two glasses of champagne over four hours and even though she was taking antibiotics it wasn't as though she'd been drinking on an empty stomach.

She sipped her champagne and smiled at him and her grey eyes shone silver. Charlie relaxed. Perhaps she was just tired. Even though it was relatively early, she hadn't long been out of hospital. But he'd have her home, in bed, very shortly. Looking at her creamy skin, her warm hair and her flushed cheeks, he thought it was a pity she'd be in bed alone.

Where did that thought spring from? he wondered. That wasn't what the evening had been about.

He'd arranged tonight as a way of repaying a debt of gratitude he felt he owed the Lockheart family and also because he'd wanted to do something nice for Bella. It hadn't been about feathering his own nest. But old habits died hard and he couldn't pretend he didn't find her attractive. Couldn't pretend he hadn't noticed Evie's little sister had grown up. But that was the problem. She was Evie's little sister. She was off limits.

Tonight was about helping make some of Bella's dreams come true but now it was time to get her home.

She was a little unsteady on her feet as they left the yacht and, as he put his arm around her, keeping her upright, he wondered again about the wisdom of mixing antibiotics with even a small amount of alcohol. He was a doctor, he'd promised to keep her safe. He hoped he hadn't failed to keep his word.

Their limousine was waiting and Charlie bundled Bella into the warm interior. There was another bottle of champagne on ice but he ignored that and poured them both a glass of water instead. Bella drained hers in a few seconds and Charlie could feel her staring at him while he refilled her glass.

'Why did you shave your head?' she asked.

Yep. He'd definitely let her down. That didn't sound like something a sober Bella would ask. It was far too personal.

'It was time for a change.' That was partially true but the whole truth was far more complicated than that and tonight was about Bella. It wasn't the time to tell her about Pippa.

'You've had a shaved head for as long as I've known you and how long's that? Nine years? You don't change things very often, do you?'

'I guess not.'

'So what was the calatyst? I mean the cat-a-lyst,' she repeated, enunciating the word very slowly.

This was a story he normally avoided telling but he figured she was going through something much worse than the drama he'd experienced.

She would probably understand—if she even remembered this conversation in the morning.

'I was on holiday in Bali, on my way home from a surfing tournament, and I was getting around the island on a scooter. The Balinese are not known for their good road safety record and I was young with a foolish sense of invincibility so I guess I was an accident waiting to happen. I got cleaned up by a truck on a mountain road and ended up in hospital with a collapsed lung and a shattered knee. That and torn cruciate ligaments put an end to my career as a professional surfer.' He spoke as though it hadn't been an extremely dark period in his life. It had taken him over a year to accept the fact his surfing days were over. The only thing that had stopped him from losing hope altogether had been going back to uni and meeting Evie. 'When I eventually got back to Australia and went back to uni I didn't want to be reminded of what I'd lost every time I looked in the mirror.' He'd lost more than his surfing career in the accident. It had also cost him his relationship with the first woman he'd ever loved. 'My hair reminded me of surfing and Bali and the accident. So I shaved it off.'

Bella reached out and ran her hand over his head. 'I think it suits you.'

Her hand was cool and soft against his skull and her touch sent a shiver of desire through him. 'You've got lovely lips too. They look sho shoft.' She was slurring her words ever so slightly and Charlie was mortified. Was she drunk? He couldn't believe he'd got her drunk. She lifted her hand again and Charlie waited, certain she was going to put her fingers on his lips, but her hand fell to her side as though she had no control over it any more.

'Didyouknow…' she was mumbling now and her words were running together and Charlie had to concentrate to work out what she was saying '…I've only been kished oncebefore. I'd like to be kished properly.'

Charlie felt Bella lean her head on his shoulder as she finished speaking. Had she just said she'd like to be kissed? He peered down at her, waiting, listening for more. But there was no more.

Her eyes were closed and her breathing was slow and deep. Was she asleep?

He shifted in his seat and turned to face her, moving his arm to wrap it around her so she settled against his chest, telling himself he was doing it because it would be more comfortable for her than bouncing around on his hard shoulder. He hoped she was sleeping because she was exhausted, not because she'd passed out. Out of habit and concern he counted her respirations and took her pulse. Both were normal and Charlie breathed a sigh of relief.

Bella's handbag was lying on the seat between them and feeling only slightly guilty he opened it, looking for her phone. He scrolled through her contacts list, looking for Lexi's number, hoping and praying she was home as he called.

Lexi was waiting at the front door when the limousine pulled to a stop. She raced over and yanked open the door. 'What happened? Is she all right?'

'She's okay, she's asleep. I'm hoping she's just tired but…' he winced as he finished the sentence '…she might be drunk.'

'Drunk!'

A wave of guilt and embarrassment swept over Charlie. 'I'm so sorry, she only had two glasses of champagne and she had plenty to eat.'

'She's not used to drinking—'

'I know,' Charlie interrupted. He knew this was his fault. 'And I know she's on antibiotics but I really thought she'd be okay.'

'That wasn't a criticism,' Lexi said. 'I was just going to say that the motion-sickness tablets she took tonight probably didn't help.'

Charlie frowned. 'What?'

'She gets seasick,' Lexi explained, 'and she took a couple of pills for that before you picked her up.'

This was going from bad to worse. 'Seasick? Why didn't she tell me? I would have cancelled.'

'That's exactly why she didn't tell you. She was so excited about tonight. It would have killed her if you'd pulled the pin.'

At least the extra medication explained why she'd been so affected by the champagne. The motion-sickness tablets would have dehydrated her more than normal and made her more susceptible to the alcohol. Perhaps he wasn't as negligent as he'd feared. 'We'll need to get plenty of water into her to counteract the dehydration from those tablets. Do you want me to organise a drip?'

'No. I'll keep an eye on her,' Lexi said, and Charlie wasn't sure if she was implying he was incapable or irresponsible or whether she thought she couldn't rely on him. He couldn't blame her, he hadn't given her a reason to think otherwise. 'Can you bring her inside?' she asked.

He scooped Bella up in his arms, surprised at how light she was, and followed Lexi up the stairs to Bella's room. Even carrying her upstairs was no problem.

'I'm really sorry, Lexi, are you sure there's nothing else I can do?'

'We'll be fine.'

'Her heart rate and respiration rate are normal but please ring me if you're worried at all,' he said as he scribbled his number on one of Bella's sketch books, which was lying beside her bed.

There wasn't anything else he could do. He let himself out of the house and climbed back into the limo for the trip home. He couldn't believe he'd let this happen; he couldn't believe he hadn't taken better care of her.

CHAPTER SIX

CHARLIE woke frequently through the night, constantly checking his mobile phone to see if Lexi had called him, but there was nothing. As soon as the sun rose the next morning he was out of bed, too restless and remorseful to sleep. He wanted to check on Bella but, if she was sleeping, which he hoped she was, it was far too early for a house call. He needed to clear his head, he needed to get into the water.

Even though his knee injury had cut short his professional surfing career he was still able to bodysurf for fun, but the surf this morning was flat and not at all appealing so he hit the Kirribilli pool. At this early hour only the keen swimmers were in the water and he joined their ranks, slipping into the fast lane and swimming hard for close to an hour. Swimming normally gave him a chance to clear his mind but it wasn't working today. Thoughts kept swirling around in his head. How could he have been so irresponsible?

There he was telling her an edited version of his life story while she was trying to combat seasickness. The tablets had certainly done their job, she hadn't shown any signs of queasiness. He smiled as he finished another lap, thinking about how much Bella had managed to eat. With everything she'd eaten he couldn't understand how the two glasses of champagne had affected her so badly. Perhaps she'd taken more tablets than she needed to?

But that didn't exonerate him from his responsibilities. He should have taken better care of her. But he'd been both distracted by her and absorbed in her and he hadn't been able to think clearly. She was virtually a stranger to him yet he felt as though he already knew her intimately through Evie. He was comfortable with Bella, he could be himself, just as he was in Evie's company, and that was a novelty for him. He was able to let his defences down. He climbed out of the pool and towelled himself dry as he wondered what it was about the Lockheart sisters that struck a chord with him.

Out of habit he scanned the other swimmers, looking for familiar faces. Finn Kennedy was just getting into the pool and Charlie nodded in greeting as he headed for the change rooms. He saw Finn fairly regularly at the pool but they rarely stopped and chatted, Finn always seemed so intent on his exercise that Charlie didn't like to delay him.

Charlie showered and changed quickly before leaving the pool. Sunday-morning traffic over the Harbour Bridge was just starting to increase as he walked out into the street and he looked up at the bridge as it stretched away overhead, spanning the water, before he turned away and headed back towards Mosman. To Bella.

The sun was high in the sky before Bella felt well enough to open her eyes properly and keep them open. Her tongue felt swollen and her lips were dry. She could remember Lexi forcing her to drink a glass of water every time she'd stirred in the night but still it felt as though her tongue was sticking to the roof of her mouth. She sat up, and she could see the indentation from Lexi's head in the pillow next to her. She knew Lexi had slept there but she was alone now. She reached for the glass beside her bed as she tried to piece together what had happened last night.

She remembered dancing with Charlie, the feeling of his strong arms encircling her, making her feel as though her feet weren't touching the floor, as though she was floating across the deck. She remembered having a half a glass of champagne as the yacht came into dock. She remembered stroking Charlie's head.

Oh, my God, I didn't really do that, did I? But she knew the answer. She could still recall just how his head had felt, the short regrowth soft and fuzzy under her hand.

She slid down in the bed, burying herself under her quilt. How would she ever face him again?

She supposed she wouldn't have to. After last night he probably wanted nothing more to do with her.

She heard her door open. She couldn't face anyone right now. Maybe she could just stay under the covers and never come out again.

'Bella? Are you awake?' Lexi's voice was quiet. 'Charlie sent you flowers.'

That got her attention. She pushed the quilt away from her face and peered out. Lexi was half-hidden behind a mass of sunny, happy sunflowers. Just seeing their cheery, yellow petals made Bella feel brighter.

'He sent flowers?'

'He brought them around this morning, while you were asleep.'

'I thought he'd never want to speak to me again,' Bella said. 'I must have looked like a complete fool, passing out like I did.'

'I think he thought it was his fault. He felt terrible because he'd been plying you with champagne.'

'Hardly plying. I only had two glasses.'

'I know. I told him about the motion-sickness tablets but I guess he still feels terrible,' Lexi said as she put the vase of flowers on Bella's chest of drawers. 'There's a card here,' she said as she removed the card and passed it to Bella. 'What does it say?'

Bella opened the little envelope and slid the card out to read the inscription. *'Ciao, Bella, I'm sorry I didn't take better care of you. Can I make it up to you on dry land? Charlie.'*

Suddenly she felt a whole lot better. He hadn't written her off, he was going to give her another chance.

'Charlie! I'm glad I found you.'

Charlie turned around at the sound of Evie's voice. She didn't look pleased to see him, she looked mad. He'd been keeping a low profile until he could organise to make up for his faux pas with Bella but he had been expecting Evie to track him down and haul him over the coals for leading her baby sister astray. He'd spoken to Bella, he'd apologised, she'd blamed herself and they'd agreed to forget about it and try a second 'date'. It would be something else from her wishlist but this time Charlie intended to keep to dry land.

Evie did not look happy. Not that he blamed

her for wanting to tear strips off him. As far as he was concerned, he deserved it, but he still thought he'd try to minimise the fallout by apologising quickly. He held his hands up in surrender. 'I know, I'm sorry, it won't happen again.'

He watched as her expression changed from cross to puzzled. 'What are you talking about?' she asked.

'I assume you want to give me a bollocking over what happened with Bella?'

'No. She's fine. She's a bit embarrassed but she hasn't stopped talking about what a great night she had, right up until she fell asleep. There's something else I wanted to talk to you about. How well do you know Finn?'

'Finn Kennedy?'

'Of course,' she replied in a voice that suggested he'd lost his mind.

Charlie shrugged. 'As well as anyone can know him, I suppose. I see him at the pool a bit but we really only exchange greetings. He's never been one to socialise much, not even with the surgeons. Why?'

'I wanted to ask his opinion about Bella but

he seems rather moody, more so than usual, as though he's angry with the world and everyone in it. I didn't know whether it would be wise, especially after what's happened today. And I just wanted to get your take on things, see if you knew about anything that might be going on that could have put him in a bad mood. See if you think I'm going to get my head bitten off for even going near him.'

'What happened today?'

'He went missing in action.'

'Finn did?'

She was nodding and she looked cross again but now it was obvious she was mad with Finn, not him. 'I had a patient who came in with a penetrating chest wound and I was trying to find Finn. I thought being an ex-army surgeon he'd be the one to call in for a consult, but no one knew where he was.'

'How's the patient?'

'We managed to keep him alive and he's gone to Theatre but it's very out of character and I'm a bit concerned. I need him to be on top of his game.'

'Why?'

'Because I need to ask him about Bella,' she replied, giving him a look that very clearly said, *Keep up!* 'And if he's got problems of his own, I don't want to risk it.'

'Risk what?' Now Charlie even felt like he was missing the bigger picture.

'Would you let him operate on you?'

'I thought Sam would do Bella's transplant...' He let his sentence tail off. He didn't want to state the obvious, which meant assuming compatible lungs were found in time.

'I was going to ask him if he'd assist,' Evie explained, finally allowing Charlie to catch up with her train of thought. 'Do you think there's anything to worry about, given that he's gone missing today and generally seems to be out of sorts, or would you let him operate on you?'

'I haven't noticed anything off. He might not be the most personable of people but he's a damn good doctor. You don't get to be Head of Surgery without being something a bit special.'

'That's what I thought but that was before he vanished in the middle of the day.'

'If you want my advice, it would be to stay out of Finn Kennedy's personal life. He may have had a perfectly good reason to take off in the middle of the day.'

'Don't you think he should have told someone where he was going? No one knew where he was.'

'And I imagine that's how he wants it to stay. You said yourself he doesn't confide in anyone. He's a loner and I think he likes it that way. I'm sure he's fine and I'm sure that even if there is something going on with him, he wouldn't let it affect his surgical skills.'

Charlie couldn't understand her concerns. In his mind they were unfounded. As far as he knew, Finn had never disappeared from the hospital before and just because Evie hadn't been able to track him down it didn't mean Finn had gone missing. He could have told someone where he was, and perhaps Evie didn't ask the right people in time.

But while he couldn't understand her concerns, he could understand her logic in asking Finn to assist with the operation. While Charlie thought

Sam was perfectly capable of performing Bella's surgery without Finn's help, Sam would need assistance and he guessed having two experts operating together was better than one. Whether or not Sam and Finn saw it the same way was something Evie would have to sort out, but until lungs were found it was all hypothetical and, in the meantime, Charlie had some plans of his own to arrange.

He had three days to organise his apology.

Bella hung her car keys on the hook and mixed herself a salt-replacement drink before wandering through to the conservatory. She'd had a long day at the hospital with several appointments all related to her transplant work-up and she couldn't afford to get dehydrated. She was exhausted and her chest felt tight but she put it all down to a long and tiring day. Rosa had pots simmering on the stove and Bella could see trays in the ovens and the kitchen benches were groaning under the weight of several other dishes covered with foil or teatowels. She lifted one corner of a teatowel. This platter held smoked salmon, pâté and other antipasto assortments. Her stomach growled with hunger but she needed to rest for a bit. She'd kick her shoes off and sit down for a few minutes and then she'd come back and see if she could sample whatever yummy things Rosa was making.

The conservatory overlooked the garden and the harbour. As Bella entered the room her attention was caught by the sight of a white marquee sitting in the centre of the lawn. That hadn't been there when she'd left the house this morning. It was the smallest of several her father had, and this one was sometimes used for garden parties. Bella wondered why it had been put up in the middle of the week. Initially all her attention was focussed on the tent and it wasn't until Lexi spoke that she noticed she was in the room.

'Good, you're back.'

Lexi was sitting on one of the day lounges, feet curled up underneath her, flicking through a bridal magazine.

'What's going on?' Bella inclined her head towards the garden and the marquee.

Lexi stood and tossed the magazine onto the

table. 'Where have you been?' she said, ignoring Bella's question.

'At the hospital.'

'I expected you ages ago. You'll have to hurry now if you're going to be ready in time.'

'Ready in time for what?' Bella had no idea what was happening. Was there a function she was supposed to know about that had slipped her mind? That would explain the quantity of food in the kitchen.

'Charlie will be here in half an hour. He's organised another date. That's what the marquee is for.'

'What do you mean, "he's organised another date"?' Bella was frowning as she was looking out of the conservatory windows. The marquee was for Charlie? 'How did he do this?' she asked, waving one hand in the general direction of the garden. 'And how do you know so much about it—did you help him?'

Lexi was nodding. 'Rosa and I agreed to help.'

'You should be spending your time organising your wedding,' Bella argued. Lexi was constantly telling her how much time it was going to take to organise the wedding so she should be spending every spare minute on that, then the wedding might actually happen sooner rather than later.

'Charlie can be very charming and persuasive when he wants to be,' Lexi replied. 'I thought this was more important.'

Bella knew she should argue but she couldn't think straight. Charlie had organised another date for them? She was getting a second chance? She forgot all about being tired as she ran upstairs to get changed. Lexi had said he'd be there soon. Bella had to get it right this time.

When she emerged from the shower she found that Lexi had selected an outfit for her. She assumed Lexi knew what the date entailed so she dressed in the clothes that were laid out on her bed. She'd chosen white cotton trousers, a white camisole and a lightweight caftan to wear over the top. The caftan was made from sheer cotton that had been printed with a pale green and white pattern with a scattering of beads hand sewn onto it. She teamed the outfit with flat sandals and put her medications into a small silver purse. She left her freshly washed hair loose, the curls cascading around her shoulders, and applied the bare minimum of make-up, mascara, lip gloss and a touch of blush.

'*Ciao*, Bella.' Charlie was waiting for her in the conservatory when she came back downstairs and hearing his familiar greeting made her catch her breath. He stood and came to meet her and she watched as his plump, juicy lips spread into a wide smile. He was casually dressed in denim jeans and a T-shirt that moulded nicely to his chest and his chocolate-brown eyes shone with good humour.

He kissed her on the cheek, pressing his delicious lips against her skin, and a tingle of desire shot through her, warming her from the inside. 'Thank you for giving me another chance. I promise to take better care of you this time,' he said.

Not for one moment had she blamed Charlie for her condition the other night. It hadn't been his fault at all but she couldn't formulate the words to tell him so.

He cocked one elbow and waited for her to

slide her arm through the gap before he covered her hand with his. She trembled under his touch.

'Shall we?' he asked.

She took a deep breath and nodded, eager to find out what lay in store for her tonight. With arms linked, they stepped into the garden and walked across the lawn towards the marquee. The grass sloped gently away from the house towards the harbour and the expanse was large enough for the water to still be visible past the marquee. Ferries criss-crossed the water, leaving a trail of white behind in their wakes, and a very slight breeze carried the sound of ferries tooting as they docked and departed from the Mosman Bay wharf to the west of the Lockheart home. The breeze also carried the perfume from the frangipani trees that hugged the boundary fence and had just started flowering. Across the water Bella could see the city lights and the shining white sails of the Opera House. The tent was enclosed on three sides and had been positioned with the open side facing the harbour. Bella knew they would have views of the city from within but the views paled into insignificance as Charlie led her around to the front of the marquee and took her inside.

'Oh, it looks beautiful,' she sighed.

The interior of the marquee had been set up to resemble a picnic. The space inside the small marquee was intimate but dominated by a massive Persian rug which had been laid out in the centre of the tent. The carpet was scattered with brightly patterned, oversize cushions and cashmere blankets, and fat candles and hurricane lamps were grouped in the corners of the marquee, casting a warm glow around the space. Fairy-lights had been strung up against the ceiling, giving the illusion they would be dining under the stars. Music was playing softly in the background and picnic baskets were lined up along one wall beside a large metal tub filled with ice that held an assortment of drinks.

'I thought we'd stay on dry land this time,' Charlie said as Bella stood, fixed to the spot, mesmerised by the colour and light and amazed by the effort Charlie had gone to. Somehow he'd managed to create a little oasis in the middle of a suburban garden in the centre of the city. 'Make yourself comfortable,' he said as he guided her towards the pile of cushions. 'I'm going to mix us a couple of baby Bellinis.'

Bella was about to protest, she wasn't planning on touching a drop of alcohol tonight, but Charlie interrupted her. 'It's okay, I'm using non-alcoholic cider, not champagne,' he said as he retrieved the peach nectar from the tub of ice. 'These will be perfect for our picnic.'

From the middle of the tent Bella could still see across the harbour but she had the sense they had the world to themselves, everything and everyone else seemed so far away.

'How on earth did you manage to organise all this?' she asked as he handed her a champagne glass.

'I can't take all the credit. I had some inside help. Evie told me you'd be out most of the day, Lexi got the marquee set up and Rosa has spent the day cooking your favourite things. I just told them what I had in mind. My only concern was that you'd be wiped out after your day of appointments.'

Her earlier fatigue had vanished in the excitement of the evening. 'I'm good, just starving,' she said as she slipped her sandals off and sat cross-legged on a cushion. Charlie stretched out beside her and his hand rested inches from her thigh. She wanted to pick his hand up and put it on her leg but before she had a chance he was on the move again.

'I haven't known you to be anything but hungry,' he said as he jumped up and searched through the picnic baskets, returning with two platters of appetisers, one warm and one cold. Pâté, smoked salmon and grapes on one, filo pastries and spring rolls on the other. Rosa must have transferred the food from the kitchen to the marquee while she had been in the shower. But surely all that food couldn't have been for them?

'How was your day?' he asked as he put the platters on the carpet between them.

'Interesting,' she replied.

'Who did you see?'

'I had a few tests, blood work, lung function, the usual, and saw Marco D'Avello and John Allen. At least John didn't tell me I'm crazy,' she said as she spread pâté onto a biscuit.

Charlie smiled. 'That would be a psychiatrist's job, John's a psychologist.'

'I know, but it always makes me nervous when someone starts delving into my psyche. It's only a matter of time before someone decides I'm a bit loopy. But he was more interested in whether I've got a good support network—although that could potentially open a whole other can of worms if he expects my parents to come to the party. Luckily I've got Lexi and Evie.'

'You're not expecting your parents to step up?'

Bella shook her head as she swallowed the pâté and biscuit. 'I've learnt it's better not to expect anything, particularly where my mother is concerned. She has very little to do with any of us. It's been that way for years. And she certainly hasn't wanted anything to do with me. I'm not glamorous enough—'

'You can't be serious,' Charlie interrupted. 'That can't be right?'

Bella shrugged. She appreciated his vote of confidence, even though she thought he was wrong. 'I'm sure it's part of it but I also think she can't handle having a sick child. Anything less than perfection isn't allowed in her world. If she could have removed me from her world, I think she would have. Instead, she removed herself from us.'

Charlie couldn't begin to imagine what Bella's life had been like. He knew she'd never wanted for material things but he could hear in her tone how much she longed just to be loved. He wondered how different her life would have been if she'd been healthy, if she hadn't been born with a defective gene. But he guessed they'd never know the answer to that question.

A fierce protectiveness rose up in him, stemming from anger towards Miranda Lockheart. Did she have any idea how her behaviour and her choices had hurt her daughters? Did she have any remorse? He knew Miranda's alcoholism was an illness but it was treatable. Unlike Bella's cystic fibrosis, Miranda could be controlled if treated if only she sought help. But as far as he knew, she hadn't tried and if she wasn't willing to do that then it was obvious her daughters were not her priority. 'What about your father? Have you been able to depend on him?'

'Financially I have, but while he's been in the picture more than Mum he's never really spent any time with me, not like he has with Lexi.' She shrugged again. 'I don't think he knew what to do with me. You heard him in hospital last week, he's used to throwing money at problems to solve them or make them go away, and if something can't be fixed with money, he doesn't know what else to do. With me, he paid for nurses and made me their responsibility so he could ignore the issue, ignore me.'

Charlie may not have had Bella's privileged background but he had a solid, tight-knit family and that included parents who had helped him find his place in the world. Even in his darkest days, when his surfing career had prematurely ended, no one could have taken his family away from him. Bella had her sisters but she deserved more, all three of the girls did.

'My life is what it is,' she said as she selected a slice of smoked salmon. 'Let's talk about something else.'

He was constantly amazed by her selfless nature. Even now she wasn't going to condemn her parents over her upbringing.

She stood up gracefully, unfolding herself from her cross-legged position on the cushion, and wandered over to the picnic baskets. 'What else did Rosa make me to eat?' she asked as she peered into the baskets.

Charlie followed Bella to the picnic baskets. Rosa had left crusty bread, sliced roast meats, mustards, salads, boiled eggs, mini savoury pastries, cheeses, fruit and a whole basket full of chocolate desserts. Looking at the amount of food, he was pleased he'd managed to organise the picnic in Bella's back garden. He knew she'd envisaged a private picnic but he hoped it was more about the company and less about the location—he certainly didn't fancy carrying these heavily laden baskets across a field to set up next to a meandering creek. This was far more civilised; he just hoped it satisfied Bella's expectations. He opened a third basket and handed her a china plate, silver cutlery and a linen napkin, and once she'd made her selection he followed suit before resuming his position on the Persian carpet.

'I put my college application in yesterday,' Bella told him as she sat beside him.

'Good girl.' He was thrilled she'd actually done something for herself for a change. 'How did it feel?'

'Terrifying,' she admitted. 'It's been years since I studied and even then I wasn't very good at it. I was eighteen when I finished school, two years later than I should have. You know Lexi and I did year twelve together and I wouldn't have got through without her help. That's why I was so reluctant to apply for fashion design, I didn't think I'd be able to do it. I still don't. But I'll give it a go.'

He was inexplicably proud of her. Tackling a tertiary degree was obviously a major hurdle for her to overcome. 'Studying a topic you love will be totally different from what you did at school.' He just hoped, having pushed her to apply, that she wouldn't be disappointed. He hoped she'd love it.

'That's what I'm praying for.'

'You're so passionate about design, I'm sure you'll enjoy every minute of it.'

'I hope so. I'm excited as well as terrified, if that makes sense, but you were right, it will be good to have something to look forward to. If I do have this transplant I can't sit around doing nothing for the rest of my life.'

'I'm sure you haven't been doing nothing,' he said as he realised she could have been doing just that for eight years. But that didn't gel with the woman he thought she was or with the woman he wanted her to be.

'I suppose not, but I can't say I've been doing anything terribly worthwhile either, although I do enjoy doing some interior decorating on behalf of the Lockheart Foundation.'

'Interior decorating?'

'Yes. Dad quite regularly buys flats around the hospital. He donates them to the hospital and they use them as short-term accommodation for country families who need somewhere to stay. I get to decorate the ones that need it and furnish them before they're handed over to the hospital. I enjoy doing that.'

'How can you say that's not worthwhile? Think of all the families who benefit from what you've done.'

'I guess, but it's not like your job. You do so much good.'

'Don't be so hard on yourself. You give people somewhere nice to stay when they're going through a tough time and once you've got your fashion design degree you'll be able to help people's self-esteem.'

'That's a lovely thing to say but it's hardly in your league.'

'Don't underestimate the power of self-confidence,' he told her. 'Your designs could give people that.'

She smiled at him. 'You have a knack of making me feel better about myself. Thank you.'

'You're welcome,' he said, as he fetched a bowl of strawberries and a bowl of dipping chocolate. He didn't know about making Bella feel better but her smile made him feel invincible. She groaned and stretched her arms over her head as he returned to the rug. 'Are you all right?'

'Yes. I think I just need to rest before I tackle

dessert,' she said as she lay back on the cushion. 'Thank you for organising tonight. No one has ever done anything like this for me before.'

It broke his heart to think of how much Bella had missed out on, how little attention she'd been given. 'I'm glad I could surprise you,' he said as he vowed to do more to help her realise the dreams she had on her wishlist.

'I feel like I've been let loose on the world. No one asking how I feel, or getting me to breathe in and out, no one taking blood samples or poking and prodding. I can pretend I'm just like everyone else,' she said as she shuffled over to make room for him on the rug.

He placed the two bowls by her knees and lay on his side, facing her. They were inches apart. He could see the faint, individual freckles that were scattered across the bridge of her nose and her grey eyes shone silver in the candlelight. She wanted to be like everyone else but she was so different from anyone he knew. And it wasn't because of her illness, although perhaps that had contributed. She had a vulnerability about her but he knew that was deceptive because he'd seen her strength of character time and again; and she had a generosity that was uncommon. She was a selfless person and she made him want to be more selfless too.

He took a strawberry from the bowl and dipped it into the chocolate. 'Can I tempt you?' he asked as he held the strawberry above her lips. She reached up and brought his hand down towards her. She parted her lips and bit into the berry with tiny white teeth.

She rolled onto her side towards him as she swallowed the strawberry. His hand dropped to her hip and then he was motionless. His other hand was supporting his head and he could feel his biceps tighten with the effort. He watched as Bella slowly, hesitantly, stretched out her hand and traced the bulge of his biceps.

In the distance a ferry tooted but the two of them were silent.

Charlie lifted his hand from her hip and threaded his fingers through her auburn curls. They were soft and springy under his touch. He shouldn't be doing this, he shouldn't be touching her like this, she was supposed to be off limits, but he couldn't resist. The movement of his arm made the hem of his T-shirt ride up, exposing his abdominals. He saw Bella's silvery grey eyes drop to his waist and follow the movement of his shirt. She removed her hand from his arm, slid her fingers under his T-shirt and traced the ridge of his abdominal muscles. Her fingers blazed a trail of fire across his skin and made him catch his breath.

He released her curls and caught her hand in his, stilling her movement as he entwined his fingers with hers. Bella held his hand and ran her thumb along his fingers. He tried to fight the attraction that was building in him. He tried to do the right thing but then Bella lifted his hand to her mouth and kissed the tips of his fingers then placed his hand over her heart, holding it against her chest. He could feel the swell of her breast under his palm. Her eyes were enormous. Her lips were parted and he could feel her warm breath on his face.

He knew he should resist but he also knew he was powerless to do so.

They were frozen in time and space. Their

gazes locked as they held onto each other, as he tried to fight temptation and tried to resist desire.

He wasn't sure who moved first but suddenly the space between them, which was infinitesimal to begin with, had disappeared. Nothing separated them. Bella's eyes were closed, her lashes dark against her pale cheeks, and then his lips were on hers. Her lips were on his.

Desire and temptation had won.

It was a gentle kiss, a soft exploration, a beginning. He shouldn't be doing this but her lips were so warm, pliable and tender and now that he'd started he didn't want to stop. But he had to stop, he needed to stop. She was Evie's little sister, she wasn't his to conquer. He pulled back, releasing her, and watched as she opened her eyes. They were dark grey now, her pupils had grown so large the silvery grey was barely visible around the edges, and he knew she'd come back for more.

Would that make it all right? If she came to him, would that make it okay?

This time he watched and waited. It had to be Bella's choice.

She closed the gap. He waited until her lips covered his and then he took over. She tasted so sweet. His tongue teased her lips open and she didn't resist. She opened her mouth to him and their tongues met. She tasted like chocolate and strawberries. Warm chocolate.

Her breasts nudged against him and he could feel her nipples, hard against his chest. Her hips pushed into his groin as she slid both her hands under his T-shirt. He felt his own nipples harden as her fingers brushed over them.

Had she really told him she'd only been kissed once before? Maybe he'd misheard her the other night. He was finding it hard to believe right now as she certainly wasn't behaving like a novice. Her fingers were trailing over his abdominals again and then all thoughts of prior conversation fled his mind as he felt her fingers at the waistband of his jeans. She broke the kiss. He could hear her panting and at first he thought she was having difficulty with her breathing but when he looked into her eyes he knew it was simply arousal.

Bella sat up and pulled her shirt over her head.

She was wearing a white cotton camisole underneath but no bra. Charlie could see the peaks of her nipples pushing against the fabric and he felt his own arousal stirring in response. She licked her lips. Her pink tongue traced the outline of her mouth and Charlie forced himself not to claim her mouth with his.

She cast her shirt aside and picked up the hem of his T-shirt, pulling it up to expose his stomach. She bent her head and kissed the warm skin on his hip bone, just above the waistband of his jeans. Charlie bit back a groan of desire. He felt her fingers slide behind the button of his jeans as her nails lightly scratched his skin.

'What are you doing?' he asked, and his voice was thick and heavy.

She poised, her fingers on his waistband, and fixed her gaze on him. 'Would you make love to me?'

He could feel her cool fingernails where they rested inside his waistband, against his stomach. He knew she was ready to flick his button undone, ready to make the decision for him, and he nearly didn't need to be asked twice. But then he remembered this was Bella, the girl he'd always thought of as shy, quiet, younger than her years. Had he got her wrong? Did she know what she was doing?

'You want me to make love to you?' he asked. His voice was thick in his throat, his words accompanied only by the sound of Bella's breathing. 'Now?'

She nodded.

'Are you sure?' He had to make certain she knew what she was asking.

'Yes.' Her voice was a whisper. 'I want you to be the first.'

CHAPTER SEVEN

HER first.

He hadn't misunderstood. She wasn't naïve but she was inexperienced.

Did he want to be responsible for this momentous event in Bella's life?

He couldn't do it. There was no way he could make love to her.

Not here, not tonight.

He knew he'd already broken the first rule. She should have been off limits entirely. But he could stop before he made things worse.

He should stop.

He held her hands in his, stilling her, and lifted them from the waistband of his jeans.

He would stop.

He shook his head. 'No.'

'No?' Bella's voice wobbled. 'Why not? Am I not your type? Am I not pretty enough?'

'Oh, Bella.' He shook his head again. 'You're beautiful. So beautiful.' He reached out and slid his fingers into her auburn curls. His suntanned hand was dark against the paleness of her cheek as his fingers rested lightly against her scalp. Her grey eyes watched him, unblinking. 'But I can't.'

'Can't, or won't?'

'Won't.'

'Why not?'

Because I'm not ready for this. He'd never thought that before but he knew this time it was true. Sex was usually about fulfilling a need, a desire. It wasn't something he thought too deeply about. But he wasn't prepared mentally or practically to make love to Bella. She had such a romantic view of the world and she would have expectations that went beyond simply fulfilling a need. This couldn't be a spur-of-the-moment decision.

She'd given up waiting for his reply. 'I know what I want. I want to experience this and I want it to be with you,' she said.

'Why?' Why on earth had she chosen him?

'Because I trust you.'

He almost groaned aloud. That made it ten times worse. It meant he had a duty of care to do it right. Still he hesitated.

'I won't regret this,' she said as he shook his head again.

'It's not because I think you'll regret this.' He'd make certain she didn't. 'But you're Evie's little sister.'

Perhaps saying it out loud would remind him to think of her only in a platonic sense. That was exactly how he used to think of her, but somewhere along the way his feelings had changed, grown and developed, and now he was having difficulty separating his conscience from his desire. He needed to remember that she was Evie's little sister. She was not his for the taking. No matter how nicely she asked.

'So? I'm twenty-six years old. I make my own decisions. Please,' she begged, 'I can't bear the thought that I won't ever know what it's like and I'm not brave enough to go looking for someone else who doesn't know me or care about my reasons.'

He couldn't imagine that either. He couldn't

imagine her in bed with someone who didn't care about her or her reasons for wanting this. She was right. Why shouldn't she experience it? And why shouldn't she experience it with someone of her choosing? Half his brain said he should tread carefully but the other half agreed with Bella. Why shouldn't she have this experience while she still could? He knew he could give her pleasure. He knew he'd be able to give her what she wanted, at least physically, but he wasn't going to rush into it. He had to have time to make it special.

He felt an incredible obligation to make it perfect. To fulfil her dreams. It was immensely important that Bella got the experience she dreamed of. Perhaps because there was always a chance that this would be her only experience, it needed to be perfect.

She was looking at him hopefully.

He nodded. 'All right,' he said as his conscience gave up the fight, 'but you have to let me do it my way.'

'What does that mean?'

'It means yes, but not tonight. I want to make it perfect for you. Will you let me arrange it?'

She smiled at him. A glorious, bright smile that turned her grey eyes silver and made him forget about all the reasons he should be letting her down gently instead of agreeing to her crazy request.

'I'm going to Brisbane tomorrow for a weekend conference,' he said. 'You could meet me there? I'll book us a suite in a five-star hotel and we'll have a weekend to remember. You can pack your red negligee,' he suggested.

It had taken all her courage to ask him to make love to her but she was determined not to die a virgin and she couldn't think of anyone better to gift her innocence to than Charlie. She adored him but, better than that, she trusted him too. She knew she might only get one chance at this and she knew Charlie was capable of giving her something to remember. Something to cherish.

But she hadn't expected him not to take advantage of the present opportunity and her emotions felt as though they were on a roller-coaster ride.

She'd gone from the high of their kiss to plummeting down the slippery slope when she'd heard 'No' but then he'd lifted her up again to a peak of expectation. She wondered where it would stop.

Brisbane sounded perfect but she couldn't do it. Her heart took another dive, colliding with her stomach, as she realised it wasn't going to happen. Not tonight. And not this weekend. Maybe not ever.

'I can't come with you.' Reality intervened and her euphoria vanished. She hoped it didn't mean she was going to miss her opportunity. 'I need to stay in Sydney in case a donor is found for me.'

'When I get back, then. The anticipation will make it even better, I guarantee it.' He smiled and his brown eyes held all sorts of promises.

He was going to grant her wish! Her emotions rocketed towards the heavens again as she felt her stomach do a lazy somersault when she thought about the things that lay in store for her. She was so close she could almost taste it. She could envisage in glorious detail how she would feel in his arms. How his skin would feel against hers, warm and silky with a firm layer of muscle underneath.

'But if a donor is found for me I'll be in hospital when you get back.'

'Then I'll let you out of our deal. If you have the surgery before we do this, you'll have plenty of time to choose someone else.'

Bella didn't want to choose anyone else but it was pretty obvious she couldn't tell Charlie that. He didn't want to hear how she'd fancied him for ever and that this was a way of making her fantasies a reality. So she had to be content with his promise for now.

'Come on, it's getting late. You should get inside before it gets too cold out here.' Charlie stood and held out his hand, pulling her to her feet. He scooped a cashmere rug up from the carpet and wrapped it around her shoulders before he walked her back to the house. He stopped at the conservatory doors and turned her to face him. He reached out one hand and cupped her chin, tilting it up until his lips met hers. Her mouth opened under his pressure and she felt herself float under his caress. A slow-burning fire was glowing in her belly, awakening every nerve ending in her body. The kiss was full of promise and expectation. It was a kiss that could change her world.

'I'll see you soon,' he said as he broke their contact. Her lips were cold without his touch. 'Wait for me.'

It had been the perfect kiss. And he was promising more. In a few days she would be in Charlie's bed.

Wait for me, he'd said.

She could wait. But only just.

Charlie watched Bella as she slept. Her auburn curls were bright against the white sheets, her lashes dark against her cheeks. He could see the rise and fall of her chest as she breathed in and out and he could see her fingers move as one hand twitched involuntarily. He wondered if she was dreaming.

Her lips were pale pink and he recalled how they'd tasted of strawberries and warm chocolate. He watched as her lips moved and he wondered what she was dreaming about. He wondered if she was making any sound at all but he couldn't tell from where he stood, separated, distant and apart from her.

It had only been three days since he'd seen her but it seemed like a lifetime. So much had changed. So much had slipped away. Would things ever be the same? Would they ever recover what had been lost, the chances they'd had? The chances they hadn't taken. The chances *he* hadn't taken.

He'd left for the conference in Brisbane full of hope. He'd told Bella that anticipation would make the experience even better and that was something he firmly believed. It was one of the things he loved about beginnings. One thing he loved about the start of a new relationship. The build-up of anticipation and expectation that culminated in a crescendo of pleasure. Once that died away he knew he struggled to maintain interest. Once the excitement of new experiences and new challenges had been tasted he had a habit of losing interest, but with Bella things felt different.

He'd spent the last nine years deliberately doing

his own thing. Avoiding relationships, avoiding commitment, making sure he always had an escape route, making sure he always had freedom, but when he was with Bella he forgot about running away. Instead, he was thinking about what he could do for her. He wanted to show her things, teach her things, he wanted to see her face light up when she tried something new or made a discovery, he wanted to see her smile when someone did something nice for her.

He was entranced by her. He felt like a different person when he was with her. He was calmer. More content. He wanted to have a connection with her. A connection that went beyond sex, and it felt good to be thinking about someone else for a change. It felt good to be looking forward.

He'd expected to come home from Brisbane to find Bella eagerly awaiting his arrival. But he hadn't expected to find her here.

He'd called her while he'd been away only to be told she was back in hospital with another chest infection. He couldn't get back soon enough.

And now he stood, watching her from the other

side of a glass window. It was fair to say things hadn't turned out quite as he'd planned.

At Sam's insistence Bella had been put into an isolation room. Her immune system had taken a hammering and she couldn't afford to get any other infections, something that was always a risk in hospital.

He watched her as she slept, although he could barely see her for all the leads and tubes she was connected to. He tried to ignore the oxygen tube, the nasogastric tube, the drip, the cardiac monitors and the oximeter. He knew she'd gone downhill rapidly over the past forty-eight hours. He knew it was critical that a donor was found for her; her lungs weren't going to last much longer.

He tried to focus on her hands, her eyes, her hair, her lips, on the parts of her that looked familiar. He wanted to go in to see her, he wanted to tell her he was back, but he wasn't sure if he should. She might not be quite as keen to see him as he was to see her.

He couldn't go into her room without scrubbing. He had to gown and glove first. He turned away from the window as he tried to decide what to do and saw Evie coming towards him.

'Hi,' she said. 'Have you just been in to see Bella?'

Charlie shook his head. 'She's asleep and I'm not sure if I should go in.'

'Why not?'

'I think I've caused enough trouble. I'm probably the last person she'd want to see.'

Evie frowned. 'What are you talking about?'

'I think I might have made her sick.' Logically he knew it was unlikely but he hadn't been able to get the idea out of his head.

'She's got another chest infection,' Evie replied. 'How is that your fault?'

'I kissed her.'

'You did what?'

Charlie cringed inwardly at Evie's tone. 'I kissed her,' he repeated.

'Why? What on earth for?' Evie sounded furious and she hadn't finished yet. 'I thought you were keeping her company, keeping her occupied so she didn't have time to dwell on things. I didn't think you had ulterior motives.'

'It wasn't like that.'

'No? She's not someone you can play with. She's vulnerable, innocent. Don't think of making her one of your conquests.'

He'd thought she was innocent too, until the other night. Now he knew she was just inexperienced and that had put a whole different perspective on things. But he couldn't tell Evie that any more than he could tell Evie how he felt about her little sister. He still wasn't sure himself.

'You'd better have a damn good reason for kissing her.'

'Bella has a list of things she wants to do,' he explained. 'A wishlist she calls it. A kiss was one of the things on her list.'

'So you were doing her a favour?'

Evie sounded sceptical and he couldn't blame her. It was a pretty lame excuse and one he didn't believe himself.

'In a way.'

'Well, don't do her any more favours. She's not worldly enough to handle you. You'll break her heart.'

'It was just a kiss. A consensual one. She asked

me to kiss her and I did,' he said with a shrug as he tried to pretend it hadn't turned his world upside down. 'I have no intention of breaking her heart.'

'No one ever intends to do that but it happens anyway,' Evie argued.

'I don't think her heart's in any danger but if it makes you feel better, I'm sorry. I didn't mean to make her sick.'

'When did you kiss her?'

'Why? What difference does that make?'

'Just answer me.'

'It was Thursday night.'

Evie was shaking her head now. 'Bella was back in hospital on Friday. It would be unusual for her to get sick that quickly, she must have already had the infection. You can't blame yourself for that, but promise me you'll keep your lips to yourself from now on.'

Charlie didn't want to make that promise. He didn't trust himself to keep it. He tried a compromise and hoped Evie wouldn't notice he hadn't agreed to her request. 'Believe me, I have no intention of hurting Bella. If there was anything I could do to help I would. I want to keep her safe. I want to make her better but it's not up to me. Do you know how that feels?'

Evie looked through the window at Bella's inert form. 'I know exactly how that feels,' she said quietly, her earlier anger replaced with a hint of regret.

Of course she would. After all, Bella was her sister. Charlie wrapped one arm around Evie's shoulders and hugged her tightly. 'I'm sorry.' He was sorry she was going through this and sorry there was nothing he could do for Evie or Bella. He hated feeling so powerless.

Evie sighed. 'I'm sorry too,' she said.

Evie was sorry for a lot of things but she wasn't sorry that Bella had Charlie in her life. Not really. But she hadn't counted on a romantic involvement between them. In her opinion that complicated matters.

Physically Bella was a mess and Evie didn't want to have to worry about her emotional state as well. With their mother's medical history there was always a chance that the girls could have issues as well. Who knew what it might take to push one of them over the edge and into the abyss if they weren't coping? Who knew if Bella was susceptible?

Evie didn't want to find out.

In Evie's mind it didn't matter what was on Bella's wishlist, Charlie should have known better. What had he been thinking? Bella didn't have the emotional strength or experience to handle Charlie.

Evie had to protect her little sister. She couldn't do anything about Bella's lungs but she'd make certain no one trampled on her heart. Not that she thought Charlie would intentionally do that but she knew how Bella worshipped Charlie. Anyone who knew Bella as well as she did would see that. And she also knew Charlie's reputation. He didn't set out to hurt women, he just wasn't prepared to invest in a relationship emotionally. He wasn't prepared for anything serious, and Bella wouldn't handle a casual fling well, not as her first experience. Evie needed to do whatever she could to protect Bella. She acknowledged that Bella's physical state was more serious at the moment than her emotional state but Bella certainly didn't need Charlie, or anyone else, throwing spanners in the works at present. She had enough to deal with.

But no matter what she thought about Charlie kissing Bella she knew he couldn't have made her sick. She'd got sick much too soon afterwards for that. Evie didn't blame Charlie for giving Bella an infection but she would certainly blame him if he broke Bella's heart.

Although he'd seemed sincere when he'd said he wished there was something he could do for Bella, and Evie knew he meant it, it was just that there wasn't anything practical either of them could do. They were both in the same situation, both useless.

Or was she? she wondered, as the lift doors opened, delivering her to the emergency department, and she saw Finn going into the doctors' lounge. Was she useless or was there something she could do?

She'd been avoiding Finn as much as possible. She was still irritated with him over the disappearing trick he'd pulled, but now she needed to speak to him. Here was her chance.

She followed him into the lounge, hoping he was alone.

As she pushed open the door she saw Finn turn away and shove something into his pocket before he turned back to face her. She glanced around and noted there was no one else besides them in the room. 'Do you have a moment?' she asked.

'What is it?' he barked at her, but Evie chose to ignore his tone. She needed to speak to him and if he was going to bite her head off, that was a chance she was prepared to take.

'I have a favour to ask, a professional favour,' she added before he had a second to object. 'Bella is back in hospital, she has another lung infection and she's deteriorated badly. She's in a critical condition and desperately needs a transplant.' As quickly as she could she explained why she was there—she didn't want Finn to have an opportunity to interrupt. She didn't want him to have time to think of a reason to say no. 'The other day you asked if there was anything you could do. I need to know if your offer still stands.'

'What do you need?'

He was rubbing the outside of his right upper arm while he was speaking to her. His movement was distracting but he didn't seem to be aware of it. She'd noticed this habit on a few occasions, usually when he was in a bad mood, and although his tone wasn't quite as angry as before it was still hardly what she'd call pleasant. But she wasn't going to let him dissuade her and she pushed ahead with her request.

'If—when,' she corrected herself, 'a donor becomes available for Bella, would you assist Sam with the surgery?'

'Why? Sam is more than capable.'

'I know, but I'd feel better if you were both in the theatre. I couldn't think of two better people to have operating.'

'Joe Minnillo would normally assist,' Finn argued. 'What do you plan on telling him? That he's not required?'

Evie shook her head. 'No. He could be there as well. I'd just prefer it if you were there too.'

'It's not all about you, princess.'

She hated it when he called her that but she

wasn't about to have that discussion with him now. There were far more important things on her agenda. 'I know that,' she retorted. She felt like stamping her foot or shaking him. Why did he have to be so pig-headed? 'It's about my little sister. Organ transplant is a massive undertaking. You and Sam together are the best in the business. Wouldn't you want to give your sibling every chance if you were in my situation?'

Finn's heart had been so badly damaged a long time ago that he was amazed it could still beat, let alone still be wounded by old memories, but Evie's words were like a knife through his heart and he could feel the air being knocked from his chest. Evie knew he'd lost his brother. How dare she use that against him like this?

The memories flooded back into his consciousness, accompanied by the sensations of a time he'd rather forget. He could almost feel the hot desert wind on his face and taste the gritty sand in his mouth, the sand that had managed to make its way into every crevice, making life uncomfortable, making working conditions even more difficult. But the heat, the noise and the sand had been the least of his problems.

Isaac's face erupted from his subconscious. He closed his eyes but that just made the memories more vivid.

He could hear the whistling of the bombs raining down onto the army base. The deafening explosions as they thudded into the buildings and the ground and the people unlucky enough to be in their way. He could feel the sensation of the earth shuddering as bombs detonated. The screams of the injured, the moans of the dying.

He could smell the scent of death, the sweet, distinctive smell of blood, the putrid, foul scent of torn intestines. He could feel the warm stickiness of fresh blood, his own blood mingling with the blood of others. He could see devastation everywhere he looked. Buildings were reduced to rubble and protruding from that rubble were the limbs of the dead and the dying.

He remembered how it felt to hold someone he loved in his arms and watch as they died. He could recall his final words, begging, pleading, for Isaac to hang on just a little bit longer, until help was at hand.

But it had all been in vain. He'd had to watch as Isaac breathed his final breath, watch as his eyes stared vacantly, seeing nothing. He remembered the awful feeling of helplessness and hopelessness, knowing there was nothing he could do.

At the time his anguish had been so all-consuming it had obliterated his physical pain. He hadn't even registered until much later that he too had been injured.

And even though his injuries had been extensive, his physical pain severe, it had been nothing compared to the pain of losing his brother.

'Finn? Are you okay?'

CHAPTER EIGHT

HE OPENED his eyes to find Evie watching him closely. She was staring at him, a worried expression in her hazel eyes, a narrow crease between her eyebrows as she frowned. She was probably wondering what on earth had got into him. Isaac had died a long time ago but Finn still felt his loss just as keenly today.

A sharp, hot pain burned into his right biceps, shooting from his neck down his arm. This pain was a daily reminder of everything he'd lost. He could feel his thumb going numb and he opened and closed his hand rapidly, trying to encourage his circulation, even though he knew it was a wasted exercise. The numbness wasn't caused by poor circulation—it was all related to a damaged cervical disc—but although the physical pain was coming from his neck, the emotional pain was coming from deep inside him. Rubbing his arm and clenching his fist would do nothing for his discomfort.

'I'm fine,' he lied.

He thought he'd done such a good job of burying his grief. He was surprised to feel the pain of events from years ago resurfacing and shocked by its intensity. He knew he would react just as Evie had in the same situation. He knew he'd try his hardest, try anything, to save his sibling.

He'd been there too. He couldn't blame her for wanting the best.

'There's no point discussing this now, not until a suitable donor is found. I'll talk to Sam then,' he said. He would speak to Sam about assisting him for Bella's operation and, if Sam was agreeable, he would help, but he couldn't see the point in making arrangements until there were lungs for Bella. The pain in his arm—and in his heart—was starting to overwhelm him.

He knew his tone was dismissive but he wanted Evie out of the room. His painkilling tablets were burning a hole in the pocket of his white coat and he needed to take them soon, before his pain worsened, before he developed a headache, but he wasn't about to take them in front of anyone. Especially not Evie. She was bound to ask questions. She didn't seem to know when to leave well enough alone.

Charlie's day had been long and exhausting. He'd had a complicated hip replacement op, which had required total concentration, but he'd found his mind had kept drifting to Bella and fighting to keep his attention focussed in Theatre had only added to his exhaustion. He was looking forward to calling into Pete's Bar for a beer before heading home but he wasn't leaving the hospital without seeing Bella first. If he had to sit beside her and wait for her to wake up, he would. Being with her gave him some respite from the madness of his days. She was always so calm and composed and he found that refreshing. He had a habit of being constantly on the go and Bella made him stop.

Usually he got his downtime in the water. Swimming laps gave him a chance to clear his head. He loved that solitary sensation, the fact that no one could talk to him or expect a conversation as he swam lengths of a pool or dived through the waves, but recently he'd found that Bella's company gave him that sense of peace as well.

He made his way to her room. Through the window he could see Evie sitting with her. A surgical mask covered the lower half of Evie's face but her eyes were puffy and her cheeks, what he could see of them, were tear-stained. She was holding Bella's hand but Bella was very still and very pale and for a moment Charlie thought the worst before he realised all the monitors were still attached and he could see her pulse and blood pressure registering on the screen.

Evie looked up and saw him standing on the other side of the glass. She stood and came to meet him, pulling the mask from her face as she came out of Bella's room.

'What's going on? Why are you crying?' he asked as the worry he'd been battling with all day came flooding back.

'She's gone downhill, I don't know what the matter is, it's almost like she's giving up.' Evie's voice caught in her throat and Charlie knew she was holding back tears.

'Why would she do that?'

'I have no idea.'

'Has Sam been to see her?'

Evie nodded. 'But he didn't have any answers. Physically he says her condition is unchanged.'

'What else has happened today? Has anything happened to upset her?'

'Miranda came to see her.'

'Your mother? Why?' Charlie knew Miranda's presence was always enough to upset any of the Lockheart sisters.

'Apparently Bella asked her to come.'

'What on earth for?'

'I don't know, she wouldn't tell me. She hasn't said anything else. The nurses told me Bella asked them to call Miranda. And now Bella's just lying there. Not speaking.'

'She's awake?'

Evie nodded. 'Would you talk to her, see if you can find out what's going on? She can't give up, she has to keep fighting.'

Charlie agreed with Evie. Bella couldn't give

up. 'Bella seems to think your mother left because of her. Because she isn't perfect enough. Is she right?' he asked.

'She told you that?' Evie's voice was incredulous.

Charlie nodded.

'We've never had an explanation as to why she left so I couldn't say if Bella's illness contributed to Miranda's problems, none of us can say, but Bella has always felt it was tied to her. I'm not so sure.' Evie was frowning. 'I can remember, even when I was small, being told she was lying down with a headache and I wasn't to disturb her. That probably started when I was five, around the time Bella was born, and I have wondered whether that was when she started drinking, but I couldn't say for certain because I don't remember anything from a younger age. I do know things escalated when I was nine. That's when Miranda left for the first time. Bella was four, Lexi was two and I was nine.

'I'm really not sure who even made the decision that Miranda would move out,' she continued. 'It could have been our father. He bought her an apartment and he still makes sure she's okay but from then on we were never allowed to spend any time alone with her, not while we were little. Any time she spent with us was always supervised by nannies. Sometimes I wonder whether that was the right decision—children need a mother— but I guess Miranda wasn't the sort of mother Richard wanted for us. Whether it was him or her who decided she'd move out, I know it was Richard who organised the supervision and none of us has an easy or normal relationship with our mother.' Evie shrugged. 'Miranda suffers from depression and an addiction to alcohol. If you want my opinion, I think Miranda would have had problems even without Bella's illness. I think she's one of those people who just finds life itself hard to cope with. Her behaviour has affected us all but in time you learn to ignore it or accept it.'

Charlie didn't think any of the sisters had accepted it and he wasn't sure how successfully they ignored it either. Particularly Bella. 'Bella's made a few references to your mother and I think it's something she hasn't learnt to ignore or accept yet. You and Lexi might have been able to do that but I don't think Bella has. I'll talk to her but there's no guarantee she'll tell me anything.'

'I know, but she's told you a lot of things lately that have surprised me and I don't have any other ideas,' Evie said as she stripped off her gown and threw it into the linen basket as Charlie started to scrub.

Scrubbed and gowned, he hesitated in the doorway of Bella's room. The room looked wrong but it took him a second or two to work out why. There was none of Bella's personality on display. There was no sketch book, no laptop, no DVDs.

Bella's eyes were still closed but some sixth sense must have alerted her to his presence because she opened her eyes as he crossed the room. The expression in them made his heart shrink in his chest. He felt it shrivel with fear. She looked crushed, exhausted, and he realised he'd hoped Evie had been wrong. But she knew Bella better than anyone so of course she'd pick up on her sister's emotions.

Bella looked defeated and his immediate thought was that he had to find a way to restore her spirit. He'd come to rely on her strength and courage and to see this expression of resignation in her eyes was frightening. He was *not* going to watch her give up. Not without a fight.

He mustered up his courage, striving to sound positive as he picked up her hand and brought it to his lips. '*Ciao*, Bella.'

She had so many leads coming off her it was impossible to get near her, and her hand was the only part of her he could get to. He kissed her fingers through his mask. As far as kisses went it was rather unsatisfactory but it was better than nothing.

He got a faint smile in response to his greeting. Her usual warmth was lacking and her smile didn't reach her eyes but he refused to give up. He sat beside her in the chair Evie had recently vacated. He didn't let go of her hand. It was silly but he felt by holding onto her he could anchor her to his world.

'I missed you while I was in Brisbane.'

'You did?' Her voice was hoarse. It sounded like her throat was hurting, which wasn't surprising given the nasogastric tube she had running into her stomach.

'You would have loved it. There was more food than even you would have known what to do with; the drug companies are very generous with their sponsorship of those conferences. I'll take you with me next time.'

'Next time?'

'Unless you've changed your mind. Is all this…' he gestured around the room '…an elaborate ruse to get out of our deal?'

She was shaking her head but even that slight movement seemed like an effort. 'I don't think there's going to be a next time.'

'What do you mean?'

There was a cup filled with ice chips on the table over her bed and she reached out and picked up the spoon, slipping an ice cube into her mouth. Sucking on it, moistening her throat before she answered. Charlie waited, still holding her hand.

'I'm tired. I've had enough.'

His heart, which was already sitting in his chest like a lump of stone, sank to his stomach. 'What? Why? What about all the things you wanted to do?'

'It's too late.'

'No, it's not. You were going to fight. What's happened? Why would you give up now?'

Bella turned her head away from Charlie but not before he saw tears in her eyes. First Evie, now Bella. What was going on? Miranda. It had to be.

He wasn't going to let her ignore him. He wasn't going to let her keep her problems bottled up inside her. That wouldn't do her any good. He needed to know what had happened. He needed to understand what was going on if he was going to be able to help. And there was no other option. He knew that keeping things bottled up allowed the hurt to fester, allowed it to feed on itself until it could take over a person's soul until you couldn't see a way out.

'Evie told me Miranda came to see you today. How did that go?'

She turned her head to face him. 'It was good.'

Charlie felt his eyebrows lift. That wasn't the answer he'd expected. 'Good?'

'I asked my mother to come,' Bella explained. 'There were questions I wanted answered, questions I've never been brave enough to ask. I told her I wanted to know some things before I die.'

'You're not—'

'Don't.' She lifted a hand as she interrupted him. 'I'm struggling, Charlie. I don't want to keep fighting for every breath.'

Charlie couldn't find the words he needed. Why couldn't he think of something to say? He should have some words of inspiration, words of encouragement, but he had nothing. Bella continued speaking as Charlie sat, mute and confused. 'I got the answers I'd been looking for. It's not my mother's fault they weren't the answers I wanted. I've only got myself to blame.'

'What was it you wanted to know?' he asked, even though he was pretty sure he knew the answer.

'I asked her why she left us.'

Bella pulled her hand from his hold to pick up the cup of ice chips. He thought she was using the cup as an excuse to break the contact but there wasn't much he could do about it.

'And?' Surely she was going to tell him the rest of the story? He could understand why she might not have shared this with Evie, particularly if the tale was unpleasant, but she couldn't leave it here. He had to know more.

'Apparently she had postnatal depression after my birth but it was undiagnosed until after Lexi was born. She says she couldn't cope with any of us, she found motherhood totally overwhelming.'

Charlie breathed a sigh of relief. PND made perfect sense and it meant Miranda's issues couldn't be attributed to Bella. 'There you go. It wasn't your fault. Postnatal depression is not the baby's fault. You are not responsible for your mother's mental health issues.'

But Bella continued as though he hadn't spoken.

'She said she felt guilty because I was sick. She started drinking after I was born. At first it was a gin and tonic when Dad got home from work, to keep him company, but then it became one late in the afternoon while she waited for him and then one after she'd picked Evie up from school. She said she tried to stop when she fell pregnant with Lexi but after a while she started again. She drank gin with lemon and soda, though, because of the side effects of tonic water.' Bella laughed, but her laugh was devoid of humour. 'Ironic, isn't it? She gave up the soft drink because of the side effects but she couldn't give up the alcohol. She would have been worried that Lexi was going to be born with CF too. I don't think she would have cared if she'd suffered a miscarriage. I think that's probably why she kept drinking. So, you see, it all started with me,' she said as she slid another ice chip onto her tongue.

Was Bella right? Had she been the catalyst? Maybe she had but he wasn't about to agree with her.

'Your mother needs to take ownership of her problems.'

'I don't blame myself for my mother's addiction but I do blame myself for her abandonment.'

'How can it be your fault? You were four when she left.'

'There's plenty more to the story. Are you sure you want to hear this?' Bella paused and didn't continue until Charlie nodded. He wasn't certain he wanted to hear what she had to say but he knew he had no choice. 'Apparently she fell pregnant again when Lexi was eighteen months old. The pregnancy was unplanned and she freaked out, worried she couldn't cope with another baby, but especially worried about coping with another child with cystic fibrosis. Genetic testing for CF was very new but she was offered the test and she had it done. The test came back positive. She was going to have another child with CF. She terminated the pregnancy. She didn't want to bring another CF baby into the world. Her depression got worse after that, she says it was the guilt. She couldn't cope with life at all without alcohol to prop her up. And then she left. She abandoned us.'

'But you weren't the trigger for her abandonment.' Charlie tried to get Bella to see reason. Tried and failed.

'Don't you see, if genetic testing had been available when she was pregnant with me, she would have aborted me. I know she would. But it was too late, she couldn't get rid of me, so she left. I always thought I was the reason she left. Now I know I was right.'

'But she wouldn't have even *known* to be tested

for CF with you. She wouldn't have been expecting it.'

'Either way, she wouldn't have wanted me. Doesn't want me. Everything started with me. It would have been better for everyone if I was never born.'

Bella was normally so upbeat, so ridiculously positive despite everything she faced, that he found it quite disturbing to hear her being so negative. Was she depressed? He couldn't blame her if she was, she was critically ill, but he couldn't understand why she was so fixated on her mother. Surely she had more important things to worry about, like whether compatible lungs would be found in time to save her life. He wondered if he should speak to Sam about getting John Allen to assess Bella again but he'd hate to find that a potential transplant was cancelled because of Bella's state of mind. He couldn't instigate something that might put her in that situation. 'How do you figure that?' he asked.

'Life would have been very different for Evie and Lexi if Mum hadn't had me. She might never have got postnatal depression. She might never have left.'

'That's a lot of "mights",' he said. 'She might have got it after Lexi anyway and from where I sit your mother clearly has a lot of issues. You can't blame yourself.'

'I've been waiting to die all my life. I never expected to live to an old age. Having my suspicions confirmed, knowing I wasn't wanted, kind of makes it all seem so pointless.'

'Hang on, your mother never actually said she didn't want you, did she?'

'She said motherhood was overwhelming.'

'I don't think she's alone in that sentiment but it doesn't mean she didn't want you. It just means she couldn't cope and unfortunately her depression wasn't diagnosed early. It's not your fault.'

'I don't care. I'm too tired to care. Lexi and Sam can get married in one week, I just want to last that long.' She'd had enough. She wasn't going to get the happy ending she'd always wanted. No one could give that to her. Not Sam, not her sisters, not her parents and not Charlie.

Her mother would be relieved she didn't have

to visit hospitals any more, her father wouldn't even notice she was gone. Her sisters would miss her but Lexi would settle down to her new life with Sam and Evie would be able to lead her own life once the burden of worrying about Bella had been lifted from her slim shoulders. And Charlie, well, Charlie would continue to live his life completely oblivious to the fact that Bella had been in love with him.

She was tired of fighting and she was tired of wishing for things that weren't going to happen.

But Charlie was distraught. Bella had to fight. If she stopped fighting, if she gave up now, she'd be lost. He knew it was only willpower that would keep her going, keep her alive. Lexi's wedding might be enough incentive to get through the next week, but then what? He had to find another reason for her to keep fighting.

'What about your wishlist? What about us? You and I have unfinished business.'

She smiled at him and his heart lifted as he caught a glimpse of the old Bella, the one who had a desire to go out and live her life. She shrugged her skinny shoulders. 'It doesn't matter any more. It'll just be something else on my wishlist that isn't done. It was a stupid list and a stupid idea. There's only one thing I want now and that's to see Lexi and Sam married. That's my last wish. My dying wish.'

CHAPTER NINE

'BELLA, no! Please, you can't give up. You have to find something worth fighting for.'

'It's my time, Charlie, I can feel it.'

'But you're not the type to give up. You just need to hold on for a little bit longer. You'll get new lungs, you have to.'

She gave the tiniest shake of her head. 'I'm so tired.' Her voice caught in her throat. 'I'm tired of fighting to stay out of hospital, I'm tired of fighting to put on weight, I'm tired of taking a thousand tablets, I'm tired of fighting to breathe, I'm tired of wanting my parents to love me.'

So that's what this was all about. He should have known. Bella just wanted to be loved. She needed to be loved.

'I know what it's like to want to give up but you can't, you have to keep fighting. Do it for the people who love you. Do it for Evie and Lexi.'

A reflex almost made him say 'Do it for me' but he hesitated and Bella picked up on his hesitation.

'Yes?'

He shook his head.

'What were you about to say?' she asked.

You're a coward, Charlie Maxwell, his conscience told him, but he couldn't talk about things he didn't understand. He couldn't tell her he couldn't imagine his life without her in it because he wasn't exactly sure what that meant and, if his words could be misconstrued, if he upset Bella, Evie would have him hung, drawn and quartered.

He'd promised Evie he wouldn't break Bella's heart so he swallowed his words and delivered some different ones. Safer ones. 'I was about to tell you a story.'

'Go on.'

He wasn't sure if she was really interested but he had one last chance to convince her to keep fighting. 'I understand what you're going through,' he said. 'I know what it feels like to want to give up but you've got to believe that this is not the end. You've got to believe things will get better. After I had my scooter accident in Bali I struggled to deal with it. I couldn't see what the point in living was once I lost everything that was important to me. At the age of twenty-three I thought my world was over. For some time I wished I'd died in that accident. It ended my surfing career but it also took away the woman I loved.'

He could tell from her expression that he'd shocked her. That was good. It meant she was listening. Maybe he'd get through to her after all.

'Was she killed in the accident?'

'No.' He shook his head. 'I'd fallen in love and fallen hard. We dreamt of travelling the world together, following the surfing tour, living in perpetual sunshine and good times. But after the accident it turned out that Pippa preferred the life of sunshine and good times to a life with me. She followed the tour and left me behind. I'd lost everything. I went home to lick my wounds, wallowing in my misery. Eventually Dad got sick of me and what he saw as my unhealthy, obsessive behaviour and convinced me to find a new interest. He talked me into going back to uni, back to medical school. He told me in no uncertain terms that I had to find a new obsession and a new way of making a living, just as he'd done. I didn't dare argue. If Dad hadn't given up after his accident, I couldn't. I let him talk me into it and I'm glad I did. Initially it gave me something else to focus on but it soon became my passion. My family pulled me back to living and once I got to uni Evie's friendship pulled me through that first year. It was tough but between my family and Evie I got back on track. Now it's your turn to look to the future.'

'But my family doesn't need me.'

'If you truly believe that then you need to find another reason to keep going. What about going to college? What about your dream?'

'There's no guarantee I'll even be accepted. It all seems so pointless.'

'Let me help you through this,' he offered.

But that wasn't enough to convince her and why should it be? He wasn't offering her what she wanted. He couldn't. He couldn't imagine his life without her in it but that wasn't the same as being in love with her. It couldn't be. People didn't fall in love that quickly.

Charlie turned and started another lap. He'd been swimming for close to an hour but his head had only just started to clear. When he'd left Bella last night he'd been upset and frustrated and he'd stopped at Pete's Bar, where he'd had one too many beers in an attempt to escape the fact there was nothing he could do for Bella. He was paying the price this morning.

He'd tried his best but it wasn't enough. He hadn't been able to get through to her, hadn't known how to, so he'd tried to forget. She was looking for unconditional love. He couldn't help her.

When he eventually climbed out of the pool and towelled himself dry, he saw a message waiting for him on his phone. A message from Evie.

His thoughts immediately turned to Bella. Had something happened?

His hand shook. He didn't want to read the message, he was terrified it would be bad news, but then his brain slowly kicked into gear and he realised she wouldn't text with bad news. But his hand was still shaking as he pushed 'open'.

'We have lungs. Sam prepping Bella now.'

Charlie started pulling on his clothes, not bothering to get properly dry, shoved his things into his bag and ran to his car. Evie had left the message a little over half an hour ago. Bella would be in Theatre now but he needed to be at the hospital. He wasn't working today but he'd wait there. He might as well pace those corridors, it was better than being home alone.

Bella was getting new lungs. It wasn't over yet.

Lexi and Richard were already in the family lounge attached to the cardiothoracic unit when Evie arrived.

'Have I missed Sam?' she asked. She hoped not, she had some urgent questions for him.

Lexi shook her head. 'He should be back soon.'

Three heads swivelled expectantly as a fourth person entered the room. But this person was wearing two-inch heels, was dressed all in black and had platinum blonde hair.

Evie froze. Miranda looked sober, but it was only early.

Richard stepped forward, and for a brief moment Evie wondered if he was going to stop Miranda from coming any further, but then she realised he was positioning himself between her mother and her as if he expected Evie to react badly. He lifted a hand and ushered Miranda into the room, settling her in a chair. 'Hello, Miranda.' His voice was tender as he greeted his wife. As far as Evie knew, neither of her parents had ever contemplated a divorce and it was obvious Richard still cared for Miranda, making Evie wonder again why he hadn't tried harder to help her. Perhaps he'd done all he could.

Miranda sat, clutching her handbag on her lap, holding it in front of her like a protective shield, but it wasn't enough to stop her hands from shaking. But Evie wasn't going to criticise her today, her own hands were shaking too.

Richard spoke to them all next. 'Do you think we could all put our differences aside, just for today at least, and focus on getting through this day? Forget the past and look to the future, one,

I hope, will include Bella.' He looked at each of the women in turn but Evie felt his message was directed at her.

Three heads nodded in reply as they all contemplated what this day might bring.

Sam walked into the lounge and if he was surprised by how quiet everyone was, he didn't show it. 'All right, I'm just about to go and see Bella before we start. Is everyone okay here?' he asked. 'Any last-minute questions?'

'Are you sure Bella is strong enough for the surgery? She's not too sick, is she?' Miranda asked, astounding Evie, who'd thought Miranda was too self-involved to even realise how sick Bella was. Had she misjudged her mother?

'This is her best chance,' Sam replied. 'What's making her so sick at present is the infection in her lungs. The transplant will get rid of that, along with her diseased lungs, and I expect she'll feel better almost from the moment she comes out of the anaesthetic.'

'Is Finn going to assist?' Evie asked. That was her urgent question. She needed to know if Finn had kept his word.

'No.' Sam gave her a puzzled look.

'Didn't he speak to you?'

Sam shook his head.

'I asked him if he'd speak to you about assisting. I wanted you both to be there.'

'I haven't heard from him,' Sam said, but he didn't dismiss her query lightly. He put his hands on her shoulders and made her focus on him. 'We don't have time to organise it anyway. I don't need Finn. Bella will be fine.'

Evie knew Sam couldn't guarantee that, she knew he was saying that because it was what they all needed to hear. At the moment she wasn't a doctor, she was Bella's sister. She too needed to believe that modern medicine could work miracles. And she knew miracles did happen. But she also knew they didn't always happen when you wanted them to.

But all she could do was wait and pray and hope Sam was right. But if anything went wrong, if anything happened to Bella, she was going to track Finn Kennedy down and flay him alive. She didn't care if he was the Head of Surgery, all that meant was that if anything did go awry the buck stopped with him and she'd make sure he knew all about it.

'What do you mean, you can't take her off the ventilator?'

After close to nine hours, Bella's surgery was over. It had gone like clockwork, according to Sam, except for one thing.

'Her new lungs are viable, they're inflating perfectly, but Bella isn't breathing independently. I'm positive it's only a temporary measure but obviously we have to keep her breathing. She's ventilated but we have her on the lowest oxygen setting so when she's ready to breathe on her own, we'll know. She's sedated now but we'll wake her for short periods each day to assess her condition.'

Charlie was stunned and judging by the expressions he could see around him the Lockheart family was just as bewildered. This wasn't how the day was supposed to turn out. Bella's life was supposed to be improving. She wasn't supposed to be in ICU on a ventilator, and to make matters worse he knew he wouldn't be able to see her today. It would be family only and even they would only be allowed in one at a time for a few minutes. He was just a family friend. He was a long way down the list.

He didn't want to be at the bottom of that list, he realised, but he couldn't do anything about it at present. He would have to be patient.

Evie visited Bella very briefly, staying just long enough to see for herself that everything was as Sam had said. Bella was fine, if you counted being ventilated fine, and at least her new lungs worked. As long as she didn't reject them, everything would probably be okay. But probably wasn't good enough for Evie. She was angry and upset and looking for someone to take her frustrations out on. She went looking for Finn. He was Head of Surgery, she'd asked him to help, and he'd been nowhere to be seen. He'd better have a very good reason for ignoring her. She could accept it if he'd said he wasn't going to help but he'd told her he would talk to Sam if lungs became available. Yet, when the time had come, when it had mattered, he'd been nowhere to be found. In Evie's opinion that wasn't good enough. Not from any surgeon and especially not from the Head of Surgery.

Finding out that Finn wasn't in the hospital, had in fact not been seen all day, didn't deter her. If the mountain wasn't coming to Mohammed, she'd have to go to him.

Her heart was racing in her chest as she knocked on his penthouse door. Visions of what had happened the last time she'd knocked on his door came flooding back. She felt a rush of heat to her cheeks as she remembered what had transpired between them then—raw, impulsive, take-no-prisoners sex. The best sex she'd ever had. She still wasn't sure how that was possible. Wasn't sex supposed to be better if there was an emotional connection? Wasn't that why it was called making love? But there had certainly been no love between them. It had simply been sex, down and dirty, and incredible.

'Princess, what a pleasant surprise.' Finn opened his door and greeted her with a voice heavily laden with sarcasm.

Once again she didn't wait to be invited in when the door swung open. 'You think,' she said as she stormed past him into his lounge, resolutely keeping her back turned to the wall where she'd let him claim her the last time she was here.

She didn't give Finn an opportunity to say any more, she didn't want to give him a chance to tell her to leave. 'Bella got new lungs today,' she told him.

'I heard.'

That took the wind out of her sails momentarily.

She frowned. 'How did you hear that?'

He raised one eyebrow in a habit she found intensely irritating but it was only one of his many habits that annoyed her.

'I *am* the Head of Surgery,' he said. 'People tend to keep me in the loop.'

Being told he'd known Bella was having surgery today and he still hadn't bothered keeping his word sent Evie over the edge. 'You said you would speak to Sam. I asked you for help.' She tried desperately to rein in her temper but she knew she could either yell at Finn or burst into tears, and she wasn't going to give him the satisfaction of seeing her cry.

'Sleeping with the head of a department doesn't grant you the right to ask favours.'

Evie clenched her fists, willing herself not to hit something. God, he was infuriating. 'You arrogant bastard, is that why you think I slept with you?'

'I don't know,' he replied. 'Is it?'

'No!' She couldn't stop herself from yelling that time. 'That was an impulsive mistake and I'm sorry it ever happened,' she lied. 'I don't have a good reason for what we did but wanting the liberty of asking favours wasn't it.'

Finn didn't react to her rising temper. In contrast to her heated tone his voice was cool, calm and measured. 'How's Bella doing?'

'You tell me,' Evie snapped. 'I thought you were "in the loop".'

'I've been out of contact a bit today. I haven't caught up on everything I should have.'

'Her new lungs are working, she's in ICU, as expected, but she's on a ventilator. This was supposed to be the start of her new life but she can't even breathe by herself.' Evie could hear her voice wobbling with emotion and she fought to keep things under control.

'That will only be temporary.'

'I know that. But somehow I think if you'd been there it might have turned out differently. If things had gone according to plan.'

'Whose plan?' he asked.

'Mine.'

Finn was shaking his head. 'I'm sorry it hasn't gone as smoothly as you hoped but I'm sure she'll be fine. Trust me when I tell you it was better for Bella that I wasn't there.'

'Trust you!' Evie retorted. 'I don't think I'll ever trust you.'

Finn sighed. 'Before you get carried away as judge, jury and executioner, there's something you need to hear.' He gestured to his sofa. 'I think you should sit down.'

Evie stomped over to Finn's leather couch. On the coffee table was a tumbler filled with an inch of amber fluid. It looked like whisky. Finn remained standing in front of her. His back was ramrod straight and his hands were thrust deep into the pockets of his jeans. Even in her irritated state she was aware of how the denim of his jeans strained across his thighs, emphasising his long, lean physique, and she was aware too of her own reaction to his maleness. It seemed that being annoyed with him wasn't enough to prevent herself from finding him attractive. Not that she planned to go anywhere near him ever again. Especially not after today.

'There's a reason I wasn't at the hospital today,' he said, and Evie had to drag her eyes away from his hips and back up to his face as he spoke to her. 'Look.' He took his hands out of his pockets and held them out to her. His right hand was shaking badly. 'I didn't avoid surgery today because I didn't want to do it. I avoided it because I didn't want to be a liability. There was no way I could have operated today. You wouldn't want me near Bella like this, would you?'

'Oh, my God!' She tore her eyes away from his hands and looked up at him. She realised the shadow in his blue eyes that she'd thought was anger was, in fact, pain. She'd marched into his home and accused him of all sorts of terrible things when he'd been suffering. She felt dreadful and for a moment she forgot the nasty things he'd said to her in reply. 'What's wrong with you?'

'I have a ruptured cervical disc at five/six.'

'When? How?'

'It happened years ago, ten years ago, when I was in the army.'

'Ten years?'

He nodded. 'But the disc has deteriorated further.'

'Tell me you've been to see someone.'

He nodded. 'I saw Rupert today.'

'Rupert Davidson, the neurosurgeon?'

Finn sat on the couch opposite her but he didn't collapse into the couch as she had. His posture remained stiff, upright and he held his head still as if even the slightest movement was painful. 'He thinks a fragment of the nucleus has broken off and is causing more C-six nerve root impingement.'

'He thinks? Have you seen anyone else, had a second opinion?' she asked, but who else would he see? Like Finn and Sam, Rupert was another one of the Harbour's surgeons who was the best in his field. 'Have you had an MRI scan?'

Finn gave her a wry smile. 'I've had about a dozen opinions. I trust Rupert. And, no, I haven't had an MRI. Remember the scar on my left shoulder?'

Did she remember? She didn't think she'd ever forget how that puckered scar had felt under her fingers or the fact that when she'd felt it they'd just made love. No, they'd just had sex, she corrected herself.

She nodded.

'I still have shrapnel in that shoulder. I can't have MRI scans.'

He had shrapnel in his shoulder and a destroyed cervical disc. No wonder he was always so grumpy. 'What are you going to do?'

'Rupert wants to operate.'

'What does he want to do?'

'He has to remove that fragment but the disc has lost its height so he's talking about trying an artificial disc.'

Evie frowned. 'Isn't that a bit experimental?'

Finn nodded.

'What does he think the odds are of it being successful?' Her earlier antagonism was forgotten as she tried to process what she was hearing.

'He has no idea. He reckons fifty-fifty that I'll even pull through the surgery and no guarantees that it will work, but I can't continue like this. If my condition deteriorates any further, I may never operate again. I don't think I have much choice. So, that's why I wasn't there for Bella today. I'm sorry.'

He was sorry? Evie felt like a complete bitch. She'd known something was wrong with Finn. She'd seen it in the way he rubbed his arm, she'd seen it in his eyes when a shadow crossed them, darkening his piercing blue irises, she'd known he suffered from migraines but she'd done nothing except badger him about her own needs.

Finn stood and Evie watched as he unfolded his limbs and rose from the couch. It seemed their little heart to heart was over. 'Don't let me keep you any longer. I'm sure you want to check on Bella.'

Evie stood too but that brought them standing within a few inches of each other. She was tempted to reach out, to try to wipe the look of pain from his face. It was etched deep into the furrows of his forehead but as if he sensed what she was about to do he took a step backwards, putting some distance between them.

'I'll see you out,' he said, effectively dismissing her.

He led her to the door but paused as he reached for the doorhandle. 'Can I ask you not to mention this to anyone? They'll all find out soon enough if I need to have time off.'

Evie nodded.

'Thank you.'

She thought that was the most sincere she'd ever heard him sound. Perhaps they could be friends after all.

'Don't mention it. I'm glad you told me,' she replied, then impulsively raised herself up on tiptoe to kiss his cheek. She didn't care if her attention was unwanted. He needed to know she would keep his confidence. He needed to know she was in his corner. 'If you need someone to talk to, I think I'm a pretty good listener.'

Finn didn't respond to her invitation but he

didn't refuse it either. He held the door for her and Evie pressed the button to call the lift, before deciding to take the fire escape stairs back down to her apartment. She didn't want to share the lift with anyone, she needed to think.

Finn had been carrying this injury for ten years. She understood that it had obviously not always been as incapacitating as it was now but how had he managed not only to keep it quiet but to continue to do the job he did? Bending over an operating table would be hell with a ruptured cervical disc, particularly at the C five/six level.

The pain would account for his bad temper and she wondered what he'd be like if he was pain free. But there was no guarantee that the surgery would be successful. And if it didn't work, what would that mean for Finn? He might lose more upper-limb function and then he wouldn't be able to operate. What would that do to a man like him? One who obviously prided himself on his skills and no doubt measured his worth by his performance as a surgeon? And that wasn't even considering the complications associated with the surgery itself.

She could see the stubborn set of his jaw and recognised in him the same traits of independence and stubbornness she saw in her mother. She knew her mother's issues stemmed from low self-confidence and self-worth. Finn couldn't possibly have some of those same issues, could he? Not someone who seemed so sure of himself.

Whatever his issues, he needed someone to be there for him and Evie would have bet her last dollar that he had no one. Could she do it? Would he let her?

CHAPTER TEN

CHARLIE sat and watched Bella as she slept. He'd been beside her every chance he'd had for the past two days but he felt he could sit there for ever. He'd be there for as long as she needed him.

'*Ciao*, Bella.'

He picked up her hand. It was cool to his touch. He rested his thumb over her wrist, over the pulse that flickered under her skin, and let the beat of her heart vibrate through him.

Her dark eyelashes fluttered against her pale cheeks but her eyes remained closed. She was still sedated. Still ventilated.

He threaded his fingers between hers and gently squeezed her hand. 'Can you hear me?' he asked as he willed her to return his pressure. Just the smallest of movements would have done but there was nothing.

He could have kicked himself for not telling

her how he felt when he'd had the chance. He couldn't believe he hadn't told her he needed her in his life. Wanted her in his life.

He couldn't bear the thought of not seeing her smile. Not hearing her laugh. Not seeing her grey eyes turn silver when she asked him to kiss her, asked him to make love to her. He couldn't bear to think he might not have the chance to introduce her to the delights of lovemaking, might not get to have her naked in his arms or take her to the heights of pleasure. That he might not get to hear her cry out in ecstasy as he tasted, teased and thrilled her.

But he didn't regret not seizing the opportunity the other night. Even if it meant he'd missed his chance, he knew the timing had been wrong. He'd wanted to give Bella the attention she deserved and he couldn't have done that. It would have been hurried and hasty, not the languorous experience that he wanted her to have. Even one night wouldn't be enough. Not for her and not for him. He wanted more than that.

If only she'd wake up he could tell her how he felt.

But he could still tell her now. He could accept the theory that comatose or heavily sedated patients were still aware of conversations, sounds and smells around them, even if they were unable to respond. He could tell her how he felt now and he could tell her again later.

He was convinced her depression was due to her mental state prior to the surgery. If she'd wanted to give up then this was a way to let go. But he couldn't let that happen. He needed to get her to fight.

He wound his fingers through her auburn curls and bent his head, burying his face in her curls and breathing in her scent. Even among the hospital odours he could smell her, fresh and sweet.

'Bella?' he whispered. 'Please wake up. I miss you.' He wanted to talk to her, wanted to hear her laugh. He could talk, he could tell her about his day, but it wasn't what she needed to hear. It wasn't going to get her breathing on her own.

He kept his back to the ICU, blocking out the rest of the world as he concentrated on Bella. His words were for Bella alone.

'I'm sorry I didn't make love to you when you

asked me to. I don't want to think we've missed our chance. Believe me when I say I was tempted, very tempted, but I wanted to make it perfect for you. You deserve that. You deserve more than a quick tumble on the grass. Not that it wouldn't have been fun,' he said with a smile, 'but I want to spend an entire night with you. More. I want you to wake up in my arms and decide to do it over again. And again. Not to end up cold and sore in the back garden, having to sneak inside like a recalcitrant teenager. I'll make it up to you. I promise you an experience to remember, but first you have to wake up.' He held her hand, connecting them. 'I want to do it properly.

'Did you know I promised Evie I wouldn't break your heart?' he continued. 'She scares me, your big sister. You didn't know I was a coward, did you?' He was only half joking. He wasn't looking forward to the lecture he was expecting from Evie but he would let her have her say, as long as she didn't try to stop him from seeing Bella.

'If you get through this, I promise I'll make

it up to you.' He lifted her hand to his lips and kissed her fingertips. 'I'll be waiting for you when you wake up.'

Bella was dozing, trying to piece together the past few days. It was still so hard to believe she'd had a lung transplant, everything felt so vague and distant. When she'd woken she'd been disoriented and she'd had to ask the nurses where she was and what day it was. Apparently it was her third day in the ICU and she'd only been taken off the ventilator that morning.

Her memory was hazy and she kept her eyes closed as she tested out her new lungs. It hurt to breathe in but it was external pain, muscular pain, not her usual tight, blocked, breathless feeling. She put her hand over the base of her ribcage where the pain was worst and felt the dressing. She followed it as it ran across the lower part of her chest and felt where the drain emerged from the dressing and dropped away over the edge of the bed.

Above the dressing, between her breasts, she could feel ECG leads stuck to her chest but there were no bandages higher up. The scar from the surgery was a horizontal one, down low, just as Sam had told her it would be. But she hadn't believed him. She'd been convinced the scar would be between her breasts, visible to everyone any time she wore a V-neck top. Sam told her that was the case for heart surgery, not lung surgery, but she'd been terrified of waking up and finding out he'd been wrong.

She took another deep breath, in, out, in, almost scared to think her new lungs actually worked. She breathed out as she heard two nurses talking as they came towards her bed. She opened her eyes, thinking they were coming to her, but they stopped at the bed beside hers, ready to turn that patient. They continued talking as they worked.

'Has Dr Maxwell been in yet?'

'No. I haven't seen him since he was at Pete's the other night.'

'I told you you should have talked to him then when you had the chance.'

They were talking about Charlie! Did he have a patient in ICU or had he been in to see her? She racked her brain, struggling to see if she had any recollection of a visit from him, but the past few days were nothing but a fuzzy jumble of images and she had no idea which ones were real and which ones were her imagination.

'I was going to but then he disappeared,' the nurse replied.

Bella couldn't believe how much the nurses in this hospital gossiped in front of the patients. They talked about their lives as though all the patients were deaf. Maybe they've forgotten I'm awake, she thought. She opened her eyes, just a fraction. She had to see who this nurse was but she didn't want them to know she was listening. She squinted through her lashes. She could just make out the name on the nurse's nametag. Philippa.

Philippa? Why did that sound familiar?

No, it wasn't Philippa that was familiar. It was Pippa. The ex-girlfriend Charlie had been talking about before Bella had gone in for surgery. She remembered Charlie talking about how he'd given his heart away and lost everything. The girl, his career, his surfing dreams. No wonder he avoided relationships.

Charlie had obviously thought he'd been helping her, telling her he knew how she felt. But all she could think about was how he'd given his heart away once and would probably never do it again.

In Bella's mind Pippa morphed into Philippa—brunette, big busted, long legs—the complete opposite from her. A woman who knew what she wanted and went after it. Not someone who'd have to beg a man to make love to her.

Bella couldn't believe she'd been such a fool. What on earth would Charlie see in someone like her? He'd even told her, more than once, that the reason he spent time with her was because Evie asked him to. He obviously thought of her as Evie's little sister, nothing more. She felt tears welling in her eyes. He'd probably had no intention of making love to her, poor, tragic, inexperienced Bella, not at any time. He'd probably just been trying to let her down gently.

She wanted to fall in love but she couldn't give her heart to Charlie. Not now. Not now she knew about Pippa. Not now she knew why he avoided relationships. That would be asking for trouble. Trusting him with her heart yet knowing he would only break it. She wanted to fall in love but she'd have to make sure it wasn't with Charlie. He'd given his heart away once before, she couldn't expect him to do it again.

Well, she decided, she'd find a way to let him out of their deal. She didn't think she could bear to hear him say no to her again.

'*Ciao,* Bella.'

By the time Charlie arrived in the ICU Bella had planned her strategy, but as soon as she heard his usual greeting she felt her resolve start to crumble.

'You're a sight for sore eyes. You're looking a million dollars,' he said.

She knew he was exaggerating hugely but his effortless charm still made her feel better. His voice was bright and cheery, he sounded happy to see her; she needed to stay strong.

He placed his hand over hers and squeezed her fingers. His hand was warm and Bella drew comfort from his strength. 'You had us all so worried.'

'I did?'

'Of course.' Charlie looked at her as if she'd gone a little mad and Bella mentally rolled her eyes. Of course people would have been concerned. 'This was supposed to be the answer for you but knowing how you were feeling before the surgery I was worried you were going to give in. But I shouldn't have doubted you—you're a fighter, a survivor.'

But she'd come close to giving up. She knew it. She normally made such an effort to be strong and to fight but she'd been so tired, she'd been almost ready to call it quits. Almost. Charlie had been right, she'd needed a reason to get through the surgery and she'd found it. She didn't need Charlie's assistance and attention any more, she was a survivor and she'd get through this too.

'I have you to thank for getting me past this,' she told him.

'Me?'

She nodded and reached for an envelope that was beside her bed. She grimaced slightly with the stretch and Charlie picked the envelope up and handed it to her. She held it up. 'In here is a letter from the college.' She couldn't stop the grin that spread across her face. 'I've been accepted into fashion design.'

She was about to let Charlie go, to let him out of their deal and possibly out of her life, but she couldn't let him go without telling him the good news. After all, she did have him to thank for it.

'That's fantastic! Congratulations.'

He leant over and kissed her cheek and Bella felt her resolve slipping through her fingers and sliding to the floor. She closed her eyes to block out the sight of him, his gorgeous brown eyes, his smooth olive skin, his perfect ears and his divine lips. But his image was just as clear with her eyes closed and his lips were soft and warm on her cheek. She felt her heart flip-flop in her chest and she forced herself to remember what he'd said about Pippa. How he'd given her his heart and she'd thrown it away. Forced herself to remember he'd said that medicine was his new passion and he didn't need relationships.

'I knew they'd love you. When do you start?'

She opened her eyes as Charlie's lips left her cheek.

'Not until March.'

'You'll be fighting fit by then?'

'I plan to be. I've got a more pressing engagement before then.' She paused and took a deep breath, still surprised at the feeling of freedom, and told him another one of her reasons for living. 'Lexi and Sam have set a date for their wedding.'

'They have? When is it?'

'In three weeks, the Saturday before Christmas.'

'That's not a lot of time. Will you be okay for that?'

'I'm going to make sure I am. Sam seems to think I have a good chance if I focus on my exercises and eating properly and being vigilant with my medication. Studying in March should be a piece of cake if I can get through the next three weeks.'

'Have you got time pencilled in for me some time after you get out of here? I seem to recall we have unfinished business.' His brown eyes were shining and Bella's insides melted as she imagined letting him take her to bed. Just once.

Was he still planning on honouring their deal?

He was grinning at her and Bella was very tempted to let their arrangement stand but she knew she couldn't do it. She wanted to be special and Charlie didn't do special, at least not for more than one night at a time. She wanted to be different and the only way to be different was to make sure she wasn't just another notch in his bedpost.

She steeled herself to stick to her plan. Now was her chance to let him off the hook before he could seduce her. Before he could reject her.

She took a deep breath, still amazed that she could actually fill her lungs, even though the wound gave her some discomfort. 'That's not a priority any more. I have three weeks to get well enough for Lexi's wedding, that's my goal.'

'And after the wedding? Are you going to keep working your way through your wishlist?'

'I have a new list now.'

Charlie frowned. 'A new list. What about staying up all night to see the sun rise? Being kissed under the stars?'

'My list wasn't set in stone. I can change it if I like, it's my list.'

'But why would you change it?'

'I've got more time now. I can look further ahead. Do you know how amazing that feels?'

Charlie was grinning at her, his eyes shining. She could tell he knew exactly how she felt. She'd bet he'd got the same thrill of excitement when he'd been surfing. 'What's on your new list?' he asked.

'I'm going to college and I'm going to travel. Halfway through next year I'm taking myself to Paris.'

'Paris?'

'I've always wanted to go to Paris but I thought it was an impossible dream.'

'You're going on your own?'

'Evie will come with me. She doesn't know it yet but she will.'

'You have everything planned but no time for me?' He actually sounded disappointed but Bella knew he'd get over it. There'd be plenty of women eager to take her place, plenty of women eager to be charmed and bedded by Charlie Maxwell.

'I don't want a quick roll in the hay,' she explained. 'I don't want to be just another notch in someone's bedpost. Not that I don't appreciate your offer,' she added, 'it's just that I want more now. I have my life back. I have time to find the things I want and I want a proper relationship. I want to be in love. I want it to be special.' Bella knew she couldn't expect Charlie to choose her over all the other women out there but she wasn't going to agree to a fling.

Movement to her left distracted her. Busty, long-legged Philippa was coming towards them.

'Hello, Dr Maxwell. I didn't realise you knew Bella,' she said as she checked Bella's monitor. She looked back over her shoulder at Charlie as she added, 'My shift is just about finished and I'm heading to Pete's. Will you be there tonight?'

Bella held her breath, waiting for Charlie's answer, as she watched Philippa making cow eyes at him. She wished she could get out of that stupid bed, out of the ICU, as far away as possible from Charlie and all the silly nurses who threw themselves at his feet. But she was stuck, literally tied to the bed by the tubes and leads and drains that Philippa had come to check, and she had no option but to lie there and listen to her flirt with Charlie.

She didn't want Charlie to choose someone else but she especially didn't want to see him do it right in front of her.

'No, I won't be at Pete's,' he said, as he stood up, and Bella let out the breath she'd been holding. He leant over and squeezed Bella's hand, 'I'll see you later,' he said before he left the ICU.

Bella and Philippa both watched him go. Charlie left and took their dreams with him. Philippa sighed in admiration but Bella felt like crying. She could only assume her dreams were very different from Philippa's.

Charlie didn't think he could do special. He'd been prepared to offer Bella amazing, incredible and delightful but only on a temporary basis. But he knew that wasn't what she had in mind. She wanted to fall in love and he couldn't do that. Love meant giving up too much of himself.

He needed to walk away. He needed to make sure he didn't hurt her. She didn't deserve that.

And Evie would kill him if he hurt Bella. For everyone's sake he needed to walk away.

He'd made himself take those steps, he'd made himself leave Bella behind, and he'd kept away because he wasn't what she needed. He wasn't even what she wanted.

But it was a lot harder than he'd expected.

He sat on the beach and let the sand trickle through his fingers as he watched the waves. The sun was warm on his back and the breeze coming off the ocean left the taste of salt water on his lips. He closed his eyes as he let his memories wash over him. Images of him on a scooter in Bali collided with images of Bella. It wasn't Pippa he pictured on the scooter with him, it was Bella. Images of Bella in hospital, her auburn curls bright against the white sheets, her skin pale, overlapped with memories of the two of them dancing under the stars, of her asking him to make love to her, her grey eyes dark like a stormy sea, her skin the colour of pearls, her lips the pink of a perfect sunset.

He'd driven down to Wollongong to try to clear his head. There were only so many laps of the

Kirribilli pool he could do before he went completely stir-crazy. The surf was good and he felt the usual pang of regret that he couldn't be out there, but this time that feeling of regret was overshadowed by thoughts of Bella. If he really wanted to, he could body-surf, but that wasn't what he needed either. That wouldn't make things right. He glanced to his left, at the empty sand around him. He knew if Bella was sitting beside him everything would be okay with the world. With his world.

He missed her. He missed the touch of her hand, her laugh, her smile when he said her name.

He wished he could teach her to surf. He wished he could share with her the feeling of freedom and exhilaration surfing could produce. He knew she would love it. But knowing he couldn't surf again was different from accepting that he couldn't teach Bella. For once he wasn't sorry for his sake, he could remember how it felt to be flying down the face of a wave, to feel nothing but the rush of wind and salt spray in his face, to feel the ocean moving under his feet, alternately lifting him up before it did its best to discard him to its watery depths, the feeling of euphoria when he bested a wave, and he was sorry he wouldn't get the chance to share that with Bella.

But there were other things he could share with her. Other things he could show her. He could take her to the ski fields. They could make love in front of a fire and drink hot chocolate while the snow fell outside. He could go with her to Paris and watch the sunset from the Eiffel Tower. They could take an early morning trip to Bondi and watch the sunrise over the ocean. They had a whole world to explore and he knew then he'd rather have that adventure with Bella than surf one more wave.

When he was with her he stopped searching for the next adrenalin rush, the next hit, the rush he used to get from taking on a monster wave and coming out of it unscathed, victorious. The rush he got from performing a difficult operation and doing it successfully. Bella gave him that same rush of excitement but she also made him feel grounded, content, happy. When he was with her he felt comfortable. He felt free.

And that was when he knew. He missed surfing but not as much as he missed Bella.

He'd offered her an experience to remember but he'd been thinking along the lines of a weekend, maybe two. But that wasn't what she wanted and he realised it wasn't what he wanted either. Could he be the man she wanted?

He wasn't sure but he was prepared to try. He wanted Bella more than anything else and he was going to make sure he got her. He stood up from the sand. He had one week until Lexi and Sam's wedding. One week until he knew he'd be seeing Bella again. There were things he needed to do.

CHAPTER ELEVEN

THE wedding was perfect, Bella thought as she watched couples moving to the music on the dance floor. Even though it had been pulled together in a hurry, every tiny element had been attended to. For the past three weeks, in between her exercise and rehab sessions, Bella had been absolutely frantic, helping Lexi with myriad details for the wedding, coordinating dresses, tuxedos, caterers, musicians, florists and the cake, but to see how happy Lexi was made it all worthwhile.

Lexi looked stunning in the dress Bella had designed for her and she watched as Sam guided Lexi expertly around the dance floor. Their eyes hadn't strayed from each other, they were caught up in their own little world, and Bella envied them.

The pale green of Evie's bridesmaid's dress

caught her eye as she glided past in the arms of Marco D'Avello. Marco was an obstetrician at the Harbour and one of several doctors Bella had seen in her pre-op work-up, but she was fairly certain he and Evie were nothing but friends.

While Lexi hadn't danced with anyone but Sam, Evie had had a stream of admiring partners. But Bella had seen her constantly stealing glances at Finn—though she could tell Evie was trying desperately to look as if she hadn't noticed him. Bella wondered what was going on between Evie and Finn. Evie was passionate in her dislike of him yet Bella could sense something else.

Finn was nursing what looked like a glass of whisky and Bella hadn't seen him on the dance floor. He looked like a man who needed a friend and for a moment she thought about going to speak to him before she realised she'd have nothing to say. The song ended and Bella saw Evie cross the dance floor and head towards Finn. She wondered if Evie was planning on rescuing him from his demons. Watching Finn with the whisky in his hand and the 'keep your distance' expression on his face, Bella hoped his weren't the same demons that her mother faced. Evie needed a new project now that Bella was on the mend; she always needed to be helping someone, but none of them had been able to help Miranda, and Bella didn't want Evie to be disappointed all over again by Finn.

She turned back to the dance floor as another song began. The wedding had been perfect and there was nothing she could do now for Evie and Finn so she might as well enjoy the evening. Charlie was in the middle of the floor. She recognised his graceful movements even before she saw his broad shoulders and bald head. His movement was fluid and rhythmical and she could picture him in his surfing days gliding down the face of a wave, at one with the power of the ocean. He looked sensational in a crisp tuxedo and she devoured him with her eyes as he moved past her.

The wedding had been perfect, everything had been perfect, including Charlie.

Especially Charlie.

She'd expected that she'd have been too busy over the past three weeks to even think about him but he'd filled her dreams every night and he'd been the first person she'd seen today as she'd entered the ballroom where the wedding ceremony was going to take place. She hadn't seen him for three weeks but she'd picked him out the moment she'd stood in the doorway waiting to walk down the aisle in front of Lexi. He'd been sitting on the left of the aisle, on the bride's side, and Bella's heart had done its funny little flip-flop thing when she'd seen the back of his bald head. He'd turned as the 'Wedding March' had started and met her gaze. He'd winked at her and grinned as if nothing had changed. As if they'd seen each other only yesterday. How was it that he could behave as if everything was the same? How was it that he could seem so calm and composed and yet her hands had started to shake and her stomach was in knots with just one look?

But if nothing had changed, why had he still not asked her to dance? She'd begun to think he was avoiding her.

Well, she only had herself to blame for that, she thought as she saw him dance past her again. After telling him about her new wishlist, there was no reason for him to seek out her company any more. At least he'd been dancing with lots of different women, at least she hadn't had to watch him pick up one particular woman at Lexi's wedding. She didn't think she could bear to sit through that.

She forced herself to look away from Charlie. No matter how tempting it was to imagine having a quick fling with him, she knew she couldn't do it. Her heart wouldn't survive. She'd made her decision and she needed to stick to it. But now that the wedding was almost over she needed something else to focus her attention on, something else to keep her mind off Charlie. Her fashion design course didn't start for another three months so she had to find something to keep her occupied.

She turned away from the dance floor knowing the only possible way to keep her mind off Charlie was to keep him out of sight.

Charlie watched Bella as she hovered on the edge of the dance floor, chatting to her father. He felt as though he'd been watching her all evening, waiting for her to be free from her official brides-maid's duties. Waiting for her to be free for him. Her auburn curls shone under the soft lights and she seemed to float against the background of the other guests. She looked divine in a dress that hugged her chest and then flared out into a full skirt that looked as light as air and floated about her legs as she moved. He recognised the outfit, he'd seen it in her sketch book.

Richard was moving away, leaving Bella alone. He excused himself from his dance partner as politely as possible and went over to her.

'*Ciao*, Bella.' He bent down and kissed her cheek, savouring the softness of her skin under his lips, the slight brush of her curls against his jaw, the lightness of her dress fabric as his hand grazed her hip. 'You're wearing the green dress.'

She smiled at him and his heart soared. 'I told you I just needed time.'

'It's perfect on you.' The pale green was a perfect foil for her colouring and she reminded him of a butterfly—delicate, ethereal and exquisite. 'Would you dance with me?'

She nodded and stepped into his embrace. She

felt slight and fragile but he knew she wasn't. She had a strength of character that belied her petite size. He held her in his arms and revelled in the sensation of having her pressed against him. They talked about everything that had happened in her life for the past three weeks—about the wedding preparations, her recovery from the surgery, her rehabilitation. He'd thought there might be awkwardness between them but they slipped easily back into their relationship as though it had only been one day, not twenty, since they'd seen each other.

Everything they discussed was important but it didn't get Charlie any closer to knowing what he needed to know. He felt they talked about everything but nothing because they didn't talk about them. And he needed to know if there could be a 'them'.

'Have you finished your official duties?' he asked as the song ended. 'Do you think anyone would notice if you sneaked outside with me?'

Her eyes sparkled silver and her pink lips broke into a wide smile. 'You're not going to drag me down to the frangipani bushes and take advantage of me, are you?'

'Not unless you want me to,' he teased. 'I have a proposition for you,' he added, 'but I'd like some privacy.'

Bella nodded silently, and then surprised him when she took control, keeping hold of his hand and leading him out into the garden, guiding him along the path. The air was heavy with the scent of frangipani flowers but Bella walked past the bushes and headed for the Moreton Bay fig tree that stood sentinel over the lawn. An old wooden swing hung from its branches, the seat big enough for two, and Bella pulled him down beside her under the canopy of the old tree.

'I'm listening.'

He wondered what was going through her mind. What she was expecting him to say? She seemed so calm. He was a bundle of nerves. It mattered so much to him to get this right. This was the most important conversation he ever expected to have.

He stood up from the swing, too keyed up to sit

still, and paced backwards and forwards, working up the courage to start. What if she said no?

He took a deep breath and began. 'This new list of yours, I was wondering if you'd share it with me, tell me what's on it?'

'What do you mean?'

'The wedding is almost over and you must have close to three months until college starts. What's next on your list?'

She'd been wondering the same thing herself just moments before. She needed to find something to occupy her time until college started otherwise she'd waste it daydreaming about things that were never going to happen.

'I'm going to go out in the world and experience life,' she told him. Being deliberately vague allowed her to keep her options open but also suited her because she really had no idea what she was going to do. 'I've been given the second chance I've always wanted. Now I can do anything, so I'm going to search out as many new experiences as I can.'

'Do you think I could persuade you to share

some of those experiences with me? I want to ask you for another chance.'

She hesitated. She wasn't sure what she'd been expecting but this declaration wasn't it. Or to be more accurate, it wasn't what she'd hoped for. She hadn't hesitated to join him outside but she knew it was because she was eager to have just one more moment with him. It didn't mean she would be okay with a casual relationship. She still wanted Charlie but unless she could have all of him, emotionally and physically, she was better off alone.

She shook her head. 'I don't think you can give me what I'm after. I don't want a casual relationship, I want something deeper. Not that I expect to find that in a hurry but I want my heart intact so that when the time is right I'm ready. I don't think I can risk my heart with you.'

Charlie sat down beside her and his weight made the swing sway on its ropes. 'Don't give up on me.' His brown eyes were unreadable in the darkness but his voice was thick with emotion. 'I promise I won't hurt you. I've already promised Evie I wouldn't break your heart.'

'I'm okay by myself,' she told him. 'I don't want you to ask me out because of my list or because you feel sorry for me or out of some sense of misguided loyalty to me because I'm Evie's little sister. I'll be fine.'

Charlie reached for her hand. 'This has nothing to do with your list and definitely nothing to do with Evie. Just because I see Evie as my little sister it doesn't mean I see you the same way. I'm asking you to let me date you. Give me a chance. Please.'

He hadn't let go of her and her fingers trembled under his touch. She yearned to give in to him but somehow she managed to shake her head again. 'I'm going to use the next few months as a chance to find out where I belong and I don't think I'll be able to do that unless I spend some time by myself. I need to learn to be independent. I need to learn to stand on my own two feet.'

'I get that, but what if I stood beside you? I want to be with you. I want to be the man you're looking for.'

'Why?'

'I've missed you.'

The way he said it, so simply, as though that explained everything, made her want to believe him and almost made her want to give in, but it wasn't enough.

'I've missed your courage and your spirit,' he continued. 'I've missed our conversations. I've missed everything about you. I've missed hearing your name on my lips, I've missed seeing you smile when I walk into a room. I've missed the taste of your mouth, the touch of your hand.' He lifted her hand to his lips and kissed her fingertips. 'I've had plenty of time to think over the past weeks and to work out what's important in my life. And I know now that it's you. I can't imagine my life without you and I want to be a part of your life. I want to be beside you when you see the Eiffel Tower for the first time, I want to be the man you kiss standing on the banks of the Seine under a starry sky, I want to drink champagne with you at midnight and stay up and watch the sun rise.'

'You want to do all that with me?'

He nodded. 'When you were in hospital after your operation I realised if I had to choose between being able to surf for one more day or seeing you, I would choose you. I'm not talking about a casual relationship. I'm ready to make a commitment to you. Not for the next week or the next month but for ever.'

He reached into the pocket of his tuxedo and pulled out a thin envelope. He opened it and removed two sheets of paper, which he handed to Bella.

'What's this?' she asked.

'Two tickets to Paris.'

'Paris? I don't understand.'

'I want to take you to Paris. In July.' He got off the swing and knelt in front of her, holding her hands in his. 'I want to take you to Paris for our honeymoon. I love you, Bella, and I want you to be my wife.'

Bella's heart was racing in her chest and her mouth was dry. He what?

'You don't need to answer me now,' he said. 'I'm prepared to wait, as long as you agree to go on another date with me. Just agree to let me love you.'

'You love me?'

'I do. And I want to be the best man I can be. For you.'

'Are you sure I'm who you want?'

'I've never been more certain of anything in my life. You have made my world a better place and you have given me the freedom to be my-self. That's something I've been searching for ever since I had to give up surfing. When you thought I couldn't give you what you wanted you didn't judge me, you left me to be my own per-son, but I found out I didn't want to be my own man, I wanted to be your man. If I could still surf I would give it up for you, I would give up everything for you, but the only thing I can offer you is my love. I thought I wanted freedom but I don't. I want you.'

The tickets to Paris were resting on Bella's lap. She folded them up and slid them back into their envelope. 'I don't need Paris.'

'But—'

She reached out and put her fingers on Charlie's perfect, plump lips, quietening him.

'I don't *need* Paris but I would love to go and I would love to go with you. I also don't need time to think about us. I don't need anything except you. I used to feel like a fairy-tale princess, locked away watching the world pass by, kept separate and apart from everyone else, restricted by my illness, but you have never treated me as a fragile invalid who needed protection. You are the only person who treats me as if I'm the same as everyone else.'

'I don't want you to feel as though you're just like everyone else. I want you to feel special.'

'I do feel special when I'm with you,' she told him. 'It's funny, I envied you your freedom but you've set me free. You're my very own Prince Charming. I've been waiting for you all my life. I love you and I know where I belong in the world. I belong with you.'

Charlie stood and lifted her off the swing, pulling her to her feet, and kissed her long and hard, and Bella knew that with Charlie by her side, loving her, all her dreams would come true.

'So you'll marry me?' he asked.

Her heart flip-flopped in her chest. 'Yes, I will marry you,' she replied.

'And we can honeymoon in Paris?'

'Definitely.'

'Then I just have one more request,' he said.

'Anything.'

'You have to throw away all your old pyjamas. You're too beautiful to be wearing them. They're not coming to Paris, they're not allowed anywhere near you. From now on it's red negligees only. Agreed?'

'Agreed,' Bella replied, as she sealed her promise with a kiss.

* * * * *

January

SYDNEY HARBOUR HOSPITAL: MARCO'S TEMPTATION	Fiona McArthur
WAKING UP WITH HIS RUNAWAY BRIDE	Louisa George
THE LEGENDARY PLAYBOY SURGEON	Alison Roberts
FALLING FOR HER IMPOSSIBLE BOSS	Alison Roberts
LETTING GO WITH DR RODRIGUEZ	Fiona Lowe
DR TALL, DARK...AND DANGEROUS?	Lynne Marshall

February

SYDNEY HARBOUR HOSPITAL: AVA'S RE-AWAKENING	Carol Marinelli
HOW TO MEND A BROKEN HEART	Amy Andrews
FALLING FOR DR FEARLESS	Lucy Clark
THE NURSE HE SHOULDN'T NOTICE	Susan Carlisle
EVERY BOY'S DREAM DAD	Sue MacKay
RETURN OF THE REBEL SURGEON	Connie Cox

March

HER MOTHERHOOD WISH	Anne Fraser
A BOND BETWEEN STRANGERS	Scarlet Wilson
ONCE A PLAYBOY...	Kate Hardy
CHALLENGING THE NURSE'S RULES	Janice Lynn
THE SHEIKH AND THE SURROGATE MUM	Meredith Webber
TAMED BY HER BROODING BOSS	Joanna Neil

Mills & Boon® Large Print Medical

April

A SOCIALITE'S CHRISTMAS WISH	Lucy Clark
REDEEMING DR RICCARDI	Leah Martyn
THE FAMILY WHO MADE HIM WHOLE	Jennifer Taylor
THE DOCTOR MEETS HER MATCH	Annie Claydon
THE DOCTOR'S LOST-AND-FOUND HEART	Dianne Drake
THE MAN WHO WOULDN'T MARRY	Tina Beckett

May

MAYBE THIS CHRISTMAS...?	Alison Roberts
A DOCTOR, A FLING & A WEDDING RING	Fiona McArthur
DR CHANDLER'S SLEEPING BEAUTY	Melanie Milburne
HER CHRISTMAS EVE DIAMOND	Scarlet Wilson
NEWBORN BABY FOR CHRISTMAS	Fiona Lowe
THE WAR HERO'S LOCKED-AWAY HEART	Louisa George

June

FROM CHRISTMAS TO ETERNITY	Caroline Anderson
HER LITTLE SPANISH SECRET	Laura Iding
CHRISTMAS WITH DR DELICIOUS	Sue MacKay
ONE NIGHT THAT CHANGED EVERYTHING	Tina Beckett
CHRISTMAS WHERE SHE BELONGS	Meredith Webber
HIS BRIDE IN PARADISE	Joanna Neil